St. Charles Public Library
St. Charles, IL 60174

NOV 2 5 2015

10616771

YOUNG

WID⊘WS

CLUB

ALSO BY ALEXANDRA COUTTS

Wish
Wishful Thinking
Tumble & Fall

YOUNG

WID⊘WS

CLUB

ALEXANDRA COUTTS

FARRAR STRAUS GIROUX · NEW YORK

Farrar Straus Giroux Books for Young Readers
175 Fifth Avenue, New York 10010

Copyright © 2015 by Alloy Entertainment and Alexandra Bullen Coutts
All rights reserved
Printed in the United States of America
Designed by Elizabeth Clark
First edition, 2015
1   3   5   7   9   10   8   6   4   2

macteenbooks.com

Library of Congress Cataloging-in-Publication Data

Coutts, Alexandra, author.
    Young widows club / Alexandra Coutts. — First edition.
        pages cm
    Summary: Tamsen married her musician sweetheart and dropped out of
high school, so when her equally young husband dies suddenly she is still only
seventeen, and totally lost—but when she is caught trespassing the judge insists
that she return to the school life that she thought she had escaped, and forced to
face the reality that her life has really just begun.
    ISBN 978-0-374-30126-2 (hardcover)
    ISBN 978-0-374-30127-9 (e-book)
    1. Widows—Juvenile fiction.   2. Grief—Juvenile fiction.   3. High schools—
Juvenile fiction.   [1. Widows—Fiction.   2. Grief—Fiction.   3. High schools—
Fiction.   4. Schools—Fiction.]   I. Title.

PZ7.C8329Yo 2015
[Fic]—dc23
                                                                            2015007198

Our books may be purchased in bulk for promotional, educational, or
business use. Please contact your local bookseller or the Macmillan
Corporate and Premium Sales Department at (800) 221-7945 ext.
5442 or by e-mail at MacmillanSpecialMarkets@macmillan.com.

For my brothers,
George and John

3 0053
01082
4707

YOUNG

WIDOWS

CLUB

PROLOGUE

IT'S ONE OF THOSE FLAWLESS, COTTON-CANDY-
cloud days.

Noah fidgets in his favorite faded button-down. We stand
near the water, the crowd a half-moon around us, blurry at
the edges. Noah smiles and holds my hands, and I forget for
a minute all the people who are missing:

My mom.

My dad.

My family.

Noah is family now.

The officiant, a shaggy-haired friend of Noah's father, says
words between other words I don't hear, words like *forever*
and *better* and *worse*. Noah digs in his pocket for the rings.
The cool gold band slides easily over my finger. His gets
caught at the knuckle. I smile and push harder.

We laugh.

Inside, I hear a voice saying the clichéd things I never thought I'd care about hearing:

We'll have our whole lives to be together.

Real life starts now.

This is just the beginning.

Over and over, as if a part of me needs convincing.

We kiss and I feel myself floating.

I see us, barefoot, pieces of our hair tangling together in gusts of the sea-scented breeze. I see those around us clapping, cheering, leaning in. I see us all like tiny figurines, trapped in a snow globe, frozen and happy, suspended in glass.

What I didn't know then was that it wasn't the beginning.

It was the beginning of the end.

.   .   .

Six weeks later, the glass is shattered.

Six weeks later, Noah is dead.

ONE

ON THE MORNING OF YOUR HUSBAND'S FUNERAL, under no circumstances should you be:

    a. Hungover.
    b. Cocooned in a sleeping bag that smells like
       Jolly Ranchers.
    c. Seventeen.
    d. All of the above.

My phone chimes, a series of cascading bells meant to lure me peacefully from sleep. I swipe groggily at the screen and the phone slips under my clumsy fingers, skidding across the floor.

I unpeel my cramped legs from the sleeping bag I found in a box in Noah's basement. It's child-size, and judging by the lingering candy scent, I'm guessing Noah hasn't used it since the summer he went to band camp in New Hampshire. It wasn't actually called "band camp," it was something fancy sounding, like Improvisational Techniques and Compositional Theory on the Mountaintops, something he won a scholarship for and pretended to hate, even though I could tell from his rambling letters and kitschy postcards that all music, all day was basically his idea of heaven.

I wonder if I could trick myself into thinking that that's where he is now. Back at camp with the Jamaican chef and the bunkmates who never showered and the endless jam sessions, where he learned to tie-dye T-shirts and start a fire and write his own songs.

The sun screams through the bare, open windows. Curtains were my responsibility. There was a time—it was just last week but it may as well have been the dark ages—when I thought about going to the fabric store and asking Noah's mother, Molly, for help with the antique sewing machine she keeps in her office. Noah insisted he'd like anything I chose. I knew he just didn't care about curtains, but I was happy to have a task. It was our deal. Noah and his dad, Mitch, would build the house. Molly would help me decorate it.

Instead, I'm stuck with a half-finished shell, a glorified cabin with windows and walls and not much else. A bed I can't look at. A bathroom with no sink. My dead husband's kid-size sleeping bag in a puddle at my feet.

I rub my fists into the throbbing sockets of my eyes and peer through the window, factory-issued stickers still glued to the outside. It's a clear shot across the pebbled driveway to Mitch and Molly's house; the Jeep is gone but Mitch's truck is still here, which means they drove together. Mitch left a note last night asking if I wanted a ride, but there was something about carpooling with Noah's parents to his funeral that felt wrong. It's bad enough I'm living in their backyard. The least I can do is drive myself.

I hurry to get dressed, pulling one of Noah's flannel shirts from a half-packed suitcase on the floor and buttoning up the faded jeans I've worn for the last four days in a row. I grab my keys from a hook on the wall, trying not to see Noah, hunched over and happily focused, as he nailed it in. Trying not to hear the soft scratch of his voice, reminding me that it's harder to lose things when you have a place to put them.

Outside, the air is sticky and full. It feels threatening, like it might rain, and I wish that it would. There's not a cloud in the sky, and it seems unfair. This day should be dark. The sun should beat it. Instead, it's showing off. An obnoxious blow-hard, a relentless, uninvited sparkle.

Across the street, a screen door slams. Mrs. Hodgson thumps across the rickety wooden deck, wrinkled hands cupped around her mouth. Her hair is wild and unbrushed, and she's wearing thick, wool socks with sandals. "Birdie!" she shouts, calling for her three-hundred-year-old fluffball of a cat. I imagine the cat, perched high in a tree, or nestled in the damp space beneath the foundation; I imagine the harried lilt in Mrs. Hodgson's voice when at last she hears a rustle; I imagine the sweet, scurried reunion they'll have on the steps, and while I'm imagining I remember, once again, how wrong it is that life is a thing that still happens.

Not my life. My life hasn't happened for days. Not since the morning Noah didn't wake up. He'd come in late from rehearsal at Max's the night before. I listened to him fumble around in the dark. I felt him kiss the top of my head. I heard him nuzzle the pillow the way he always does—did—to find the place where his head fit the best. And at some point between then and when I found him, after breakfast—half a banana on toast with peanut butter and honey—his heart had stopped beating.

Most of the time it feels like mine stopped, too. But I'm still here. Mitch and Molly are still here. Mrs. Hodgson, Birdie, sleeping bags, Jolly Ranchers. All of it still exists in the universe, pointless and oblivious and taking up space. I start Noah's car and listen to the engine wheeze, thinking for the thousandth time this week that I'd happily trade it all in. I'd live in an empty cardboard box and never see another person again if it meant I could go back to the way things were, when Noah was alive and I could sleep and the rest of the world wasn't such an asshole.

•   •   •

The church lot is packed. Hatchback Subarus and rusty pick-ups and older-model Volkswagens are shoved up against each other, scaling the grassy hill and clogging the narrow roads. I do a lap, give up, and find a spot at the playground across the street. The park is also jammed—the early Saturday morning crowd. A couple of kids are swinging and two boys in matching fleece coats are pushing the empty carousel while their parents sit on benches and ignore them.

Ahead, I see Ross and Eugene loping across the church gardens. They're each wearing pieces of what looks like the same suit: sweaty gray herringbone that definitely doesn't belong to either of them. But they look okay. Better than I do. Better than any of us should after staying up all night in Ross's basement, pretending to rehearse but mostly just staring at our hands and talking about how disgusting it is that Noah's gone and we're not.

Traffic slows and I cross the street without looking. Anybody who is supposed to be here is already inside. The rest of the cars are blatantly rubbernecking, curious drivers biting their nails, shaking their heads. I can practically hear them telling each other whatever they think they know, in hushed, capital-letter tones. *Did You Hear? Mitch Connelly's Kid. Was It Drugs? Just Awful. Can. You. Imagine?*

Gossip on an island bounces around like pinballs in a machine, fact and fiction whipping up and down and around. As a former-runaway-turned-teen-bride-turned-widow, I'm something of an expert on gossip: how it starts, when it's real, and when it's a convoluted mess of nothing even resembling an original kernel of truth.

The truth, in this case, is unbelievably dumb. Noah's heart stopped beating. That's it. He didn't have a "condition." No drugs or abnormalities were found in the autopsy, which, it turns out, is a thing that happens to real people, not just the unlucky victims on *Law & Order: SVU.* The on-call emergency room doctor, a lanky man with a wispy comb-over, explained that it was probably something called Sudden Arrhythmia Death Syndrome. *SADS.* That's the official acronym. There was no way of knowing, and nothing that could have been done. It was, as far as we know, just SAD.

The inside of the church is quiet and smells like coffee and gardenias. Flowers are everywhere, exploding in large bouquets from the end of each pew and potted at the front on either side of the coffin. My knees get tingly, and I think for a second that I might pass out and also that I wish I hadn't worn jeans. Nobody else is wearing jeans, and the last thing I need is another reason to be stared at.

Noah would have worn jeans. Noah always wore jeans. Secondhand jeans, with rips and tears and awkward hemlines, that somehow always fit him just right. He wore jeans to our wedding. They were his Fancy Wedding Jeans. We got them together at the J. Crew outlet on the mainland, dark wash with white stitching on the pockets. He pretended he was going to iron them. Nobody we knew owned an iron, but he kept the jeans folded over a wooden hanger in our makeshift closet, before and after. He never wore them again.

I look for a seat in the back but there isn't one. There isn't an open seat anywhere. People are stacked three deep against the walls, and I think about squeezing between them, but the first person I see is Miss Walsh, my old AP English teacher. Not *old* like she's old, she's actually really young and has this amazing curly red hair and I probably would have liked her and her class if I hadn't been so committed to dropping out of school altogether. But I was, and when I told her she did a lot of squeezing my shoulder and looking disappointed and asking if I was sure, and now I can't imagine having to stand in the same room with her and all of these other people and a coffin.

Pastor Paul is hunched over Mitch and Molly in the front row, and all three of them turn to wave me up. I haven't been in a church since Dad and Juliet got married, and even then I spent most of the ceremony outside.

Nothing in me is prepared for the long, silent walk up the center aisle, my stupid flip-flops slapping against the dull wooden floor. It feels like a nightmare where you're naked in front of a bunch of strangers, only instead of strangers it's everyone I've ever known, and instead of being naked I'm just a girl in flip-flops who wants to be dead.

Last Saturday Noah and I went out to breakfast, the two of us. Molly usually makes a big deal out of weekend breakfasts, but we wanted to do something special. We were celebrating our one-month wedding anniversary. We went to the Tavern, got cinnamon French toast and eggs Florentine and shared them both. We said we'd make a weekly thing of it. A Saturday breakfast date.

Mitch shuffles on the bench and makes room for me beside him. He's wearing what appears to be every article of black clothing he owns, all at once. A black vest and a black turtleneck and black dress slacks. Molly sits to my right, swathed in a black skirt and black sweater and even sheer black pantyhose, as if the neutral tone of her bare legs would have been an insult to the memory of her son.

For some messed-up reason this almost makes me laugh. I don't laugh. I sit, and Molly hands me a crumpled tissue and I look at the open casket for a second to make sure all of the laughing feelings are gone. From this angle I can see only the tops of his hands, folded over his belt in a way that looks uncomfortable and absurd, probably because he never, ever wore a belt. I can almost see the glint of his ring, and my jaw goes slack and I think I might puke. I look away and force myself to believe in a parallel universe, where Noah and I are holding menus and ordering coffee and thinking about all of the Saturdays we have left.

Pastor Paul walks to the podium and says something that sounds like a greeting and something else about these difficult times. He says it's okay to have questions for God, but I don't have any questions. What I have is a half-used tissue and two dangling flip-flops and a lump in my throat the size of a small continent.

I swallow, but instead of going away the continent morphs and gets bigger, like it's oozing between my lungs and up into my throat, and suddenly, too late, I know that it's not a lump. It's puke, actual puke, and it's not going away.

I claw at my mouth with my hands and I shuffle back down the aisle, trying not to run or make too much noise or throw up on my flip-flops, which are flipping and flopping so obnoxiously that I think Pastor Paul stops talking, though I'm sure I couldn't hear him even if he didn't.

I stare ahead at the swirled stained glass of the chapel doors and push through them, the idiot sun mocking me all the way to a cluster of soon-to-be-sullied hydrangea. I fold in half and let it all go, or what I hope is all of it; anything that was ever a part of me today, proof that this happened, this is happening, a record that I'm here: I bend and I retch and I heave, until it's gone.

TWO

Six Months Later

"WELL THAT WAS A BUST." MY HALF BROTHER, ALBIE, straddles the arm of the sofa, chocolate frosting crusted on his chin, a plastic bow and arrow balanced menacingly across his lap.

Dad and Juliet's living room, normally catalogue-ready with embroidered pillows and matching throws and color-coordinated toy bins stacked neatly in the corner, is now a mess of discarded party hats and scraps of wrapping paper, the carcass of a lobster-shaped piñata spewing candy guts across the geometric pattern of Juliet's favorite rug. The detritus of a six-year-old's birthday party.

"Looked like fun to me," I say, wading through a valley of plastic toy guns that, along with the bow and arrow, I know will be quietly spirited to the basement later tonight after Albie is asleep.

"It wasn't," Albie says. "It was too crazy. I already forget what happened."

I wad up a handful of wrapping paper, bears in bow ties riding unicycles, and toss it into the open trash bag I've been dragging around the wreckage. Upstairs the bath is running, and Dad is trying to convince Gracie not to wear her tutu in the water. The tutu was a gift from Albie, in the sense that Juliet bought it and wrapped it and made Albie give it to her first thing this morning, an attempt to ward off any sibling-birthday envy. Apparently this is something Juliet and her three sisters all did growing up. The kid with the birthday gives the other kids presents before opening up his own. I was an only child, at least until Albie and Grace came along, so maybe I just don't get it, but it seems like a weird and unfair tradition to me.

"I have an idea," I say, as Albie strings the bow and arrow and aims it directly at my face. I gently nudge the rubber tip away. "Let's get ready for bed and you can tell me all about it."

"All about what?" he whines, releasing the arrow with a *thwang* into a rumpled cushion on the couch. "You were here."

I grab him by the waist and haul him off, sideways, toward the stairs. "I know," I say. "But sometimes it helps to remember things that happened when you say them out loud."

Albie rights himself and stomps up to his room. "That's dumb, Tam," he says. "That's so dumb I can't even think about it anymore. It's making me dumber."

"Albie!" Juliet barks from the kitchen, elbow-deep in a sink full of dirty frozen pizza dishes. "Listen to your sister. And don't talk back."

I follow Albie to his room and help him into his Spider-Man pajamas. He lists off roughly thirteen edible plant species while brushing his teeth, and then I tuck him in before Dad shows up to read him a book.

"Tam?" Albie shouts as I reach the hallway. I poke my head back in. "Remember when you came over for breakfast and Mom made crazy eggs because they're my favorite and you ate them even though you hate crazy eggs because it's my birthday?"

"Yup," I say. Crazy eggs are regular scrambled eggs doused in ketchup, which Albie requires in epic proportions on pretty much everything he eats. "I remember."

"Okay." He waves at me dismissively and stretches across Dad's knee for a book. "This one, please," he announces, selecting a hardcover picture book about picking blueberries in Maine. "It's for babies, but I find it soothing."

Dad playfully rolls his eyes at me over the cake-crumbed mop of Albie's dirty blond hair—no baths on birthdays—and I start downstairs, catching the tail end of "Minkle, Ninkle, Litta' Stah," as Gracie sings herself to sleep.

"He loves having you here," Juliet says, her back to me as I collapse at the kitchen table. "It's all we'll hear about for the next two weeks."

There isn't any rule, or schedule, about how often I come over for dinner, but it's worked out to be just about every other Sunday (with exceptions for holidays and birthdays). Dad or Juliet will call on Thursday or Friday and act casual, like it's just occurred to them that they haven't seen me in a while, and make up some excuse about why one of the kids needs to see their delinquent half sister. I don't mind; it's nice not to have to think about making dinner by myself, for myself, which is both depressing and a pain.

It was Mitch's idea for me to stay in the house that he'd built for me and Noah. I hadn't really given it much thought. After the funeral, it took me a few weeks to start thinking about anything again, other than how to tape towels to the windows to block out the sun, or how to survive on seltzer water and crackers. Mitch came over one night with a foil-covered plate of leftovers—a rotating crew of well-meaning friends brought them dinner every afternoon, for what seemed like an eternity—and said that they'd talked about it. He'd finish insulating the basement and get me a space heater. As long as I was warm enough, I could stay.

Juliet folds a dish towel in thirds and loops it over the oven handle as Dad shuffles in behind me. He opens the refrigerator and rummages for leftover pizza. "Anybody else?" he asks. With a houseful of hopped-up six-year-olds, none of us had a chance to eat much besides stolen handfuls of Goldfish and maybe a spoonful of frosting.

"No thanks," I say, even though I'm headed to Max's to watch the guys rehearse and I won't have time to eat. "I should get going."

"Hang on a minute," Dad says, one long leg unfolding like a gate across the kitchen floor. Chicken legs, Mom used to call them, long and spindly. I definitely inherited his height, which I'm grateful for most days, but also Mom's curves, which, usually, I'm not. Looking older helps get me into bars and clubs, but otherwise I'd happily trade in my "womanly figure" for a typically compact teenage physique.

"We've hardly had a chance to chat," Dad says, gnawing on an edge of cold crust.

"Chat?" I smirk. Dad and I don't chat. We yell—or at least we used to, before he married Juliet and everything got so civilized. Mom was a yeller. Some of my earliest memories are doors slamming, walls shaking, and the long, teary hugs that followed. Juliet prefers to talk everything out in measured tones, and I played by her rules for as long as I could. I didn't yell when she moved in. I didn't yell when they got married. I didn't yell when Dad cut his hair, or shaved his beard, or started wearing button-down shirts to his new job at the bank.

I didn't yell again until Noah asked me to move in with him. To marry him. Even then, I didn't think I'd have to. Dad married Mom when they were both nineteen, a year older than Noah was when he asked. And I still don't think it was the marrying or moving-out part that really bothered him. It was school. He didn't like the idea of me dropping out, even though, once again, he had done exactly the same thing.

"Yeah. You know. Catch up," Dad says, still straining for nonchalance. "How is everything?"

"Everything is fine," I say carefully. "How is everything with you?"

"Good. Good. You know." Dad pushes a piece of crust into a puddle of marinara sauce on his plate. "What are you up to? Still working for Max?"

Working for Max is code for pushing around a mop at the one bar on the island that isn't completely lame, the bar where the band rehearses, the bar that's owned by Dad's former best friend. (Former because Dad no longer has friends, he has Juliet, and two little kids, and pressed khaki pants, and a job at the bank.) It's hardly work and I hardly get paid—Max sometimes throws me a few twenties and always feeds me when I'm there, but it's nothing formal.

"Yup," I confirm. "He says hi, by the way." This is a lie. Max never asks about Dad anymore, I think because the answer's always the same. Ever since "The Great Reformation," as Max calls Dad's post-Juliet life, they haven't had much in common.

"I keep meaning to get down there." Dad shakes his head, as if time just gets away from him. As if he still leads a life in which heading into town on a weeknight to see a friend's new band makes sense. "One of these nights, right, hon? Get a sitter? Hear some music?"

19

Juliet is busy rebuilding the living room and offers a phony "Sounds fun!" in response. The house is a disaster, sure, but all of a sudden I notice there's something stark and pointed about Juliet's absence. She's shuffling back and forth, close enough to hear what's happening, but she's clearly giving us space. Almost as if the whole thing has been prearranged. Planned out. Suddenly, I know exactly where this chat is headed.

As if sensing I've been spooked, Dad leans quickly forward, rapping his knuckles on the table with a new sense of urgency. "Listen, Tam," he says. "It's been a while since we've talked about . . . things. I've . . . we've . . . wanted to give you time, but . . ."

"Time for what?"

"To figure things out on your own. I know this year hasn't been easy . . ."

I look down at the chipped linoleum floor that Mom picked out. She thought it was retro. Juliet says it's tacky and is always trying to get Dad to put in tile. "Not exactly," I say, barely above a whisper.

"I know," Dad says warmly. "But . . . you can't just . . . I mean, at some point, you have to . . . you know . . ."

"No. I don't know, Dad," I say, feeling the old, familiar shouty voices clawing at my chest. "Really, I don't. 'At some point I have to' . . . what? Please. I would love it if somebody could tell me. What comes next?"

I stare into Dad's watery blue eyes and hold his gaze as long as I can. I'm not sure if it's a sign of our failing relationship or just the awkwardness of the situation, but we still haven't had "the talk." The talk where Dad tells me he "knows" how I "feel." The person he was in love with, the person he thought he'd spend the rest of his life with, she died suddenly, too. Maybe it's because he knows I'm not the biggest fan of the way his version of the story turned out. If his advice is going to be "Change everything about the person you once were, and find somebody who is the polar opposite of the person you lost," then it's probably better that I don't hear it.

Dad sighs and runs his hands through his thick, sand-colored hair. "I don't know," he finally says quietly. "I have no idea. But I do think you should go back to school."

The chair squeals as I push it back and stand up.

"Tam," he says. "Wait. Just hear me out."

"I don't want to talk about it, Dad," I say. "Really."

"I'm sure you don't," he says. "But you're not thinking this through. Say you don't go back to school. You don't graduate. You don't go to college . . ."

"And I end up just like you?" I yell. I see Juliet's shadow jump as she busies herself by the fireplace.

"Tam," Dad says; his warning voice.

"I'm sorry," I say. I push through the narrow hallway, ten pairs of baby Grace and Albie eyes staring at me from the gallery wall near the stairwell. I feel Juliet, frozen with a broom in her hand, just a few feet away. "Maybe I shouldn't come back for a while."

"Tam!" Dad follows me out of the kitchen. He shoves one hand into the pocket of his chinos and slumps against the doorjamb. There's always a moment like this: the instant when he starts to look familiar again, like the Dad I used to know. The Dad who used to let me stay up late, watching old movies and eating baked beans from the can. The Dad who let me wear whatever I wanted to school, even if it was pajamas, and learned to braid my hair just the way Mom did, high pigtails with elastics that never matched. The Dad who tried everything to hold it all together, after his world—our world—was broken. Only mine was broken twice. "I just want to talk."

I grab my coat from the rack near the door, Noah's coat, the one that still smells like him, still has his receipts in the pockets. Iced tea and a chocolate croissant. *Rolling Stone* and three Twix bars, his late-night favorite.

"You're still my daughter," Dad says when my hand closes on the doorknob. "I know you don't think that means anything anymore, but it does."

I wait for a minute before I pull the door open, a wet blast of winter air rushing at my face. "Bye, Dad," I say into the biting wind, and the door slams shut behind me.

THREE

THE LINE AT THE ROYAL IS LONG FOR A SUNDAY. I snake my way through to the door and strain to catch Max's eye. He's perched on the stool as usual, doing a cursory check of IDs and collecting the five-dollar cover, his long, graying hair twisted in a braid down his back.

I wave and try to shuffle past, so as not to hold up the line, but he pulls me in for a quick hug. His beard is reddish and scraggly and tickles the side of my face. He smells exactly the way Dad used to: warm and earthy and weirdly sweet.

"How ya doing, Pickle?" he asks. "All good?"

Max is the only person who still calls me Pickle, the nickname Mom gave me when I was born. ("I ate so many before you came, I thought for sure you'd be one.") I used to hate it, but now I don't mind. Sometimes it feels like everything that happened before happened in a different life, to a different person. It's nice to know I didn't make it up.

I nod and half shrug at the same time, which is basically my preferred shorthand these days for "You know. Getting by."

Max shifts on his stool as a group of carpenter types, stocky and gruff in full-body Carhartts, fumble with their wallets. "They're in the back," Max says to me, nodding toward the beaded curtain beyond the throngs of people swaying to the old-timey bluegrass band on the run-down stage in the corner.

"Thanks," I say, and begin to make my way through, waving quick hellos to the regulars.

I'm not sure if it's possible to be "legendary" by the time you're seventeen, but if it is, I may just be the island's most legendary groupie. Before Mom died, we used to go out to the Royal almost every night, to hear whatever collection of her and Dad's ex-hippie friends was taking the stage. We'd go right after dinner—usually a one-pot, cumin-scented vegetarian dish Mom had concocted—and post up at a table near the back. It was a half-booth and perfect for me to fall asleep in during the band's second set. By now I can see how not-normal it was to put your six-year-old to bed in a bar, but I didn't know any different at the time.

Plus, I loved it. I loved the dark wood and sticky floors and plastic baskets of peanuts. I loved watching my parents dance, the way they swayed and looked so happy. I loved that everyone knew my name and I loved the way they'd point me out when I stood in front of the stage with my arms crossed, staring.

But mostly, I loved the music. It didn't matter what kind. Since these were my parents' friends it was usually folksy, but there were a few really funky groups that played songs I adored, songs by James Brown, Otis Redding, that kind of thing. Those were my favorite nights, when everyone got on their feet and nobody noticed if I stayed up past the encore.

Max grew up with my dad in New York, in a small town on the Hudson River, and after high school they packed up Dad's van and moved to the island, in search of a "simpler life." Until I was about five, we all lived together, us and Max and the rotating cast of girls he was seeing, plus Skip and Diane and their daughter, Lula Bee. I guess it was kind of like a commune, except that it was just an old, run-down house by the water that belonged to Max's grandmother, and none of them paid for anything, I don't think.

Max drove my parents to the hospital on the night I was born, in his '76 Volkswagen Golf at an alleged ninety-five miles per hour. He has known me longer than anyone I'm not related to and doesn't care that I'm technically too young to be in here. We have an agreement—as long as I don't try to buy drinks or get in any trouble, I can hang out and listen to music and eat all the peanuts I want.

The guys are still setting up when I finally push my way through the curtain. Ross is tinkering with levels on his B3 organ, his tall, wiry body curled in a giant C as his feet work the pedals below. Teddy sits behind his drum kit, tongue stuck through the gap in his two front teeth, a messy mop of yellow curls shielding his face. And Eugene, as usual, picks out notes on his towering upright bass, his face to the wall, pretending he's alone.

There was a time when Ross and Eugene still talked about going on tour, and I still planned on going with them. Early last year, right around the time Noah asked me to marry him, the guys had been signed to LoveCraft, a new indie label out of Detroit. It was the perfect fit for them, small but not too small, lots of personal attention but also some big names to back them up. The label guys said they'd foot the bill for the tour if we planned it. "We" meant me, the de facto band manager, the only band girlfriend crazy enough to spend hours on the phone with venues and motels, shipping off demos and stalking everyone from bookers to bartenders online.

After Noah died, we got a call from the label telling us they were sorry for our loss, but we'd been dropped. Noah was the heart of the band, the label guys said; he was the whole of the "image" they signed. No one really knew what to do after that. We still met at Max's once a week, the guys going through the old songs and vamping underneath the parts where Noah was supposed to come in. It was enough to just be together, playing something.

Ross takes a solo on the keys and it goes on for so long that I almost forget which song they're playing. It's one of the poppy ones that Noah wrote when he was listening to a lot of Beach Boys, called "Sunday Sun." Ross's fingers fly over the keyboard so spastically that the original melody is almost unrecognizable, just a flurry of notes and the occasional heavy chord.

"You made it."

I hear an unfamiliar voice behind me and turn to see Simone, Ross's girlfriend-of-the-moment. She was a junior when I was a freshman, and then, as now, wore only floral prints. Floral sundresses in the summer, floral jumpsuits in the fall. A long black coat embroidered with a loud floral pattern all winter long. The coat is currently draped over her knees as she leans against a broken amp, floral tights peeking out from under the hem.

"Hi, Simone."

We watch the guys play. It's too loud to talk, which is fine; we've never had much to say to each other anyway. Simone started hanging around a few months before Noah died. He called her the Predator. She always seemed like she was circling something, waiting for the right moment to go in for the kill. Ross was easy prey; he's a serial monogamist. None of his relationships last very long, but he bounces from one to the next like he's got a list. He probably does; there's never any shortage of skirts swaying nearest his corner of the stage. But Simone's stuck around longer than any of us ever thought she would, which is both awkward and kind of sweet.

After a few minutes, Ross stretches and lumbers over to say something to Teddy. Teddy gives him a thumbs-up and nudges Eugene, who finally turns around, his choppy black hair stuck in sweaty patches against his forehead. Ross puts a hand up over his eyes—the lights are bright back here, to keep the "stage" authentic—and I notice a sharp shift in his posture when he sees me.

"Tam," he says, loping toward me. "I didn't think you were coming."

I slip my arms out of Noah's coat and hold it to my chest. I'm still wearing the dirty jeans and too-big flannel I wore to Albie's party, and suddenly, wedged up against the ever-blooming garden of Simone, I feel like a grubby street urchin.

"Why not?" I say. "I'm here every week."

Ross scratches the back of his bald head—the ratty dreadlocks he wore in high school took their toll on his hair-line, and now he shaves it clean. His mouth twists into an anxious knot.

"What's wrong?" I ask. Simone gracefully pulls herself up to her feet, doing some kind of yoga stretch that involves one foot perched against the inside of her thigh, her hands clasped at her heart in silent prayer.

"Nothing, nothing," Ross insists. Teddy coughs behind him, and Eugene pretends to fiddle with a knob on the pegboard. "It's just—well, we told Simone she could sit in tonight. You know, give it a shot."

I look sideways at Simone, whose eyes are now closed, her lips quietly moving as she fakes her way through a Sanskrit chant.

"Give what a shot?" I ask, although my heart has already dropped into my stomach and is churning around with the answer.

"I thought it might be cool if she sang with us," he says. "You know, just for fun."

Simone's eyes flutter open and she smiles at me. "Just for fun," she repeats, giving my arm a quick squeeze. She skips up to the stage and stands behind the microphone, her loose auburn curls falling to one side as she taps the mike with her fingers.

"Tam, I'm sorry," Ross says, quieter now, leaning against the wall. "I would have told you, but I didn't think you were coming. You said you had that birthday party, I . . ."

"He's six, Ross," I mutter. "Did you think it would go all night?"

Ross looks at the scuffed toes of his high-top sneakers. "I'm sorry," he says again. "But we need to get serious about where we're going. Right? I mean. We can't do this forever. We need a singer. And it sure as shit isn't going to be me."

Ross chuckles hopefully, searching my face for some sign that it's all going to be okay. "You're welcome to hang out," he says. "If you're up for it. I'd love to know what you think."

My mouth goes dry and there's a pounding in my temples, but I manage a quiet nod. "Sure." I swallow, forcing a tight smile. "No problem."

Ross wraps an arm around my shoulder and gives me a squeeze before shuffling back behind the keys. I lean against the wall and take a deep breath as they throw out ideas for what tune to play next. I knew it would happen eventually. The band couldn't go on without a lead singer forever. But Simone? We could hold auditions for years and still not find a person less Noah-like on the island. Possibly even the planet.

"How about 'You and the Rest'?" Ross calls out.

Simone swoons, her hands clutching her heart. "Oh, can we please?" she begs. "I adore that one."

Eugene picks out a few notes before launching into the song's signature bass line, a staccato climb that ends with Teddy coming in strong on the drums. "You and the Rest" is one of the few songs Noah wrote before we got together that the band still played regularly. It's about an older girl he liked who worked at the record store in town, before it closed for good.

Simone starts singing and my throat gets tight, like breathing is suddenly a challenge. She's not bad, her voice is sweet and mellow, but it all just feels so wrong. To her, the lyrics are just words. She has no idea what they mean, what they meant to Noah when he wrote them. There's a buzzing in my brain and I feel like screaming, or at least covering my ears and rocking back and forth like a baby. Anything to make it all go away.

Instead, I turn and push back through the curtains, jostling against the warm, clumsy bodies of the drunken crowd, and find my way to the door.

FOUR

"TAM, WAIT UP!"

I'm winding my way through the narrow side streets in town, the icy wind stinging my nostrils. I don't realize how fast I'm running until I turn to see Eugene, sprinting to catch up. I turn back and keep running, hoping to lose him around the corner.

Across the street, beyond the vast, open green, lit up by a half circle of streetlamps, I see the silhouette of the weather vane, spinning at the top of the Howard's tallest spire. The Howard House is one of the oldest buildings in town, and by far the most ornate. It's like a gingerbread house on steroids, with fancy, curlicue moldings and red and white frosting trim.

I sprint across the green and Eugene strides to keep up, his short legs cutting across the grass in hurried slices. At the sidewalk I duck immediately between a row of prickly hedges, into the overgrown garden. The gate, knotted iron with a rusted latch, is locked, but it's not a bad climb. I've done it before.

After graduation, Mitch talked Noah into helping out with some roofing jobs. Noah hated it—hated the burnt smell of asphalt in the sun, hated being up so high—but it was good money. Money we needed to save up for tour. And every so often they'd get to work on something special, usually the stately summer home of some old-moneyed family that visited only once or twice a year. The Howard was Noah's favorite.

He took me here the night he proposed. We snuck onto the back porch and climbed up to an open balcony and stayed nestled there for hours. Noah brought take-out Chinese and made me eat my cookie first. On one side of my fortune, scrawled over the factory type in ballpoint blue, it said: "Marry me?" On the other, the Chinese characters for dumpling.

Getting married wasn't something we'd ever talked about. And Noah wasn't really the crazy-impulsive type. But the band was gearing up for their first big tour and I would only be going to the first few shows, the ones that were nearby. He wanted me to know I was his family, he said. He wanted me to know that he would always come home.

When he asked, that night on the balcony, I didn't cry. I didn't shout or squeal. I kissed him. I said yes. Because as crazy as it was—the idea of being married before I turned eighteen—I knew it was supposed to happen. I knew I wanted to spend the rest of my life with Noah. Why wait?

I look up at the balcony as if they might still be there, the best versions of who we were, so certain that we could tackle the future together. So certain we *had* a future. I scramble to the top of the arched metal gate and throw one leg over a spiky point.

"What are you doing?" Eugene asks. I feel a sharp tug at my ankle. "Tam. Come on."

I jump down to the other side, my knee turning and throbbing in quick, hot flashes. "I'm fine," I shout over the gate. "Just go back, okay? Everything's fine."

There's a long pause and then a shuffling, and at first I think he's leaving, going back to report that there was nothing he could do. *Tam's lost it,* he'll tell them. *She's finally, totally lost it.*

But then I see two sturdy hands gripping the top of the gate, one laced-up combat boot kicking over the metal knobs.

"What is this place?" Eugene asks, rubbing his palms as he lands beside me with a thud. The yard is manicured and dotted with topiary—strange, shy figures that loom almost demonlike in the darkness. I stay close to the side of the house and climb quietly up the steps to the back porch, a broad wooden deck that's shaped like the prow of a ship. Thick, painted columns are wrapped in ivy, and a hose snakes from an outdoor shower across the wooden planks. Empty clay pots are stacked upside down by the sliding back door, and I stand on one to peer inside.

I push past Eugene toward the door and jiggle the spiral brass handle. The door is latched so I try a window. The two in the kitchen are locked, but there's a smaller one that's open just a crack. I drag an empty pot beneath it and throw my weight against the sill. It's stuck.

I look back at Eugene, leaning against a column. "What?" he asks.

"If you're going to follow me, the least you could do is help." I jump down from the pot and stand beside it.

Eugene glances around the yard. He sighs and steps carefully on the pot, reaching up to the casing and easily shoving the window open. He runs one hand along the side of the screen, popping it out and resting it against the outside wall.

I shove past him and lift myself up on my elbows, squeezing inside. The window is in a small guest bathroom, over a toilet. I knock the lid down with my foot and jump to the tiled floor. I stumble through the darkness, bumping into a tall wooden chest, and reach the open kitchen. Moonlight pours in dusty shafts through the windows, over a deep farmhouse sink. I feel for a bolt on the back door and twist it open, leaving the door shut.

I pad across the kitchen to a long hallway that leads to the foyer. I hear Eugene slowly creeping in behind me. Where the hallway opens to the rest of the house there's a stairwell, and beneath it another small door. I pull it open and a blast of warm air escapes. The smell of chlorine is sharp and familiar.

When Noah told me about the indoor pool, I didn't believe him. That's the thing about vacation homes on the island: people are so obsessed with history and maintaining these crumbling, storybook facades, while at the same time insisting on every modern convenience inside.

I fumble along a wall for the lights. The lap pool glows in shimmery neon blue, a row of buoys bobbing between two lanes. A smaller, kidney-shaped Jacuzzi bubbles to life beside it. "No way," Eugene says. "How'd you know this was here?"

"Don't worry about it," I say, kicking out of my boots. The room is damp and sticky. I peel off my coat, then my flannel, and quickly unbutton my jeans. Everything lands in a heap by the shiny metal ladder. Wearing only my bra and underwear, I stand at the edge for a long moment, staring into the still, quiet water. Then I dive in. The water is sharp and bracing.

I stay under for as long as I can. I open my eyes, the distorted light fixtures rippling against a wavy pattern of blue and white tile on the slick pool wall. I hear a high-pitched whistling, a steady underwater gurgle that is interrupted, suddenly, by the muffled alarm of Eugene's voice. There's a tightness growing in my chest that swells to an ache. I wait until it really starts to hurt, until my eyes burn and it feels like my ears will explode, before I kick up through the shimmering surface.

There's a puzzling splash and I feel some part of Eugene's body tangling in my legs. He pushes up behind me, his black hair stuck to the sides of his face. "What the hell?" He spits, his thick lashes dripping, his blue eyes big and frantic. "I thought you weren't coming up."

I swim to the ledge and lean my forearms against it, gasping for breath. Eugene slaps at the water around him, like he's mad at it. He's wearing all of his clothes, and his heavy wool coat balloons up under his arms. "Jesus, Tam," he says. "What is this?"

"What do you mean?" I ask. I dip my head back and smile up at the mural of dolphins and mermaids painted on the ceiling. "You don't like swimming?"

"I like swimming," he says. "I don't like breaking into people's houses and jumping in their pool with my clothes on and potentially dragging you out of some suicidal stupor."

"Nobody told you to follow me," I say. He swims up beside me, flopping his arms up onto the ledge.

"I know." Eugene shrugs. "I just . . . I wanted to say . . . I'm sorry. I know it sucks, getting somebody new, but . . ."

I take a breath and plunge back beneath the blue. I push off the wall and glide from one side of the narrow pool to the other. I keep my eyes closed, feeling ahead with the tips of my fingers, waiting to touch the stubbly, underwater wall. But all I feel is floating, weightless nothing, and I wish I never had to feel anything else.

There's a dull thudding sound, and when I finally come

up for air, a swirl of lights on the wall. At first I think maybe I've done it. I've stayed under so long that the world is different. Magical. Far away.

But the voices are real and gruff and Eugene is splashing around for his coat, which floats beside him in a puddle, clawing at my arms and dragging me toward the ledge.

"Great," he whispers.

Two fat cops are swinging flashlights from the bottom of the stairwell. One of them flips a switch, turning off the Jacuzzi, and the room plunges into a cold and unforgiving silence.

"Party's over," he says.

FIVE

JULIET STARES AHEAD, THE WINDSHIELD WIPERS slicing back and forth, a relentless, rhythmic squeal. It started to hail when we got to the station, hard, sharp pebbles pelting our necks as we walked in handcuffs toward the door.

I turn back to look at the dim yellow light of the office, where Eugene still sits, slumped against the wall. Eugene is twenty-one, which means he's legally been an adult for years and has to spend the night in jail before we can be arraigned in the morning. "Jail" on the island is a two-room office with a dinky little cell in the back, but still. It's my fault we're here, and I—because I'm seventeen and still straddling the line between juvenile and adult—get to go home.

Home.

Juliet stabs at the radio console with her manicured fingers, attempting to shut off the all-Disney sound track that is constantly on loop in her bulbous, immaculate minivan. Somebody at the station must have called the house. She was here before I was processed, and I watched her from behind the glass half-wall, perched on a stiff plastic chair and clutching her purse to her lap.

I've never been arrested before. I've never been in real trouble before. The whole charade felt so over the top and ridiculous that I had a hard time not laughing. While a female intake officer was pressing my finger into a rectangular pad of ink, I asked if we were on a school field trip. She pressed a little bit harder.

"Did you hear me?" Juliet asks. She stops at an intersection and tilts her head to one side. I can see the charms on her bracelet glinting in the headlights from an oncoming car. It's a thick silver chain that Dad gave her just before they got married, adding a charm on every special occasion since—a heart for their anniversary, initials when the babies were born, a dog that looks just like her tiny, lunatic terrier, Mac. Either she sleeps with it on, or she took the time to search for it in her jewelry box before coming to get me. I'm not sure which is weirder.

"No," I say. I tuck my fingers into the pockets of Noah's coat. My hair is bunched inside the collar, still wet and dripping in an icy stream down my back.

"What happened?" Juliet repeats. "What were you thinking?"

I stare at the tops of my boots and shrug. *What was I thinking?* For the first time in months, I wasn't thinking. And it felt great. "Where's Dad?"

Juliet holds in a tight breath. "He needed time to cool down," she says, which makes me feel strangely pleased. I imagine him sitting up in bed when the phone rings, shouting obscenities at the wall. I imagine him stomping around the room, fumbling to get dressed in the dark, Juliet insisting she should go instead. Before I know it, I'm laughing again, a strange, gurgling chuckle.

"None of this is funny, Tamsen," Juliet says as we pull into the driveway. Albie's tricycle is on its side near the garden, and I watch as Juliet eyes it with growing irritation. There's a light on in the kitchen and I can see the gleam of the countertops, the alphabetized spice rack, the fruit bowl with a neurotic pyramid of clementines on top. Pre-party order, restored. "I'm not staying here," I say.

Juliet turns off the engine. "Tam, it's late." She slips the key from the ignition and clutches it in her slender palm.

I stare at the glove box and try to guess what's inside. Manual. Registration. Neat stack of napkins. Packaged snacks for the kids.

"Why don't you sleep in your old room?" Juliet puts a hand on my knee, Grace's G charm resting on my thigh. "We can talk more in the morning."

I turn to her, my eyes heavy and tired. "We're not talking

about it in the morning," I say. "I'm done talking. Can you both just try to understand that?"

Juliet opens her mouth to say something, but I push the door open with my knee and slam it shut behind me. The wet snow falls in angry sheets and I can hear Juliet calling my name. She opens her door and her voice gets louder, but I'm already sprinting, already halfway down the block. I run through a yard across the street and into a wooded trail that cuts away from the road.

．　　．　　．

The sleet turns to a soft rain, and I walk for an hour in the cold and dark, out of town and deeper into the part of the island that's nestled in thick woods. Noah's neighborhood is full of winding dirt roads and tucked-away houses. At the bottom of the driveway I'm careful not to trip the floodlights, on a sensor from the roof of Mitch's house. I follow the crooked stone path that winds behind the garage to the little A-frame cabin in the back of the lot.

I climb up two cinder blocks and push open the front door. The chemical smell of oil and primer stings my nostrils. There's a table saw in the living room and a towering pile of two-by-fours stacked in the kitchen where the breakfast bar was going to be.

Noah insisted we move out here as soon as the bedroom

upstairs was finished, or finished enough to put a mattress on the floor. Before he died, we lived out of suitcases and showered outside. I got sort of addicted to seeing the sky while I rinsed my hair, and it took me a few days after the plumber showed up to stop taking my towel outdoors.

I step over a multicolored web of extension cords and carefully climb the staircase, which is, at this point, a glorified ladder. The upstairs loft is buried beneath a tarp, and it looks like Mitch has been painting. I vaguely remember being asked last week about colors, but it was hard enough to care about that stuff when Noah was around. Mitch chose something innocuous in the taupe family, which somehow still doesn't feel right.

Mitch announced that he was giving us a piece of his land right after we told him we were engaged, and before the guys left for tour. The timing was not a coincidence. Mitch would never dream of telling Noah to stop playing music—nothing made him prouder than hearing his son sing the songs he'd written himself, seeing his picture in the paper, collecting flyers from the shows he'd played—but it was no secret he was terrified. Terrified that Noah would leave one day and never come back. Terrified that music would open his world up so big that the island would disappear inside it.

There was always something about the idea of building a house that made me feel a little off-balance, like we were on a train that had suddenly, without warning, switched tracks.

Making our world bigger was exactly what we wanted. It's what we'd talked about practically every night we'd spent together, starting that first night on the roof of the Howard House. Touring was our ticket out of here—or Noah's ticket, at least. I was just along for the ride.

But I knew that saying no wasn't an option. Noah could see how much it meant to his dad, not just the promise that a piece of him would always be next door, but the process of building something together. Mitch had never looked happier than when he showed up every Saturday morning, two steaming mugs of coffee in his hands and a tool belt sagging around his hips, ready to work.

And it was hard not to be a little bit excited. We were getting married. After I left Dad and Juliet's, I had assumed we'd stay with Mitch and Molly whenever we weren't traveling. But now we were going to have a place of our own. A place to come home to, after months of living on the road, sleeping in seedy motels or on the retired school bus Ross was converting into a rustic RV to take us all cross-country one day.

There's a twisting near my heart. So many things have died. None of them hurt as much as Noah, but together, they add up. Everything we wanted to do. All the plans we made, the cities we'd see, the parks we'd camp in, the food we'd eat. Every hour I spent researching routes, making notes in my planner about famous diners or must-see roadside attractions, like the dinosaur park in California or the imitation Stonehenge made out of junked cars. All of it is gone. None of it will ever happen the way it could have happened, the way it should have happened, when Noah was here and we were just getting started.

In the bathroom, I peel off my clothes and leave them in a damp heap on the floor. I turn on the shower, as hot as it will go. I stand beneath the scorching spray and feel my bones start to tingle, thawing one by one.

I thought I could do it. I thought I could stay. I was starting to get used to the strange and solitary life I had accidentally carved out for myself, my own little Young Widows Club, Membership: One. A few nights a week, I'll hang out with the band, or check in with Max at the Royal. But usually it's just been me, all day, all night, binge-watching Noah's favorite shows and listening to songs that he wrote, over and over again.

But now it seems so obvious. There's no reason to be here anymore. I live in a house with no furniture. Dad has a new family, a new life. The band has no use for me. I could go anywhere. Nothing is holding me back.

I dry off and pick out one of my old T-shirts. I look at the bed and for a second I think I'm so tired, so physically spent, that I could do it. I could climb in. But even six months later, one pillow is still creased with the vague imprint of Noah's head. I haven't touched that bed since the paramedics pulled his body out. I fumble for the sleeping bag and spread it out beside the bed. At first, sleeping on the floor every night made my back ache and my shoulders throb, but now I'm used to it. I curl my legs inside the slippery bag, and sleep creeps in like a fog.

SIX

"DOUGHNUT?"

Mitch knocks the truck into reverse and we back out of the bumpy driveway. Dad must have called him; at eight-thirty Mitch was at my door, with coffee in to-go cups and a greasy bag of doughnuts, insisting on driving me to court. Molly was still asleep, which is how she spends the bulk of her days now, when she's not shuffling around the house, flattened out by a cocktail of Valium and vodka tonics. Usually Mitch keeps busy, working on the cabin or staying late at job sites, which is pretty much how it's always been. He seems to think Molly just needs more time. I try to give them both their space—or as much space as I can while squatting in their backyard—and I mostly just hope that he's right.

"No thanks," I say quietly. I can feel my cheeks glowing

red and I want to apologize again, but it's pretty much all I've said all morning. Mitch is a man of very few words and he's already way out of his comfort zone, driving his dead son's wife to court for acting like a moron. Silence, I decide instead, is golden.

We park behind the courthouse and walk the concrete path to the imposing double doors. I look around for Eugene, but there's no sign of him anywhere. I wonder if he's already been arraigned, what kind of sentencing he got. There's a lurch in my gut and I squeeze my eyes shut. Eugene is the last person who deserved this. He worshipped Noah. He would have done anything to help him, and, by default, me. He followed me because he was worried, and, as an extra-special thank-you gift, I got him locked up.

My lawyer is waiting by the soda machine. His name is Gerald Something and he grew up down the street from Juliet. She and Dad show up a few minutes later, after waiting for Albie's bus and dropping Grace at day care; there's a purple pipe cleaner stuck inside the sleeve of Juliet's coat. Juliet and Gerald do most of the talking, in hurried whispers, while I feed the machine crumpled dollar bills in exchange for a Diet Coke.

"Everyone knows the situation here," Gerald is saying. He has thick, bushy eyebrows and boxy shoulders, and looks more like a car salesman than an attorney. In his lap there's a yellow pad with my name and the date written across the top. His handwriting is worse than Albie's. "Try not to worry," he says, pawing at my knee with one gigantic, hairy hand. "I have a feeling we'll be in and out pretty quick."

Gerald ushers us past the open courtroom and across the hall, into a small corner room that looks like a library or personal study.

"We do the juvenile hearings in here," Gerald explains. "Very informal." He gestures at an empty seat on one side of the desk and takes the upholstered chair beside me. Dad and Mitch and Juliet sit on a bench behind us, in front of stacks of bookcases filled with matching leather-bound volumes that look lawyerly and important.

A side door opens. A tall woman with wiry black hair, cut to the end of her square chin, enters. She's wearing a striped pantsuit and holding a dark robe over one arm. She hangs it on the back of the door after it closes. I have the vague sensation that I know her from somewhere, but can't remember from where.

"Good morning," she says pleasantly without looking up. She fidgets with the rolling chair behind what appears to be her desk—there is a framed photograph of her with another woman and two Asian children, smiling among pumpkins and bales of hay.

"Good morning, Judge Feingold," Gerald says. There's a chorus of mumblings over my shoulder.

"Let's see. Tamsen Baird. Seventeen?" She looks up at me and takes in the row of spectators for the first time. "Baird. I thought I recognized that name." She smiles at Dad. "Stephen. How are you?"

"Lori," Dad says quietly, before clearing his throat. "Judge Feingold."

Judge Feingold tucks a thick section of curls behind one ear and appears momentarily flustered. Suddenly, it all comes back. Parties in Max's backyard, "Lori" in a sundress, tangled, wavy hair and a loud, commanding voice. "It's been a long time."

I glance again at the photo of her family and try to remember how long she and Max were together. I wonder if she knew she was a lesbian even then. There was always something temporary about her, as if she knew she was just pretending at Max's way of life. Then again, none of Max's lady friends lasted much longer than a few months at a time, so it's not like she was an exception.

"Tamsen." The judge says my name again, and I realize she's staring at me. "Do you remember me?"

I look up and nod, but she seems to be waiting for something more, so I say: "Yes," and then I add, "Your Honor," because that's a thing that happens on TV. I pull my limp blond hair over one shoulder and try to sit up straighter.

"Your Honor, this is Miss Baird's first offense," Gerald interjects, pulling one ankle up over his knee. He's wearing tan suede loafers with white athletic socks, and a patch of furry skin peeks out from beneath the bottom of his hitched-up trousers. "She's here today with her father and stepmother, as well as her father-in-law. Tamsen was married to Noah Connelly, who, I'm sure you'll remember, passed away about six months ago."

Dad coughs behind me. Judge Feingold looks back at her notes. She picks up a pen and scribbles something in the margin. I try to guess what it could be. *First offense.* Or: *Husband. Dead.*

"All right," she says. "And what happened, exactly?"

Gerald leans in toward the desk. "On the night of the twenty-first, Miss Baird was out with—"

"I'd like to hear from Tam, if you don't mind."

Gerald sits back, tugging at the hem of his pants. My heart pounds in my chest. I squeeze my knees together and take a breath. "Um," I say, like an imbecile. "Okay. You mean, what happened . . ."

"Just tell me why we're here." Judge Feingold takes off her glasses and sits back in her seat.

"Okay," I say quietly. "Well. I guess . . . we're here because I was swimming."

"No." She shakes her head once, like the question was a test and I've failed it. "We're here because you were trespassing. You broke into a home that does not belong to you, and you were found, after midnight, in somebody else's pool." She stares at me unflinchingly before holding a piece of paper to her face. "Is this correct?"

I swallow. My eyes find the yellowing tassels of a dark

Persian rug, caught beneath the knobby foot of her desk. My heart is a drum. "Yes," I finally whisper.

I feel the judge's eyes on the top of my head. "As I see it, we have some options here. Normally, I would order that you be taken into custody, spend some time in a juvenile facility on the mainland, or—"

"Uh, Judge?" Mitch coughs behind me. We all turn as he shifts forward on the bench. "I'd just like to say that, well, I've known Tam . . . Tamsen . . . for a while now. She's a good kid. She's kind, she's smart . . ."

"She's not smart," the judge interrupts. I hear Juliet pull in a quick breath, and a flash of fire burns my cheeks. "If she were smart, we wouldn't be here. If she were smart, she'd still be in school."

"Your Honor," Gerald says, placing a burly hand on my shoulder. "Tamsen and her—and Noah, they were musicians, and . . ."

"You're a musician?" She ruffles dramatically through my folder, as if searching for a missing detail she already knows she won't find.

There's a soup of rage boiling in the pit of my stomach. "No," I practically spit. "I'm not a musician."

"So you dropped out of school because your boyfriend was a musician."

There's a heavy silence, and I feel Gerald staring at the side of my face. A clock on the wall dispassionately ticks off the seconds.

"He wasn't my boyfriend," I hiss. "He was my husband."

Judge Feingold swivels in her chair and I hear more scratching of pen on paper. "All right," she says, staring pointedly over my head. "Here's the proposal: Tamsen agrees to go back to school."

"What?" I sputter. *School?* What does any of this have to do with school? "No! That's not—"

She holds up her hand. "She also agrees to attend a monthly support group for young widows. I have a pamphlet here from Community Services. By the time she graduates in June, if she has successfully attended all sessions and managed to stay out of trouble, the charges will be dropped from her permanent record. Does this sound agreeable to everyone?"

I feel my mouth hanging open in an unattractive gape. I turn back to Dad, to Mitch and Juliet. Juliet is nodding and Mitch is looking at his hands, caked in asphalt and gripping the tops of his boxy knees. Dad clears his throat and leans forward. "Judge, Lori, if I could make one more suggestion?"

She twirls the pen in her hand. "Yes?"

"For the past nine months, Tamsen has been living with the Connellys. Mitchell and Molly have been incredibly generous, and they've allowed her to stay, even now that Noah is . . . gone. Given the . . . circumstances . . . I think it would be best if she moved home, with her stepmother and me."

There's a scratching sound as the judge rolls back in her chair. "Mr. Connelly?" she asks. I stare at the faded tops of my jeans. "Do you have any objections?"

There's a long, excruciating silence. Mitch scratches his elbow. "No," he finally mutters. "If that's what everybody wants, I guess it's how it should be."

"Good," the judge says, and stands. She holds out a sheaf of stapled papers for Gerald to take. "I'll expect this behavioral contract signed by both your client and her legal guardian, and on my desk by the end of the day."

Gerald nods as Judge Feingold pulls her robe from the hook on the door. I stare at her feet as she slips it on, the dark heavy fabric bouncing around her shins. "Nice to see you all." She nods before turning to me. "And Tamsen"—she closes one hand on the doorknob—"I sincerely hope not to see you in here again."

SEVEN

DAD AND JULIET INSIST ON DRIVING ME BACK TO
Noah's. It's a Monday, but they've both taken the day off work,
I guess to help me move my things and get me settled. I don't
have very much stuff—what random furnishings we had were
Noah's, mostly on loan from his parents' basement—so be-
tween the three of us and Mitch, it doesn't take long.

The final trip I make alone in Juliet's van, putting together
a box of smaller possessions: photos in handmade frames,
single earrings, old notebooks and journals. I thumb through
one of the books, cringing at the pages of X-ed out song lyrics I never showed to Noah, sappy stuff he would have pretended to like. There's also a section of notes I made on a few
shows we did in Pennsylvania. Late each night, while the guys
partied or Noah slept (he was a master at sleeping anywhere
on tour) I would scribble down thoughts on all the other

bands we saw. What I liked, what I didn't, the importance of live music in the digital age, *blah blah blah*. I didn't share this stuff with Noah, either. I didn't share it with anyone. It always felt like something I did for myself, just because there were too many ideas to keep track of in my head for too long. Now I toss the notebook on top of the box and lug it down the stairs.

On my way to the car, I see Molly hovering over a frost-mangled hydrangea bush. She's wearing Mitch's brown canvas coat and sweatpants tucked into fur-lined boots. It's the first time I've seen her out of the house in weeks.

"That's the last of it," I say, gently shutting the trunk.

Molly looks up from the broken branches and smiles. "Isn't it amazing?" she asks, her eyes vacant as she stares through me, to some dark place I can only begin to imagine. She snaps off the end of a dry branch and shakily holds it out. "You think they're gone. You think they'll never come back. And every year, they do."

Molly was—is—a landscape architect, and occasionally her midday reveries wander into the world of horticulture.

"Bye, Molly," I say, bending over to give her a hug. I try not to think of the open, loving woman I used to know, the one who accidentally walked in on me in Noah's bathroom after the first night we spent together, and invited me to stay for breakfast without missing a beat. Noah would sometimes talk about "the bad old days," back when his mom was still drinking, but it always seemed like he was remembering somebody else. Now I see how easy it is to quietly sink into an unreachable place, especially when there doesn't appear to be a compelling reason to climb back out.

"Tam, wait up," I hear Mitch calling as the screen door slams. He jogs down from the house and stops beside my car, hugging his arms to his chest in the cold. "You got everything?"

"I think so." I nod. The back of my throat throbs, and I try to think about anything other than what's happening. This is not goodbye. This is not me leaving the two people who have treated me like family from the moment we met.

"Don't be a stranger, okay?" Mitch grabs one of my arms and then the other, as if he's going to pull me in for a hug. Instead, we just stand like that in the driveway, his hands on my elbows, while Molly wanders around the dormant gardens, talking to the plants.

"It's still yours, you know," Mitch says through my open window, after I've climbed in the van. "The house. I'll finish it up and it's yours. Whenever you're ready. Whenever you get the go-ahead. All right?"

Mitch drums his fingers on the roof of the car and gives me a sad, hopeful smile.

I nod. "All right," I say. "Thanks. For everything."

Mitch salutes as I pull out of the driveway, and somehow I wait until he's just a blur in the mirror before I start crying.

. . .

The next morning, Dad drives me to school on his way to work. He doesn't even suggest the bus, perhaps because he doesn't trust that I'll stay on it. To be honest, I don't have the energy to think about running away. Nothing seems worth the trouble anymore. I feel far away from the person who broke into a stranger's house, like she's been sucked from my body, leaving a lazy, lumbering shell behind.

Instead of dropping me in the parking lot the way most parents do, Dad pulls right up to the yawning double doors, in line with all the buses, which is seriously frowned upon. Dad willfully ignores the honking of the two buses behind us. I think about suggesting an alternate meeting place for pickup, but decide I don't care enough to bother. "Have fun," he encourages halfheartedly, before swinging the car lazily away. "See you tonight."

I stand alone on the pavement for a few quiet seconds, until the buses unload and I'm swallowed into the fray of backpacks and headphones and shuffling Ugg boots and sneakers.

It's still early. I slink past the entrance and around the corner, over to the deserted patch of grass behind the cafeteria. I imagine it was, at one point, supposed to be some kind of outdoor dining space, but now it's just a sorry square of balding lawn, littered with cigarette butts and grimy plastic furniture.

I perch on the damp corner of a wobbly table and take out my phone. I scroll through old text messages from Noah, hoping to avoid the muddled morning energy on the other side of the cafeteria walls, and the possibility of actually having to speak to someone. I've been too numb to feel nervous, but now, suddenly, I am. It's like I've completely forgotten how to do it. How to be here and walk fast and know where I'm going. It used to be as natural as breathing, and now I feel like a foreign exchange student, or a visitor from another, exclusively homeschooled planet.

I used to love school. I'm not really sure when things started to change, but by the beginning of last year I'd just sort of checked out. It was supposed to be the time when I was really "buckling down." There were college applications to think about. Committees to join, fund-raisers to plan, and so forth. All signs pointed to riding out my AP classes, getting into some small liberal arts school, maybe somewhere in Maine or Vermont or the Pacific Northwest. But somehow, the course changed. I didn't care about college anymore. All I cared about was getting out.

It didn't help that, by this point, Noah had graduated. All I wanted to do was be with him. All day, every day. But I didn't drop out of school for Noah. And it had nothing to do with the fact that he was a musician. In my head, at least, I was already long gone.

I dab at a wet spot on the back pocket of my jeans and tug Noah's shirt down over it. The entrance is quieter now, and I slip through the front doors undetected. The buzz from the cafeteria is frenetic and palpable. I start down the long hallway toward the office.

Miss Kelley isn't at her desk. I scan the bulletin board on the wall behind it, plastered with multicolored posters for musical auditions and swim team tryouts and the spring formal. ("This year's theme: *The Great Gatsby!*") The copy machine grumbles in the back room and a woman I've never seen before walks carefully in my direction. She pulls out Miss Kelley's gray swivel chair and sits down with painstaking precision.

"Yes?" she asks. Her voice is frail and warbling. "May I help you?" She is elderly and impatient and wearing a lopsided beret. I tell her my name and she says Mr. Peterson is expecting me in his office. I'm surprised and a little bit sad that Miss Kelley, the old secretary, is gone. I always liked her, mostly because she famously overlooked things like the millions of forged doctor's notes and early dismissal slips I laid on the mind-scrambling clutter-field that was her desk.

On second thought, I guess I'm not all that surprised that she's gone.

Mr. Peterson is the guidance counselor/building trades instructor/tennis coach. I knock on his open door and he waves me in. He starts by explaining block scheduling, which is new this year and has apparently been met with some pushback, given the long-winded and weirdly defensive pitch I receive on its behalf.

"I mean, essentially, all we're dealing with here are classes that are twice as long and meet half as often," he says, while pacing in front of a window that overlooks the faculty parking lot. He tosses a tennis ball up in the air and catches it with a loud and satisfying *pop*.

Mr. Peterson doesn't believe in sitting, so there are no chairs in his office. While he paces I stand awkwardly by the door, fidgeting with the buttons on the sleeves of Noah's shirt, my canvas tote bag sagging over one shoulder. I grabbed it at the last minute this morning and stuffed one of my old journals inside, so I could at least pretend to be writing things down.

"I've printed out a schedule for you, and a calendar of SAT test dates and review groups. We've decided it makes the most sense for you to catch up on what you've missed this semester, and then we can talk about summer school." He hands me a bunch of stapled papers, still warm from the printer, and stops pacing. He twists his mouth and uses the ball to scratch a spot on the back of his head. "Also, uh, you know, if you ever want to talk about anything . . . I mean, about your friend . . . what happened . . . you know . . ."

Here's where I should nod or thank him or at least clear my throat, anything to save him from whatever he imagines to be the end of this sentence. Instead, I just stare.

"So," he says, at last trailing off. "Yeah. So we're good?" He tosses the ball and catches it behind his back.

"We're good," I sigh, and fold the papers into my bag without looking at them.

• • •

60

I spend the rest of the day, as promised, in chunks of ninety-minute classes. I also spend it pretending not to notice that every time I walk into a room the weather changes. Everything freezes. People stop talking, or start talking in quieter tones. Some of them hover at my shoulders and make uncomfortable eye contact and stutter and repeat themselves. Others hang back and say "Noah" to each other like they knew him.

For the most part, it's the people I'd most like to ignore that insist on real conversation. Like Addison and Ava, two shiny-haired girls I hung out with for five minutes at the beginning of freshman year. Addison finds me at lunch, in the long, snaking line for the register. I stare with fake concentration at the colorful posters on the pillars, urging me to EAT LOCAL and advertising today's menu of free-range chicken fingers and seasonal kale soup. Addison tucks her arm into mine and I can feel Ava brushing up behind me. Each of them probably weighs a whopping ninety-five pounds, but I feel suddenly cornered. I try to take long breaths and focus on one of the cafeteria ladies as she replenishes a plastic bin of beat-up apples.

"We are so glad you're okay," Addison whispers conspiratorially into the air beside my face. She is taller than Ava and has such severely short bangs that it looks like she trims every morning. I still can't see Ava but I imagine that she's nodding, which is what she usually does when Addison is talking. "I mean, not *okay* okay. But here. We're glad you're here. I just can't imagine . . ."

Ava ducks ahead of me in line and grabs a bag of baked potato chips from a plastic display tower. "I *cannot* imagine," she agrees, nodding.

"Shit like that is not supposed to happen." Addison shakes her head as we inch toward the glass-covered case of hot entrées. "You know?"

I swallow and delicately wriggle out of her clutches. "Yeah," I manage. "I know."

"If you ever need anything," Addison says. "I mean, *anything*. Like, if you need to talk, or you just want to hang out, or whatever . . ."

"Anything." Ava nods.

I stare at the tops of their boots, scuffed suede cowboy boots for Ava and black chunky motorcycle boots for Addison. I try to imagine what it would look like, hanging out at one of their houses. It's not like it would be terrible. Ava doesn't live too far from Noah's parents, and there's a path that runs from her house straight to the cove. We'd probably go for a walk and share a cigarette and they'd ask lots of questions and tell me what everyone's been saying. I'm sure they'd try to be nice. Friendlike, even. Only we're not friends. We have nothing in common. It's nobody's fault. It just is.

"Thanks," I say. I slide out of line and buy a granola bar and an Odwalla smoothie and take them to the long hallway outside the Family Center. The Family Center is the faculty day care staffed by students on the early-education track. On days when I wasn't sneaking out to meet Noah for lunch, this was where I used to eat. I'd usually convince myself it was because the benches here are more comfortable than the rigid, Ikea-esque chairs in the Caf, but really I think the chorus of sporadic squealing and the musical singsong of toddler play gear somehow made me feel less alone.

My last monstrous class of the day is Senior Social Sciences. It is notoriously a joke class, sort of a cross between Intro to Behavioral Psychology and a full semester of Truth or Dare. Mr. Alden, the doughy, goateed man who has taught the class for the past twenty-seven years, briefly and unnecessarily alerts the class to my sulking presence and passes me a heavy blue paperback book with EMOTIONAL INTELLIGENCE printed in red block lettering across the front. On the board he writes the words *Empathy* and *Sympathy,* and asks Leon Bucknell, captain of the wrestling team and the one kid in the class least practiced in either emotion, to differentiate.

My eyes settle on the back of Lula Bee's head. She showed up soon after I did, tossing me her trademark half sneer / half smile as she plopped onto a purple beanbag near the corner of Mr. Alden's desk. There are no desks in Senior Soc., just a giant circle of chairs and cushions, presumably to promote intimacy and to make us forget we're being graded.

Lula's stick-straight hair has most recently been dyed a deep crimson color that has started to fade to a watery orange at the roots. People used to mistake us for sisters, our wispy, white-blond locks often twisted into pigtails with matching bows.

63

I manage to stay tuned out while Gigi Wong explains to Leon and everyone else why empathy is the superior emotional response. I watch Mr. Alden settle into the rolling chair behind his desk, his feet propped up on the windowsill. There's a plastic container of chopped cantaloupe open in his lap, and every so often he reaches in to grab a slimy chunk.

I am suddenly filled with a dark and whirling energy, like a battery has been replaced, or I've been abruptly wound up from a spring in my back. All of this, every single thing I've done today, feels so completely disconnected from reality. Not just my reality, but the actual real world, the place on the other side of these concrete walls where people have free will and responsibilities and beating hearts in their chests. It feels like I've been swallowed into a vortex of arbitrary scheduling and assignments, where some of us exist solely to tell the rest of us what to read and how quickly.

I fidget in my seat, trying to find a comfortable position, but my legs are throbbing from sitting so long and my head splinters and aches. I flip open the textbook, hoping to focus my eyes on something harmless and distracting, but the blur of text only makes me nauseous. I need air. Real air—not vented, oxygenated stuff that's recycled through hundreds of pairs of adolescent lungs each day, breathed in and out to the rhythm of announcements and page limits and insidious, brain-busting boredom.

Before I can talk sense into my feet they are carrying me along the periphery of the circle. My shoulder jostles a poster of a drunk-looking Albert Einstein and that stupid quote about gravity and falling in love that I'm sure he never said, and my hands push heavily into the door. I hold my breath and hurry down the hallway, my boots squawking on the slick, abandoned floor, and turn into the first door I see. It's a dank stairwell that leads downstairs to a utility closet and another, heavier door, a fire exit that leads, thank God, outside.

The afternoon sky is mottled and dense, the sun is deep in hiding, but I'll take it over the seizure-inducing fluorescent flicker of the lights in Alden's classroom. I find an obscured spot on one of the JV soccer fields, behind the trainer's office, where I can wait for last bell and watch for Juliet.

"That's it?"

The wind, brisk and punchy, carries a voice from the edge of the parking lot. I squint to see Lula Bee rolling toward me on a fat-tired mountain bike plastered with angry-looking stickers that are mostly the names of late-eighties punk bands.

Her lips are stained bloodred, her eyes drawn heavily in charcoal liner. It's hard, sometimes, to reconcile her face with the little girl I used to know. As she pedals closer I try to remember the last time we exchanged words directly. I'm pretty sure it was in the eighth grade, right after I started officially going out with Noah. This was way before the dyed hair and tattoos, when Lula was just a shy kid in homemade jumpers with a shaggy, bowl haircut and an endlessly drippy nose.

We did everything together when we were kids, even after we stopped sharing a room. Dad started building our house close to town, and Lula's parents moved to a farm up-island, where Lula and I would spend our afternoons taunting the pigs or tricking out the chicken coop, building new levels with hidden rooms and stairs made out of twigs. From my house, we'd ride our bikes down the secret path to the beach, where we'd pretend to be archaeologists, hunting for arrowheads and shark's teeth, clues from a primitive past.

But things changed when I started hanging out with Noah. After school, instead of taking the bus to Lula's house, I'd walk over to the high school and wait for Noah to get out of class. On weekends, I'd ride my bike to wherever the band was getting together (back then it was usually somebody's garage). I still tried to see Lula when I could, but it was suddenly hard to care about livestock or buried treasure. It was like I'd snuck through a trapdoor, to a different universe, and the old one didn't make sense anymore.

Now, I sit slack-jawed and stare as she skids to a stop where the grass meets the pavement. *That's it?* Her words echo inside me. "What do you mean?" I ask.

"One day and you're done?" Lula pulls her hair back into a messy bun, revealing two shaved stripes on each side of her head and a long sequence of bone-shaped studs glistening along the rim of one earlobe. "Seems sort of dramatic."

I stare at the flimsy buttons of her black trench coat, the

scraggly laces of her vintage Dr. Martens. "Whatever," I mutter.

Lula pumps the handlebar brakes with her wrists, a trail of short, sturdy muscles in her forearms tightening beneath the loose cuffs of her coat. Lula has always been both solid and tiny. There's a picture of the two of us when we were five or six, and even though I'm a full head taller than she is, she's holding me on her hip, like a doll.

The cold breeze is whipping through the open collar of my shirt, and I tuck the fraying lapel up closer to my cheeks. "Did I miss anything?" I ask.

Lula pivots her backpack, black with a giant metallic X duct-taped from top to bottom, around on one shoulder and unzips one of the front pockets. She pulls out a piece of paper folded into fourths. "It's a group project," she says. "We're working together. It was Alden's idea, I guess because neither of us was paired up. Try to contain your excitement."

She hands me the paper and I start to flip it open but she keeps talking in this loud, frantic voice, so I stop. "I'm not thrilled about it either, but it's not like it's a big deal. Just some stupid research, social constructs, adolescent identity, blah blah. It's all right there." She gestures at the paper.

I glance quickly at the printed handout and see something about "exploring the foundation of modern teenage life," and a mandate to "Think Outside the Box!" at the bottom. "Oh . . . well," I finally manage, but Lula has already reholstered her backpack. She kicks at the ground and the wheels of her bike spin forward. "I don't know if—"

"You got a problem, take it up with him," she says as she rolls away. "Later, Pickle."

I watch as she veers into a line of traffic, causing a brief commotion of startled, staccato horns. One newly licensed junior gives her the finger and she returns the gesture with a goofy, cheerful wave, before turning into a wooded path that cuts away from the road and disappearing deep into the maze of forest.

EIGHT

THE YOUNG WIDOWS SUPPORT GROUP MEETS ON
the first Thursday night of the month, in an old, neglec-
ted theater space adjacent to the town hall. I arrive early,
because "New Dad" builds in extra commute time even to get
from the front door to the mailbox, and climb up the shallow steps to the dimly lit stage, where a small group is already
gathered.

A plump woman with thick silvery hair sits cross-legged
at the edge of the stage, her back to the darkened rows of
crimson-cushioned chairs. Her name is Beatrice, but I have
been ordered to call her Bunny. She reads from a plastic-
covered library book with a picture of doves on the cover. As
she reads she clutches the endless folds of her quilted skirt and
rocks gently back and forth.

" 'Grief is like the weather,' " she intones, in a voice that is a cross between Maya Angelou and a pack-a-day smoker's husk. "'It is constant, and constantly changing. It has the ability to affect our mood, our perspective, the very essence of who we are on any given day. Grief is in the air and we are given no choice but to breathe it.'"

The grief in the air I'm currently breathing smells heavily of patchouli and blueberry mini-muffins. The muffins are part of a sorry-looking spread laid out in the center of the circle, along with two plastic jugs of apple cider and a jar of salted nuts. I clench my fists into tight knots and dig my fingernails into the fleshy part of my palms, wondering how many bathroom breaks are acceptable over the span of two hours.

The dense quiet in the room is punctuated by rough, phlegmy sobs. A red-faced woman on the other side of the circle blows her nose into a stiff wad of paper napkins. She used to work in the library of my elementary school and is, at the very least, pushing fifty. I wonder if there's an Old Widows Support Group and just how old you have to be to make the cut.

Bunny examines the thick, open pages of her book before slamming it shut and tossing it to the floor. It skids across the circle and stops in front of a fit, dark-haired woman in a down vest and yoga pants.

"Liza," Bunny says, nodding her wobbly chins. "What's your grief forecast like? Sixty-five and sunny? Cloudy with a chance of precipitation?"

Liza half smiles and twists the sparkling diamond rock on her ring finger. I glance quickly around the circle. All of us still wear wedding rings of one variety or another. There are bejeweled engagement rings and bands of simple, hammered gold. The one man in the group, a preppy-looking guy probably somewhere in his late twenties, the type of gentleman that Noah would have mockingly called a "Chad," wears a thick, platinum ring on his right hand instead of his left. As far as I'm concerned, it still counts.

Aside from Chad, everyone else in the group is squarely middle-aged. There's the librarian, and Liza, and two other less-trim versions of Liza. I've been told I missed the first session, and I'm wondering if we're going to do that thing where we go around and say our names and why we're here. It seems unavoidable, though I guess the "why we're here" part is sort of a given.

"We have a new soul joining us today." Bunny smiles at me, revealing a jumbled assortment of stunningly white teeth. In my experience, extra-white teeth also tend to be freakishly straight. Not so with Bunny. Hers are as gleaming as they are crooked, with perfect, pointed canines jutting out at dangerous sideways angles. "Tamsen. Do you like to be called Tamsen?"

I zip and unzip the bottom of my striped hooded sweatshirt. "Tam is fine," I say, staring at a tattered piece of blue electrical tape stuck to the stage near one of Bunny's leather clogs.

"Tam," Bunny repeats deliberately. "Everyone, let's welcome Tam."

Bunny totters forward and waggles her fingers, as if she's casting a spell. She looks around at the rest of the group. A few people mutter "Welcome, Tam," and the librarian flutters her fingertips lazily in her lap.

"Come on, friends," Bunny urges. "We'll need to do better than that. Tam is one of us, and she's taking a big step today. Tam, if you don't mind, we usually start by saying a little bit about ourselves. Where we're from. Who we've lost. Whatever you feel comfortable sharing."

Bunny smiles at me, warm and encouraging, and all of a sudden I feel dizzy. I'm ten years old, on a leather couch in a sunlit home office. Dr. Pepper (his actual name, though he insisted on being called Dr. P) was the child psychologist I saw once a week the year after Mom died. I liked him right away; liked the books in his office, the way he listened and took notes at the same time, the way he chewed the eraser of his pencil while he watched me play games that were supposed to be somehow revealing of my emotional state. I liked him so much I wanted him to think I was A-Okay, and it didn't take me long to figure out the words I had to say to get him to give me a glowing report. The last thing I wanted was something else for Dad to worry about, so early on I decided I would be a dream patient. A recovery superstar. And it worked.

The same do-gooding instincts take over and I feel myself leaning forward. "Sure," I say. "I'm Tamsen Baird. I've lived on the island all my life." Bunny raises her eyebrows, as if this is a feat for which I'm somehow personally responsible, and motions for me to go on. "The person I—I'm here because of Noah. He was my . . . my husband. We just got married last summer. He died in his sleep." More nodding from the group and a tentative hand on my knee, an older woman with a blunt, blond bob. "It's been a tough few months. I just try to stay positive. I'm back in school—I was out for a while, but now I'm back. I think it will be good for me. I think I just need a new routine."

The words feel awkward and foreign coming out of my mouth—it's been a long time since I've had to use my Therapy Voice. Dr. P was huge into routines, and I can see that Bunny is, too. "Excellent, Tam," she says, beaming. "And welcome. We send you light and healing."

The light and healing arrive in the form of six sets of wiggling fingers and a slightly more heartened chorus of greetings. I glance up and see that Chad's eyes are closed.

Bunny claps her hands together and a clear echo bounces around at the top of the arched theater walls. "Now," she says. "As I mentioned last week, this will be our final circle group. No more readings. As a grief counselor I've done the work for you, I know what's out there. And as a human soul who, like each of you, has experienced life-changing loss, I can tell you that most of it is a pile of garbage. Are we clear?"

Bunny looks deeply into our eyes, slowly scanning the circle. She is one of those people who insists on meaningful eye contact at all times, I can tell. When she gets to me, I hold her gaze with confidence. "Next week, we'll begin our off-site adventures, but for today, we'll be jumping feetfirst into Stage One of Active Grieving. Who wants to fill Tam in? Colin?"

Bunny turns to Chad. *Colin.* I hear Noah laughing in my ear. *Close enough.*

"I guess so." Chad/Colin straightens. The stiff collar of his checkered button-down shirt is tucked inside a soft navy blue sweater. He shakes a heavy watch down on his wrist. The only other person I've ever known who wore a watch was my dad, and that was only because Mom found it at a flea market and loved the inscription. "Make time," it said. It never worked.

Colin looks up at the intricate tangle of stage lights and wires that hang in crowded clumps from the ceiling. "Let's see," he says, his voice quiet and slow, like he's just waking up. "Bunny wants us to act out our grief, in all of its stages. The five stages of grief are as follows: denial, anger, bargaining, depression, and acceptance. Bunny believes that grieving is not a passive endeavor. Bunny feels feelings with her whole body. Did I leave anything out?"

Bunny laughs, the loose skin on her neck jiggling as her broad shoulders jump up and down, ruffling the front of her multicolored knit poncho. "Wonderful." She smiles. "Very good. Lesson One: The world will not stop being funny. Whether or not we are in a place to appreciate humor matters little to the universe. Humor, grief, suffering, love, it's all a part of the game. Thank you, Colin. I honor your experience."

Bunny bows deeply in his direction. Colin chews at the skin around his thumbnail. I look down at my own gnawed cuticles and wonder if nail-biting is a condition common to all widows. And widowers.

"Denial!" Bunny exclaims, as she pushes herself up to her feet with great, wheezing effort. "According to the Kübler-Ross model, denial is the first stage of grief. Now, it is my professional opinion that a 'grief scale' of any kind is mostly a bunch of petrified bullcrap, but it does serve as an excellent jumping-off point. Shall we?"

Those of us still seated glance around the circle with uncertainty. "Shoes off!" Bunny bellows. She removes her clogs and paces the edge of the stage, the uneven hem of her thick skirt swishing against the floor. "What is denial about? Why do we refuse to accept certain events or outcomes as *real* in our lives? We are sad. We feel hopeless. We no longer find enjoyment in the things that used to bring us pleasure. And so, we create new realities. Realities in which our partners have not left us. Worlds in which we are not alone. We are, in a sense, playacting."

Bunny stops pacing and faces us, her eyes and lips contorted into what is probably meant to be a display of wonderment and/or whimsy, but actually more closely resembles gut-wrenching constipation.

"Playacting!" she repeats, this time with a grand, sweeping gesture of poncho wings. "Today, we will build worlds for each other, free from the self-imprisonment of denial. If we want to be . . . giraffes . . ." Bunny stands on her tippy-toes and stretches her thick neck up to an imaginary tree branch. "We will be giraffes! If I want to be a schoolteacher, and I want, hmm . . ." I feel Bunny's eyes landing on the top of my head. "Tamsen—excuse me, *Tam*—to be my student, then I will be a schoolteacher." Bunny crosses her arms beneath her chest and peers over the rim of her invisible spectacles. "And, Tam, who will you be?"

I stand for a moment with arms unmoving at my sides. There's a quick flash and I see myself from the outside. I wonder how I got here. How did I go from doing nothing but exactly what I wanted, every second of the day, to being ordered to sit through classes that have no value, to do group projects, to playact my emotions?

"Tam?" Bunny prompts. "Your turn."

Suddenly, I'm squatting, as if my body has decided to intervene without consulting my brain. I'm pretending to be seated at a make-believe desk. I open and close a fake book in my lap. "Your student," I say, my voice clear and loud. "I'll be your student."

Bunny applauds. "Brava!" she calls out. "You've got it! Now, I'll need just a few volunteers to start. We're spelunking in an underwater cave. Liza, you be the jellyfish."

·   ·   ·

The group ends early, and I wait in the cold for Dad. One by one, the older women shuffle slowly to their cars, some still sniffling with damp tissues clenched in their fists. After the improv games, Bunny asked us to come back to the circle and close our eyes. We were supposed to imagine the faces of the people we've lost. She told us to pretend we were sitting across from them at the kitchen table, or lying beside them in bed. She asked us to have a conversation with them, to tell them whatever we thought we hadn't said when we'd had the chance. If we wanted, she said, we could even move to different corners of the theater and actually speak out loud. Nobody moved, which disappointed Bunny, but she sat up straighter and tinkled a rusty bell she held nestled in her lap.

"Begin," she whispered.

I tried to see Noah. I imagined we were at our kitchen table in the cabin, the table he grew up with, the round wooden surface chipping along the edges from where he'd picked at it as a kid. I could see every pale spot where the wood had peeled back, every crack, every missing spindle of the beat-up chairs, covered in years of basement dust and sticky spots of forgotten food, that we'd spent hours wiping down. I saw it all, but I couldn't see Noah. Maybe it was because we never actually ate at the table; we'd only lugged it up a few days before he died, and even then, we'd opted for the couch.

At one point my eyes felt jumpy and tight, and I opened them briefly just to give them a stretch. I glanced around the circle, my eyes locking abruptly with Colin's before I quickly squeezed them shut again.

Outside, Bunny checks in to make sure I don't need a ride before plopping into her dusty red-brown Omni, a tangle of beads and what appear to be tarot cards hanging from her rearview mirror. "Nice work today," she says before she drives off. I smile and stuff my hands into the pockets of Noah's coat, scanning the lot for signs of Dad approaching.

"Do you smoke?"

I turn to see Colin perched on the concrete steps in front of the town hall. The doors are closed and the building seems haunted and abandoned.

"No," I say, glancing over my shoulder. He pushes a pack of cigarettes into the pocket of his dark gray peacoat and holds one out to light it.

"Me neither," he says, muffling a cough as he exhales a thick white cloud, a mix of cold and chemicals.

I raise an eyebrow at him, adding a skeptical smirk as I lean against the metal railing. "Really."

He shrugs. "They're not great for you, I hear?" He tilts his head to one side and peers up at me, as if waiting for confirmation.

"So it's just the look you're going for, then," I joke. He holds the burning cigarette at an awkward distance from his face, a ribbon of smoke drifting in the still winter air.

"No," he says. "I'm working up to it. Today, I light it. Maybe tomorrow I'll take a hit."

I tuck my long hair into the collar of my coat. "That makes sense," I say drily. I shape my hands into frozen fists in my pockets and stand on my toes to see beyond the curb. A car putters toward us but doesn't slow down.

"It's this thing I'm trying," he says. "Not making sense."

I study him as he switches the cigarette from one hand to the other, the orange tip glowing behind a length of ash. His jeans are crisp and look expensive, his leather boots shiny and un-scuffed. "Why?" I ask.

He shrugs again. "Why not?"

I scan the mostly empty parking lot. "Don't you have a car?" I ask. "Or is not-smoking in the freezing cold part of your *thing*, too?"

"It's my mom's car," Colin says, gesturing to a retro-looking BMW with an array of yuppie-liberal bumper stickers on the back. "She only drives it when they're here in the summer, but she's got a nose like a shark."

"I didn't know sharks could smell," I say. "I mean, like, famously."

"A shark can smell a drop of blood in two hundred and fifty thousand gallons of water," Colin answers automatically. I must be staring at him funny because he shrugs and adds: "I spend a lot of time on Wikipedia."

I smile. "I can see that."

There's a low sputtering and I watch as Dad's truck swings

slowly into the lot. I hop down the steps and hug my coat closer to my waist. "This is me," I say, over my shoulder. "See you next time."

"How do you do it?" He hurries to call out after me.

I stop with one foot on the curb. "Do what?"

"Put on such a good show," Colin says. He leans forward so his elbows are resting on his knees and flicks the untouched cigarette to the concrete.

"A good show?" I repeat uncomfortably. I'm not sure why, but hot, anxious splotches are quickly spreading across my cheeks and neck.

Colin stamps the cigarette out with his boot and throws me a strange, knowing smile. "You weren't talking to anybody, in there. And you don't really believe in *new routines*, do you?"

Dad pulls up beside me. He honks unnecessarily and squints through the darkened window. I hesitate for a moment, a fast-burning fury heating up my belly. This guy, this *Chad*, who couldn't even be bothered to participate in the group in any meaningful way, is criticizing *me*?

"Try inhaling next time," I say, rolling my eyes at the littered butt by his feet.

The door sticks and I tug it open, climbing into the truck and staring straight ahead. I pretend not to see the shadowy shape of Colin in my periphery as Dad pulls away.

NINE

"ANYONE SITTING HERE?"

It's just before the lunch bell, and I'm taking advantage of the empty cafeteria and a free study period to cram for my first calculus test. School has taken some getting used to, but it wasn't long before my feet fell into a new, zombie rhythm, marching me every ninety minutes from World History to Organic Chem and back over to the vocational wing for International Cuisine. But I've missed six weeks of this term, not to mention all of the last, and whenever I'm not hunkered down in the library, or in my room poring over textbooks and trying to catch up, I'm sitting, stone-faced, in a classroom, pretending I already have.

The big highlight is that I've started eating lunch in the cafeteria again. This is a highlight mostly in the sense that I can tell it makes everyone else feel comfortable, and that's pretty much the endgame these days. The more comfortable everyone else seems to be, the less they try to talk to me about things like Noah and how I'm feeling and what the plan is for the rest of my life. Which I prefer to the alternative, so eating at a corner table by myself, surrounded by the rest of the floater misfits, is a significant but worthwhile concession.

Miss Walsh is really the one who puts the kibosh on the sad-solo-lunch-in-the-hallway routine. She also convinces me to switch into her creative writing elective. She says I've got potential, which I think just means she feels guilty about not doing more to keep me around the last time, given how wonderfully that all worked out. Either way, switching classes gets me out of gym, so I'm not all that opposed to the idea.

But today it's all about calculus, and I'm so lost in derivatives and differentials that it takes me a second to realize that somebody is trying to get my attention.

"Hello?" I hear the voice again and look up. I'm surprised to see that it's Eugene, hovering near my shoulder.

"Hey," I say, quickly shutting my notebook. "What are you doing here?"

Eugene and Ross took turns calling and texting the first few days after court. I was too embarrassed to answer. The messages said I should stop by rehearsal that week, and again the week after, and I kept telling myself that one day, soon, I would. But every time Sunday night rolled around, I came up with an excuse to stay home. Too much studying. Something good on TV. The truth was, it was all just too weird. I knew the band had to move on, but I wasn't sure I could be there to see it. I know I should have at least called Eugene. Now it's been weeks, and I'm not sure which is worse: the shame I feel about acting like such a freak on the night we got arrested, or the fact that I still haven't apologized for it.

Eugene flops his fake-leather messenger bag on the long orange table and pats it with one hand. "I'm subbing for the composition teacher," he says. "Haven't been back to this place since I graduated. Smells the same."

"Yeah." I smile. "Cajun fries and hormones."

Eugene has always had a funny laugh, this abruptly startling giggle that seems too big for his delicate frame. "Exactly," he says. He looks over my shoulder at my textbook. "How's it going? Weird being a kid again?"

"Kind of," I say. "It sucks."

"At least you're almost done, right?" he tries. "I mean, it's not like you had to start over."

"Might as well have," I say, gesturing to the closed textbook. "It feels like everything I read is in some code and I've forgotten how to crack it."

Eugene nods and drums his fingers on the table. There's a heavy pause and then the words are pouring out of me like lava.

"I'm sorry, I'm so sorry," I blurt. "I mean—you never should have gotten in trouble. That was all totally my fault. I tried to tell them that you didn't do anything. I did everything I could to—"

When I look up, Eugene is smiling. "Don't worry about it." He shrugs. "I got five hours of community service. Built a fence in the state forest. It was nothing."

I stare at him for a moment and see the quiet, awkward kid Noah overheard in the band room, dwarfed by his hulking upright bass and playing along to some old Miles Davis records he'd brought from home. Noah and Ross had just started getting serious about playing together, and they were looking for people to fill out the band. Ross thought Eugene was too "straight," which just meant his jeans weren't skinny enough or his hair was too clean. But Noah fought for him from the beginning.

"It's not nothing," I say under my breath. "You were just trying to help."

Eugene shrugs. "I should have minded my own business," he says. "Anyway, that's not why I'm here."

I look up to see that he's opening his bag and pulling out a flyer for a show. It's a group of shows, actually, a festival; one I remember researching last year online. "Home Grown Hillbilly," it's called, for Boston area alt-bluegrass bands, and it happens each winter.

"It's in three weeks," Eugene says, pointing out the date. "We've been practicing a lot, and Ross thinks we're ready. We want to try to get in."

"Cool," I say, trying to sound nonchalant. Now that the band is moving on, it's hard to know how excited to feel, or where and how I fit in.

"We need your help," Eugene says. "Ross says it looks better when we don't make the call ourselves. And you know the bookers—you got them to let us play that festival on the Cape last summer, remember?"

I nod. It was a week before our wedding. I had hopes of sneaking off to a hotel after the show with Noah—we didn't have money for a honeymoon, and I knew it would be our only chance to get off-island for the summer. But we ended up cramming into a single tent with the rest of the band, and Simone, and some girl with a pet parakeet that Teddy picked up in line at the merch tent. It wasn't exactly a romantic evening for two, but it was an adventure. Everything with the band was an adventure.

"I know you feel weird about Simone," Eugene says carefully.

"I don't feel weird about her," I lamely protest.

Eugene gives me a knowing look.

"Fine, I feel a little bit weird about her," I admit. "But what does it matter what I think?"

"That's what I'm saying," Eugene insists. "It does matter. We need you. We need a new label, and we're not going to find one without you. Have you ever heard Ross on the phone? He turns into some kind of robot salesman. And me? I practically start to stutter."

I laugh. It's true. As crazy-gifted as they all are, the guys are not exactly smooth talkers.

"So what do you say?" Eugene asks. "Come back? You can

85

think of this as a trial run, if you want. We'll go to Boston, see what happens. If you hate it, you're done. Okay?"

I stare at the web of numbers and equations on the cover of my textbook. I'm supposed to be starting over. Concentrating on school. But he's right. It's only one show. And even if it goes well and the band starts getting more gigs, nobody said I couldn't finish school *and* manage them at the same time. I could even still go to the sad widow meetings—although the thought of sitting across from judgy, smirking Colin and talking about my feelings makes my insides squirm.

I squint and squeeze the sides of my knees, pretending like my mind hasn't been made up from the moment Eugene asked. "Okay," I say with a tentative smile. "I'm in."

• • •

After school, I toss my tote bag, bulging with library books and half-finished makeup tests, on the floor of my room and collapse on my unmade bed. My history textbook is where I left it this morning, tangled in the sheets from some last-minute brain-bending, and I toss it loudly to the ground.

I lug one of the smaller boxes I brought back from the cabin up to my lap and start rummaging inside. A framed photo of me and Noah at our "wedding dinner," fried clams and lobster rolls at the docks with the band and Noah's parents. I pull out handfuls of scarves and a tangle of necklaces and the iPod dock we used as an alarm clock, always set to our favorite song: Leonard Cohen's "Hallelujah," the Jeff Buckley version.

Finally I find what I'm looking for: the binder. Noah laughed when I brought it home. He said we'd be the only band on the road that carried a dorky Trapper Keeper from gig to gig. But it's where I kept notes on everything, from contacts to accommodations to van rentals, lists of friends we'd made in other cities with couches we could crash on, set lists, newspaper clippings . . . everything. Ross called it the Band Bible. We never traveled without it.

I plug in the iPod dock and reset the clock. The familiar, dull red lights transport me back to our cabin, and for a moment my heart aches. In another world, Noah and I are talking about what to make for dinner. Noah's playing around with a new song while I look up a recipe online. The guys are probably over, too, lounging on whatever secondhand furniture we've managed to find, calling out requests for food and tunes.

I rifle through the binder, trying to find the flyer from last year's festival. I remember getting the private cell number of one of the bookers from a mutual friend. The only way I'm going to get the guys—and Simone—a decent billing at such late notice is by pulling some strings, not that I am sure I have any left to pull.

There's a knock on the door and at first I ignore it; Albie usually loses interest if my door is closed and I don't respond right away. But it pushes open a crack, and I'm about to yell out when I see Dad's loafer wedged in the corner.

"Hey," he calls from behind the door. "Okay if I come in?"

One thing about Dad and Juliet is that they're big on personal space. They never barge into my room without asking, not before I left and not now that I'm back.

"Sure," I say, just as I find the flyer. I turn down the corner and close the binder, quickly stashing it beneath my pillow. I reach for the history textbook on the floor and flip it open on my lap as Dad walks to the foot of my bed.

"Homework?" he asks. He leans into the bedpost, the one missing the pineapple-shaped knob on top, and the frame creaks and groans. The bed is an antique; it was Mom's when she was little, and my grandmother's before that. I used to hate it—all the high-pitched squeals as I tossed around in the middle of the night made it seem haunted—but now I realize how much I missed it while I was gone.

"Yeah," I say, trying to sound fatigued as I hold up the faded textbook. "Big test tomorrow."

Dad nods, impressed. "You're really taking this seriously, huh?" He smiles.

"I wasn't aware I had a choice," I say.

Dad sits carefully at the edge of my bed. "Dinner's almost

ready," he says, looking around at the posters on my walls, which have been there since the eighth grade, when I started dating Noah. A cartoon rendering of Bob Dylan and Joan Baez from a concert in 1965. That hand-drawn Decemberists album cover showing a strange-looking couple, arm in arm. A black-and-white poster of a woman holding a trumpet and a suitcase, peering around a corner. That one's called "The Trumpeter's Wife," and it's always been my favorite. I love her secret smile, and have always imagined that she's waiting by the curb while her husband, the famous jazz musician Donald Byrd, does his best to hail a cab.

"I'll be down when I'm done," I say, flipping randomly to a page on the Great Schism of 1054, which I certainly hope isn't on the test, considering I have zero idea what it is.

Dad nods and scratches a spot on his head. "I actually wanted to talk to you about something alone, if that's okay," he says. "I know this has already been a rough few weeks, and I really don't want to throw anything else on your plate, but I've decided . . . Juliet and I have decided . . . we're selling the house."

"What house?" I ask, pretend-studying. *Eastern Orthodox. Roman Catholic.* Persecution, controversy, et cetera, et cetera.

"This house."

I look up quickly from the book. "Our house?"

Dad rubs his hands against his knees. "We met with the

89

contractor this morning, and it turns out this place needs a lot more work than we thought," he says. "And Juliet thinks we'll need something bigger, as the kids get older."

"Juliet thinks?" I prod.

"We both do," he says firmly. "I know this is a big deal, Tam. I don't want to sugarcoat it or try to make it any easier. You grew up here. You have a lot of memories in this house. Your mom . . ."

"Whatever," I say, leaning back against the pile of pillows, the book across my folded knees like a shield.

"Whatever?" Dad sits up straighter, pushing his thick hair away from his forehead.

"You've made up your mind, right?" I shrug. "I mean, it's not like this is a discussion. You had news. You shared it. What else is there to say?"

Dad holds my gaze for a few moments before slowly standing up. He turns at the door and clears his throat. "In the next few months, people may be coming by. To look at the house. One of Juliet's friends is a broker, and she said it would help if the place was kept . . . tidy."

I laugh, a hard chuckle. So that's what this is about. Cleaning my room.

"Yes, sir."

I mock-salute his back as he pulls the door shut. I glance quickly at the corners of my room, the room I slept in from the time we moved out of Max's. I look at the walls, the same light purple Mom chose and painted herself, wearing Dad's dirty overalls and a scarf in her hair.

I take the binder out from under my pillow. It doesn't matter, I think. What difference does it make where we live? And besides, as soon as I finish school and the band is signed, we'll be on the road again anyway. For good.

TEN

"THIS IS ABSURD."

Lula Bee lies on the floor of her room, staring at the fading glow-in-the-dark stickers that plaster the ceiling. Her wool coat is bundled up beneath her head, and perched on her abdomen is a pair of painted figurines from *Doctor Who*, which, I have already been scolded, I am a "pitiful philistine" for not yet watching. The assignment for our Social Sciences project rests against her folded knees, and she pelts the plastic figures at it, one by one.

" 'The Princess Effect and Disney Movies'? Who cares? Here's an idea: don't watch them," Lula huffs, crumpling the paper into a ball and tossing it under the bed.

I stretch my legs out across her bed and close my eyes. Everything about Lula Bee's room is different from the way I remember it: where there used to be Winnie-the-Pooh slippers in her closet there are now rows and rows of grungy low-top sneakers, and the Harry Potter posters on the walls have been torn down and replaced by graffiti-covered photos of the Sex Pistols and The Clash. But somehow, the room smells exactly the same: burnt popcorn, dirty laundry, and a subtle hint of incense, probably seeping in from her parents' room across the hall. "We have to choose a topic," I say finally. "And we have to do it soon."

Our project proposals are due on Monday, and so far all Lula Bee and I have managed to agree on is how much of a joke the class is, and that we'd each rather be working alone. It's not like I don't have plenty of other things I should be doing; there's an ever-growing list of calls to make for the band, and rehearsal at Max's in less than an hour. But the proposal deadline has been looming over my head like a cartoon storm cloud, and part of me is wondering if I should ask Alden to be paired with somebody else. That part of me grows exponentially when I hear an electronic ding and open one eye to see that Lula is turning on her computer.

"What are you doing?"

"What does it look like I'm doing?"

She clicks around on her laptop on her desk, opening iTunes. "It looks like you're watching a show about a time-traveling alien in a phone booth, which, believe it or not, has nothing to do with our project."

"Pick a topic, any topic," she says, clicking through her library of saved episodes. "It doesn't make any difference to me."

I haul myself up from the bed and attempt to smooth out the crumpled assignment. She's right; the suggested topics are terrible. I throw the paper back on the floor and browse Lula's bookshelf. She reads everything: classics, thrillers, graphic novels. When we were little, we would pile in Max's hammock and she would read to me from her favorite fantasy books. I could never get into them, could never keep all the worlds and characters straight, and she would get red-faced and flustered when I asked too many questions. For her eleventh birthday Mom helped me buy her the complete Harry Potter series, which she'd checked out from the library so many times she was put on a temporary lending block.

I see the box set now, on a top shelf, wedged beside a clear display box of beach treasures: shark's teeth, sea glass, and arrowheads we'd found together as kids on the cliffs. I take the box down and open it. My collection is in the basement somewhere, in a box of crap that Juliet cleared out of my room when I moved out. I can't remember the last time I held an arrowhead, its uneven edges cool and sharp in my palm.

"What about the island?" I murmur, mostly to myself.

"What about it?" Lula asks, ominous electronic theme music blaring from the flickering blue screen.

"Maybe we could do something about the island. Research the effects of growing up here, versus the mainland."

"What's to research?" Lula scoffs. "It sucks. The end."

I close the lid on the box of treasures and tuck them back on the shelf. "I mean, more than just annoying boat travel and no strip malls. Like, maybe it creates a certain kind of student?"

"Sure." Lula nods. "The kind of student who doesn't see first-run movies in the theater until they're already out on DVD."

"I'm serious," I say, leaning against the desk between Lula and her screen. "Maybe we're all hardwired to do things differently, to be different, than kids who grow up somewhere else."

Lula pretends to ignore me, but I can see the wheels turning. It almost looks like she's going to say something when a voice calls up from downstairs. "Lou! Tam! Grub!"

Lula rolls her eyes and flips the laptop shut. She starts toward the door and looks at me from the hall. "Coming?"

"Oh," I say, hurrying to gather my coat and bag from a pile on the floor. "I actually kind of have to be somewhere."

"Where?" Lula asks flatly, arms crossed over her small chest.

"Rehearsal," I say. "The band. I'm managing them again."

"Why?" she asks.

"Because they asked me to."

Lula runs her hands through her strawlike hair, a stack of silver snake bangles jingling down to her elbow. "Suit yourself," she says with a sigh. "But you're going to have to break it to Diane. She's been waiting for you like the Second Coming all week."

I follow Lula Bee downstairs and into the kitchen, where

Diane is standing at the stove, stirring a pot of something that smells like melted chocolate. Her hair, as always, is in a thick braid that grazes the tops of her hips, only now the chestnut brown is threaded with delicate strands of gray.

"Tamsen Baird," she says when she sees me. "Get over here."

I squeeze past Lula in the cramped kitchen—every surface is covered in dirtied mixing bowls, ceramic jars of all sizes, spices in little plastic baggies with scrawled labels on each side. Diane opens her arms and pulls me in for a long hug. There is nothing like a hug from Diane, and I feel myself melting into it, smelling the warm, familiar scent of her mix with the fragrant steam from the stove.

"It is disgusting how long it's been since I've seen you," she says, pushing me away to get a better look. "Look at you. You're a woman. You have tits."

"Mom," Lula barks.

"What?" Diane waves her off. "Did I say something we don't all know? A gorgeous feminine figure will not go unnoticed under my roof. And that's a promise."

"You're a menace," Lula says, opening the refrigerator and taking out a large glass jar filled with an unidentifiable brown liquid that could be anything from home-brewed kombucha to a woman's placenta; Diane works as a midwife and home birth advocate, and, beyond that, she loves to rile people up. "And don't get too carried away. She's not staying for dinner."

Diane drops her wooden spoon dramatically onto the antique stovetop, sending an abstract splatter up against the stucco walls. Lula's house is a hodgepodge of architectural styles; each room was designed at the whim of whatever Skip's mood happened to be at the time. The living room feels like a ski lodge, the kitchen like an adobe hut. It's disorienting, but somehow, all together, it works.

"This is a joke, right?" She turns to me with a pained grimace. "I made tofu mole!"

"It's pronounced mo-*lay*, my love," a piercing tenor interjects from behind me. Skip, layered up from feeding the goats, turns on the faucet and runs his hands beneath the water. He reaches around Diane's sturdy hips and gives her a squeeze; she's a good six inches taller than he is, a fact that both of them seem to relish. "Tamsen." He nods to me with a small bow. "What a treat."

"She's not staying." Diane pouts. "Which is *fine*. I made homemade tortillas, but we'll have to enjoy them ourselves."

"She's entitled to her own plans," Skip says lightly, winking at me. "How goes the project?"

"Swimmingly," Lula deadpans, grabbing a stack of plates from an open shelf on the wall.

"It's not so bad," I offer. "I think we finally have a topic, if Lula Bee would stop sulking for five minutes."

"Good luck," Skip says to me. "And hasn't she told you? It's *Lou*, now. Just *Lou*."

"I miss *Lula Bee*," Diane muses, reaching into the oven and pulling out a heavy dish stuffed with rolled tortillas and cheese. "It suits you."

Lula unfolds a handful of stained cloth napkins and tosses them in a heap on the table. "It suits a four-year-old in a dandelion costume," she says. "Or a braless folksinger from the sixties. It does not, in any way, suit me."

"Bras are overrated," Diane counters, serving up heaping mounds of the thick, sweet-smelling sauce. "What do you say, Tam?"

"Oh. Um. Bras?" I stammer. "I could take them or leave them, I guess."

"No, silly," Diane chortles. "Dinner. You're sure you can't sit down with us? Eat fast and skedaddle. That's what *Lou* does, anyway."

My stomach rumbles, and I think about the prospect of grabbing a yogurt at the convenience store next to Max's before rehearsal. Even a greasy plate of fries at the bar pales in comparison to Diane's feast. I feel Lula pretending not to look at me, pretending not to care what I decide.

"I'd love to stay," I say, draping my bag and coat over the back of a tall wooden chair.

Diane grabs my face in her hands and plants a wet kiss on my forehead. "There's my girl," she says. "Now, be a doll and finish setting the table. The forks are all dirty, just give them a rinse."

ELEVEN

WHEN THE FIRST THURSDAY OF THE MONTH ROLLS around again, Dad drives me to town for the meeting of mostly middle-aged widows, which is what I now call them in my head. Bunny left a voice mail this morning about a change of venue, but the message was garbled and pretty much the only thing I could decipher was something about Spring Street and an order to wear "leisure clothes."

Dad drops me off in front of the fudge shop. I look up and down the street for familiar faces. There are a bunch of people filing into the alehouse on the corner, hamming it up over who gets to hold the door open and who should walk in first. I glance down at my baggy jeans and one of Noah's zip-up sweatshirts. Pretty much all of my clothes have turned into "leisure clothes" lately, so Bunny's directive was convenient.

"Tam, right?" I hear a voice and spin around. One of the younger women from the group is sitting on a bench outside a storefront with a cramped-looking window display, featuring everything from skin care products to vacuum cleaners to dead-eyed stuffed animals. In typical island fashion, it's a store that took in a bunch of other stores when they were in danger of closing: toy-store-meets-hardware-store-meets-women's-boutique.

"Liza," the woman says, holding out her hand. I sit beside her and shake it awkwardly, that thing that happens when you run out of personal space but have already committed to the gesture.

"Hey." I smile. "Is this where we're supposed to be meeting?" I ask, looking over my shoulder. In addition to being a completely inappropriate location for a support group session, the mishmash museum also appears to be closed.

"No. The gym across the street," Liza says, glancing across a row of diagonally parked cars. At the end of the block is a thick wall of windows, revealing a mirrored room stuffed with shadowy hulks of fitness equipment. The glass is plastered with a peeling decal of a man's steroidal biceps, above the words ISLAND FITNESS: GET PUMPED! On some level it feels impossible that I've never noticed the gym before. I wonder if it's new, but the dingy, wall-to-wall carpet and the poster advertising an expired membership special tell me it's been here a while.

"We're meeting at a gym?" I ask. I wonder with a dull panic

if we'll be doing more playacting, perhaps improvising roles as coaches and trainers. I am momentarily terrified that this is an extension of the tiresome, endorphin-boosting argument: *Exercise! You'll feel better!* The last thing I feel like doing is working out with Bunny and a roomful of sad strangers.

Liza crosses her legs, clad in shiny spandex, and jiggles one snugly sneakered foot against the other. "Apparently," she says with a warm smile. "Bunny's kind of a trip, huh?"

I smile again. I take my phone out of my pocket and pretend to scroll through voice mails. Liza gives my shoulder a soft nudge. "I'm so sorry about Noah," she says.

I must do something weird with my face, because she starts apologizing more. "Sorry, sorry, that's probably creepy," she says. "I work with his mom's cousin. Marie? At the RE/MAX in the Plaza." My mind quickly scrolls through blurry faces of distant relatives until I remember Marie from the wedding. She gave us a set of margarita glasses and a big, colorful pitcher, and was mortified to remember that neither of us was yet of drinking age.

"Oh, right," I say. "Thanks. And you, too. I mean, sorry about . . . your . . ."

Liza smiles in a way that lets me know it's okay to stop. Her cheeks get full and cherublike, and a sharp, half-moon dimple plunges into one of them. There's a buzzing inside her purse, a canary yellow tote with big, silver hardware. She reaches into a small pocket for her phone and looks at me apologetically. "It's my kid," she says. "Just a sec."

She swipes at the screen and smiles. "Hey, buddy," she says. "What's up?"

I shift the angle of my hips to give her the idea of privacy, despite being practically in her lap. Liza chats with her kid about homework and sanctioned TV time, and at some point I decide that I like her. I think it's her smile. It's warm and genuine, and totally unnecessary given the fact that she has not only lost a husband but the father of her child. And I like that she's put together, but not in a way that makes me feel bad about my scrubby sweats. Her manicured nails and sleek ponytail appear to be part of her survival plan, and I respect her for having one.

"Sorry," she says again, once she's tucked her phone back into the outside pocket of her purse. "Logan. My youngest. He's decided he can't deal with my mother today, so I'm fielding all sorts of emergencies."

"How many do you have?" I ask.

"Emergencies?" She smirks, the dimple squirming back into place. "At least six. Daily."

"N-no," I stutter. "I meant kids."

"I know," she says. "That was me, trying to make a joke. Out of practice, I guess. I have three kids. Logan's five, Theo's eight, and Caitlin's eleven."

I do some quick and shoddy math in my head. "Wow," I blurt, still subtracting. "You don't look . . . I mean . . ." I realize there's no inoffensive way to remind her how old she already knows she is.

"Got an early start," she says. "Mike enlisted right after high school, so we got married before he shipped out the first time. My parents were thrilled."

"Yeah," I say. I look quickly down at the pavement, the mysterious sparkling flecks glinting in the glare of the Brewery's patio lights. "I know something about that."

The words are barely out of my mouth before I want to lasso them back in. Obviously, I meant the part about her parents. I have no idea what it's like to be married to a soldier. I've heard of a couple of island kids who went off to Afghanistan, but I've never known any of them personally. At the end of eighth grade we got a new principal, and he'd just done a tour in Iraq. He was always a little far-off in the eyes, like he was constantly tuned in to a different frequency than we were, but he never talked about it. The "war" has come to seem less like a thing that happens in an actual place, and more like a state of being that some people disappear into forever.

"Mike had cancer," Liza says. "A tumor on his spine. I always feel like I have to explain, because otherwise people think he died over there. And that's like, this whole other thing . . ."

I look up to see that she's flipping her hands over in her lap, again and again. It's stupid and petty but I find myself wondering if she's disappointed. Would it have been easier if he had died *over there*? Or would that have been worse?

I think about that, sometimes. I wonder if things would have been better or worse if Noah had been sick. Lots of people—at the funeral, Molly's friends who stopped by every afternoon, even teachers at school—seemed to think the abruptness was some sort of gift. "At least he didn't suffer," they'd all say, with the same hopeful, silver-lining looks on their faces: wrinkled foreheads, pursed lips, usually followed by a quick exhale and slight, knowing tilt of the head.

Part of me knows they're right. I know, deep in my bones, that it would have been excruciating to watch Noah go through something like that. But another part of me wants to kick those people in the head, or at least ask them what they think each day is like for us now. For Mitch and Molly and me and anyone who thought he would be here for six to seven more decades. Just because we didn't see it coming doesn't make it any less horrible. Or any more fair.

"Here they are." Liza stands, hoisting her bag over her shoulder. I follow her gaze to the front of the gym, where Bunny, in a neon windbreaker and billowing parachute pants, is greeting a group of women in Capri pants of varying lengths. She pops open the trunk of her toy-size Omni and lugs out an enormous drawstring sack, which she leaves on the ground to paw each of the women into a dramatic hug.

Behind them, I see a figure trudging up the street, and before I've even fully registered his face I know that it's Colin. He wears knee-length basketball shorts and a gray hooded sweatshirt with the words HARVARD LAW printed in maroon across the chest. On his head is a striped knit hat with a pom-pom on the top. There's something about him that looks old and young at the same time, and there's a faraway sadness in his eyes when they meet mine. I'm trying to decide whether to stare back or look away when Bunny tosses the bulky bag in his direction. He catches it with automatic ease.

The lobby is a closet-size room with a desk on one side and a series of yellowing anatomy posters on the other. Colin drops the bag with a thud and Bunny peers around a corner. "Anthony!" she calls out. "Yoo-hoo! We're here!"

Liza gives me a look and Colin clears his throat. Karen, the school librarian, studies one of the skeletons on the wall and wraps her wool coat tighter around her wide hips. A stocky, dark-haired man in a cutoff T-shirt and warm-up pants is suddenly standing in the doorway.

"There you are!" Bunny exclaims, closing him in a hug before he can protest. He pats the backs of her shoulders awkwardly with two hands, crinkling the shiny polyester of her coat.

"Hey, everyone," he says. "Welcome to Island Fitness. Bunny's brought some groups here before and we always have a good time."

Bunny beams and the rest of us trade uncertain glances. *A good time?* Doing what? I stare at Bunny's pants, which appear to be nautically themed, with purple and magenta wheels and anchors stamped on all sides.

"You brought the stuff?" Anthony asks vaguely. Bunny nods at the bag by her feet and he scoops it up, motioning for us to follow him out of the lobby. We walk through the "gym," which is really just the one empty room with rows of elliptical machines and Stairmasters and tiny TVs perched high in the cobwebby corners. Anthony ducks into a darkened doorway across from a pair of treadmills and pulls a cord on an exposed bulb hanging from the ceiling. There's a windowed door that he opens, and we huddle around behind him while he flips a series of switches on the walls.

The room is heavy with the unmistakable aroma of grimy socks and man sweat. The lights buzz and flicker, illuminating a giant boxing ring in the middle. *"Tada,"* Anthony says, with what is probably supposed to be fanfare. "This is where the magic happens."

"Boxing?" Karen crosses her arms on top of her peacoat, puffing air into the crest of her fluffy, rolled bangs. "You can't be serious."

Bunny claps her hands together and motions for Anthony to open the bag. "Welcome to Active Grieving: Stage Two," she says, as Anthony pulls out dusty black boxing gloves, Velcro-ed together in bulbous pairs. "Who knows what Stage Two is? Martha?"

Martha, a quiet woman with a blond bob and translucent skin, fidgets with her black-rimmed glasses. "It's anger, isn't it?"

"Anger!" Bunny booms. She tosses a pair of gloves to Martha, who bats them around in a slight, bewildered panic, before letting them drop to the floor. "First, we deny. We tell ourselves stories. We invent excuses to get away from what

106

we're feeling. And when that doesn't work, what happens? I'll tell you what happens. We get seriously, royally pissed."

Bunny plants another pair of gloves firmly in the middle of Colin's chest. He takes a few startled steps backward, into a wall hung with plaques and framed photos of dueling men in spandex. "I don't know about you," Bunny muses, "but when I lost my Rodrigo nine years back, I got pretty tired of talking about how *mad* I was feeling. Oh, everyone said it was okay. They said it was all right to feel angry. They told me to 'let it all out.' But I didn't feel like talking. I felt like hitting something. Or someone." She looks at each of us with a wild glint in her eyes. "So one day, I got the idea to call my old friend Anthony here, and see if we couldn't work something out."

Anthony has grabbed a broom from some hidden corner and is busy sweeping the ring. He gives a wave of acknowledgment and snaps the elastic barrier, a cloud of dust rising up around him.

"Don't worry." Bunny smiles. "Anthony's a pro. He won't let you get hurt. This is just about blowing off some steam. Moving around. Feeling something new."

I look from the pile of gloves to the ring. The clean yellow floor has started to shine and look almost magical. I can't explain it, and it sort of freaks me out, but I'm drawn to it, somehow.

"So who's first?" Bunny looks around at us. She kicks the final pair of gloves over to my feet. "Tam? You look pissed. Are you pissed?"

All eyes turn to me. There's a strange stirring in my veins, and I don't realize I'm laughing until I hear an unfamiliar chuckle bubbling up from my lips. "Yeah," I say finally. I reach down and grab the gloves, slipping my hands into the cool weave of the fabric. "Sure. I'm pissed."

"Good." Bunny nods. "You should be." She stuffs her hands into the pockets of her windbreaker and slowly turns her head to the rest of the group. "Who wants to spar with Tam?"

I look from one middle-aged woman to the next, feeling a sudden wave of regret. I imagine a lot of careful sidestepping and halfhearted bats to the shoulders.

"I'll do it."

Something catches in my throat, and I turn to see Colin wrapping on a pair of gloves. I look back to Bunny, certain she'll intervene. It's not that he's all that big or imposing—he's probably five feet ten or so, average build, shoulders slightly too broad for his frame—but, really? First, he confronts me after group for no good reason, and now he wants to fight?

"That's the spirit, Colin," Bunny cheers. I start to wonder about her credentials. What kind of grief counselor encourages a bunch of bereaved people who can barely get out of bed into hand-to-hand combat?

Anthony separates the elastic ropes and helps me up. I squeeze through the opening and Colin crouches up behind me. Anthony leads us to the center of the ring and stands with his hands on his hips.

"Okay," he says. "Either of you done this before?"

I shake my head.

"Not since I bit that guy's ear off," Colin mutters under his breath, which I guess is supposed to be funny because Anthony and Bunny laugh in short, loud bursts.

"Right," Anthony says. "So we're going to start with some footwork. This is how you want to be facing each other, yeah?" Anthony steps behind me and angles my shoulders so that I'm facing Colin from the side. "Now punch."

I look up quickly. "What?" Wasn't there supposed to be some kind of instruction happening? "That's it?"

"No, don't punch *him*, just punch." Anthony gestures to the air. "I gotta know your dominant side."

"Oh," I say. I try not to think too hard and stab my right fist forward. "That one, I guess."

"Good." Anthony nods. "So you want your other foot in front."

Anthony runs Colin through the same routine and soon we're hopping around in a circle, taking practice shots at the space between us. It feels completely ridiculous and also like the best thing I've done in months. It's like my muscles, which have all but disappeared into early retirement, are actually relieved to be doing something productive again. Soon I'm out of breath, but I keep bouncing around like a doofus, my eyes glued to the blurry black targets of Colin's covered fists.

"Good," Anthony shouts. "Gloves up. Keep your head and

neck protected. Little jabs with your left hand, that's just to get some space. Like you're saying, 'Back off, buddy.'"

I look up over the humps of my gloves to see that Colin's eyes are narrowed, and this sort of magnetic amber brown. He's shifting side to side, and all of a sudden he juts his front fist forward, giving my shoulder a gentle shove. It barely even registers but I pull in a quick breath, shocked to feel the cool, vinyl weight of the fabric on my clothes.

"Nice one, Colin!" Bunny shouts out from the floor. I see her clapping and nodding to the others in a failed attempt to rile them up. "Let's see it, Tam. Show him what you've got!"

I roll my eyes and keep bouncing. After a few turns of the circle dance, I push my left hand forward. It lands lightly near Colin's neck, higher than I'd hoped. "Sorry," I say reflexively.

"No you're not," Colin shoots back, a goading sparkle in his eyes.

I take a step away, feeling the muscles in my face tighten, a knot of tension growing between my shoulders. He leans forward to jab me again, this time near the ribs.

"Yeah! That's better," Anthony chimes in. "Next is the cross. When you're ready, you're gonna take your dominant hand, and you're gonna throw it across your body, connecting with your opponent wherever he—or she—is open. Got it?"

Colin dances around me, small beads of sweat forming on his hairline. He takes a few swipes and I duck, still holding myself at a careful distance.

"You think I don't know what you're doing?" he whispers, drawing himself up taller as he pushes into my space. "I mean, seriously. How long are you going to keep this up?"

"Keep what up?" I spit, between jagged breaths.

"Colin? You first," Anthony says. "Just to get a feel for the motion. You don't even need to make contact. Just work on the arc."

Colin nods and hops a few times before swiftly thrusting his back arm forward. It swipes the air in front of my torso. Instinctively, I hop back. I let out a lungful of air I didn't know I was holding. My pulse is now throbbing in every imaginable place—my chest, the veins on the side of my neck, my forehead, even the tips of my fingers, huddled together in the warm cocoon of the gloves.

"This little game of yours," Colin says, towering over me. He's so close I can smell him, detergent and shampoo mingling with new sweat. "It's a waste of time."

Without thinking, I lower my gloves to my sides. "Whose time?" I seethe. "And what makes you such an expert? You spent all of the last meeting practically asleep!"

Colin takes the opportunity to lunge forward, his back arm swinging in a clean, slow arc until it meets with my shoulder. It doesn't hurt, but it feels like he wanted it to.

"Nice, Colin!" Anthony cheers, and the crowd claps and hollers behind us.

Bewildered, I bob closer to the sides of the ring. "Okay,

Tam," Anthony says. "Your turn. Just the basics. You want to keep your abs tight, your shoulders loose. Like your arm is an extension of your core."

Anthony's voice mellows to a buzzing drone in the back of my head. All I can hear is my heart, the wheezy tunnel of my breath. My mind replays our last exchange, and I focus on the sharp twinges between my ribs as I fight to pull in more air.

Colin bounces toward me, holding his gloves in front of his face and peering out from behind them. "At least I'm being honest," he says. "What kind of a person cheats at therapy?" He lowers his fists to reveal a knowing half smile.

I feel my eyes turn into slits, my jaw lock tight. I wind up and throw my weight forward, a guttural groan pushing up from somewhere hidden and dark inside me. My fist lands on a soft patch of cheek first, but sinks quickly into a wedge of fragile bone. There's a crack—not a loud one, more like the splintering echo of ice at the top of a thawing pond. Colin yelps, and I lower my gloves, my eyes wide and unbelieving. Fat drops of blood splatter the neck of his clean sweatshirt, and Anthony is on him at once, with a towel.

"Jesus!" Colin shouts. My stomach turns. I shuffle back toward the corner of the ring, my pulse drilling in my ears. I keep my head down. I'm afraid that if anyone looks too close, they'll see it. They'll know. They'll know what I didn't, until it was too late. It wasn't an accident.

I wanted it to hurt.

TWELVE

THAT NIGHT, JULIET MAKES MY FAVORITE, FALAFEL
from a box and cucumber salad, but I barely eat a bite. My
arms and shoulders are throbbing, and every time I blink I
see the lingering shock on Colin's face as he stumbled back
into the ropes. He excused himself early and I sat in the corner, watching as the rest of the class took tentative turns in
the ring, but there was something spoiled in the air. It felt like
everyone was looking at me, waiting for me to do or say something crazy. Seven-thirty couldn't come fast enough.

After dinner, I curl up with my laptop in bed. I check my
e-mail to see that the booking agent for the festival has finally written back. He got the demo I sent last week and the
band is in, scheduled for a five p.m. slot on one of the smaller
stages on Sunday. I immediately call Eugene to share the good
news and set about making travel arrangements.

First, I book us a boat reservation online. We'll take Ross's dad's work van so we can all cram in, but it means we'll need to pay extra. I put it on my emergencies-only credit card, deciding to explain it to Dad later, but I realize when I'm trying to find a return trip that we'll need to stay in the city overnight. There's no way we'll make it back before the last boat.

Quickly, I find us two rooms in a cheap motel near the venue, typing in the credit card info again before I can change my mind. The guys are usually good about paying me back, I'll just have to keep track of expenses. I start a table on an empty page in the back of the binder and make two columns. My brain works quickly, my fingers struggling to keep up. It's been so long since I've done this, part of me was worried that I'd forgotten how. That I'd be too distracted by how weird it felt, organizing a band trip from my childhood bedroom, without Noah hovering at my shoulder, double-checking my every move. Instead, it feels immediately natural, like trying on a favorite pair of old jeans and discovering that they still fit.

My phone buzzes on the bedside table and I reach for it, still adding up the figures in my head. It's a Boston number, one I don't recognize, so I assume it's festival-related and answer in my "manager" voice.

"Tamsen Baird," I say, wedging the phone between my neck and shoulder.

"Colin Corwin," a flip, familiar voice answers on the other end.

I let the binder fall from my knees and sit up straighter. "Colin?" I check the clock across the room—9:57. "How'd you get this number?"

There's a long, staticky pause, and then a beeping sound, like a car door left open with the engine still on. "I did some snooping," he says. "Told Bunny I was worried about you, wanted to check in."

I roll my eyes and flip the binder shut. "Good to know where she stands on the issue of personal privacy," I mutter.

Colin laughs. "I'm pretty sure she felt bad for me," he says. "Bloody nose and everything."

I take a deep breath and stand in front of the full-length mirror on the back of my bedroom door. My hair is longer than it's been in a while, inches past my shoulders, and has assumed the lifeless, dirty-dishwater color it takes on every winter. "Is that why you called?" I ask. "You want me to apologize?"

"No," Colin says. There's a door-slamming sound and then a crunch of footsteps. "Plenty of time for that. I called because I'm downstairs."

"Downstairs where?" I ask quickly, before hurrying to my window and peering into the darkness. The sky is black and moonless, but I can just barely make out the shape of a person huddling at the edge of the floodlight's glare, on the sidewalk.

"See me?" He waves a hand over his head.

"What is this?" I ask, a timid tremble creeping into my voice. "She told you where I *live*, too?"

"No." I see him shaking his head. "You're in the phone book. Only Baird on the island, as luck would have it."

"What do you want?" I say, turning my back to the window, as if maybe, if I can't see him, he's not really there.

"Ice cream."

"What?" I scoff. "It's like seventeen degrees."

"So?" he asks.

"Right," I remember. "Not making sense. Your *thing*."

"You're a quick study." Colin laughs into the phone.

I look again at my reflection in the mirror. I'm dressed for bed, one of Noah's old T-shirts and black leggings. "It's late," I say. "Nothing is open."

"Planned ahead," Colin insists. "Check it out."

I peer back from behind the curtains to see Colin holding up a refrigerated bag from the convenience store, the one island establishment open past eight o'clock. "What do you say?" he asks, waving the bag back and forth. "I've got options."

I let the curtain fall and stare at the lacy trim for a long minute, suddenly paranoid that Colin can see me standing there, a conflicted silhouette, weighing pros and cons. I jump away from the window.

"My dad's home," I say. "You can't come in."

"Then come out," Colin counters.

I roll my eyes at my reflection. "Fine," I say. "There's a tool-shed behind the garden. I'll meet you there."

"Nothing says late winter like ice cream in a toolshed," Colin jokes.

I end the call and grab a long, tunic-like sweater from my closet. Over that, I snap on my blue puffy vest and add a checkered wool scarf. I push the door quietly open and tiptoe down the hall, listening for the TV in Dad and Juliet's room. Juliet is always asleep by nine, in order to effectively manage predawn kid wake-ups, and Dad rarely tears himself away from whatever late-night movie he's found on basic cable. Downstairs, I pad across the kitchen in my socks, slipping into my winter boots by the door. I noiselessly slide open the side door, nearest the garden, and step out into the night.

The yard is silent and creepy, old piles of slushy snow still blanketing the grass in random patches. My boots crunch quietly over the ice-crusted lawn as I walk toward the dark figure leaning against the shed.

"Hey," Colin says, too loud.

"Shhh!" I order, creaking the shed door open and pulling on the string attached to a bare lightbulb. Broken lawn mowers and rusted rakes cast eerie shadows on the paneled walls. I close the door behind us and clear a basket of gardening tools from one of Dad's old sawhorses, left over from the days when he actually did things around the house himself.

"Sit," I command, making room for myself on the dusty windowsill. A cold draft stings the back of my neck, and I wrap my scarf high around my cheeks.

"Yes, boss," Colin replies. He's wearing a North Face parka and cargo pants, for a combined total of about three hundred unnecessary pockets. The pants are rolled up over his leather boots to reveal a thick, flannel lining. In the dim yellow light of the bad bulb I see the beginnings of a giant purple bruise beneath one eye, and a swollen red spot near the bridge of his nose.

"Jesus," I mutter. He winces as he opens the white paper bag, pulling out two pints of Ben & Jerry's: Tennessee Mud and my all-time favorite, Cherry Garcia.

"It looks worse than it feels," he says, holding out a pair of plastic spoons.

"Really?" I ask, unable to mask the relief in my voice. I take a spoon and grab for the Garcia. Mom and I used to polish off pints by ourselves, sometimes skipping dinner in favor of a couchside splurge.

"No," he says. "Not really. Hurts like a bitch."

I push the toes of my boots against the bottom of a box of old beach toys. A battered striped umbrella leans out of the top, and a stack of plastic buckets is wedged against the wall. "I didn't mean to do it," I say. I peel off the top of the carton and scrape my spoon against the frozen surface.

"Sure you did," he replies lightly.

I scoop a cold bite and roll it around on my tongue. "Yeah," I mumble. "I did. But I didn't know I would hit you so hard."

"I deserved it." Colin shrugs. "I shouldn't have said what I said."

I swallow and feel the cold spreading across my chest. My eyes get narrow and the weird flip-flops are back in my stomach. Despite the fact that I basically broke his face, Colin went out of his way to bring me ice cream. It's confusing.

"Which is not an apology," he clarifies. "I meant every word. I just maybe could have said it in a way that was less—"

"Dickish?" I supply.

Colin nearly chokes on his Tennessee Mud. "Sure." He smiles. "Less dickish."

I swallow another spoonful and try to shake off the impending brain freeze. It's totally bizarre, eating something so cold outside in the middle of March, but it also feels sort of daring, and surprising. It makes me wonder if this is what Colin is after, with his strange "no sense making" agenda.

"I don't know," he says, tugging at the front of his light brown hair. There's a patch in the middle that looks thicker and darker than the rest. It sticks up in all directions like a stubborn cowlick and seems to be the perfect length for distracted twirling. "I know I'm not exactly a model support group member, but I could tell you were . . . From the minute you started talking, at the first meeting, it was like some sort of challenge. Like I was on this mission to get you to do something real."

I force a hard laugh. "Mission accomplished."

Colin nods, but he still doesn't look satisfied. He stares through the shed's one window, dark and layered in a grimy sheen. "You were right," he says eventually. "I have no idea how this stuff is supposed to work. Who am I to say you're doing it wrong?"

His eyes get that lost, cloudy look again and for a second it seems like he might keep talking, but he shovels in another bite instead.

"I don't think there's a right way to do it," I offer, after a pause that feels too long. "If that makes you feel any better."

Colin looks at me for a moment before breaking into a smile. I'm not sure I've seen him really smile before, and it does something dramatically goofy to his face. Maybe it's just the bruising, or maybe it's that the rest of him looks so serious, so proper and refined. "Not really," he says. "But thanks."

I laugh, resting the frosted pint on the sill beside me.

"Can I ask you something?" Colin starts. He leans against the wall, making room for his head between two mesh clamming nets that probably haven't seen the bottom of a pond in a decade.

I stuff my icy fingers in my pockets to warm up. "I guess."

"Were you really married?" Colin looks at me intently, his light eyes swirling in the glare of the bulb. "I mean," he continues, "I know you're still in high school, so I'm guessing you're not as old as you look."

"I'm seventeen," I say.

"Seventeen," he repeats. "And you were married?"

"Yes, I was married," I say firmly. "For six weeks. But we were together forever. He was older."

"Wow," he says. "That's . . . that's really cool."

"Is it?" I ask. "Didn't work out so well."

"True." He nods. "But at least you got that time together, you know? Almost like you knew you had to make the most of it."

I feel around for the cool band of my ring with my thumb. I've tried taking it off a few times, but it never lasts long. My finger, my hand, my whole body feels missing without it. "Never thought about it that way," I admit.

"Anyway." Colin shrugs. "I'm impressed. When I was seventeen I was still operating under the kindergarten philosophy of 'Girls have cooties.' I mostly just did a lot of pissing them off."

"Sounds familiar," I say.

Colin raises his spoon to his lips and holds it there. "I guess old habits die hard." He smirks. "I'll bring it up with my therapist."

"You have a therapist?"

"Yeah," he says. "Don't you?"

"No," I say. "Not anymore. I used to, when I was a kid." I can feel Colin's questioning glare. "My mom died when I was ten."

"You're kidding," he responds, dropping the spoon in the half-eaten pint in his lap.

121

"Be a pretty weird thing to joke about."

"No, sorry." Colin leans forward, as if to touch my knee, but pulls his hand away. "I just meant . . . that's a lot of shit luck for one person."

I shrug. "It happens," I say. "You adjust."

"How'd she die?" he asks. "If you don't mind . . ."

"Car accident," I say. "Hit and run off-island. Never found the guy."

"I'm sorry," he says. I expect him to say more—people usually find the need to relate the experience back to themselves, tell me about the person they've lost, or a friend of a friend who died the same way—but he doesn't. He shakes his head and picks up his spoon and keeps eating.

"So why are you here?" I ask abruptly. "On the island. I mean, you must have a job or something."

"I took a leave of absence," he says. "My parents have a beach house. It's empty all winter long. They thought I should . . . regroup."

"How's it going?" I press.

"Well it was going great," Colin says. "Until I got jumped in the alley. Some angry young-widow type."

I laugh. It's one of the first times that it's happened naturally in a while, and it sort of catches me off guard. I clear my throat. "Sounds scary," I say.

"What about you?" he asks. "Your parents—your dad—is he on you all the time?"

"Sort of," I say. "Moving back home was an adjustment. But I'm starting to work again, which helps."

"Work?"

"I manage a band," I say. "It was actually . . . Noah . . . my husband, it was his band. I've been helping them out since they started."

"Helping how?" Colin asks.

"Just organizing things, going with them to shows." I shrug. "Whatever they need."

"What about school?"

"Haven't really figured that out yet," I say. "Their first show is on Sunday. I'm not sure I'll make it back in time for classes Monday morning . . ."

Colin nods. "And this way it's like nothing's changed."

"What do you mean?"

Colin drops the spoon into the bag and stuffs the ice cream on top. "Just that it's a way for you to keep pretending that everything is the same as it was," he says. "I tried it for a while, too." He nods. "Doesn't work."

I look up quickly and catch Colin's eye. He holds my gaze, another challenge. I force a smile and pass him back the ice cream. "Thanks for the tip," I say. "I should go."

"Hey." He stops me with an arm on my shoulder. "I'm sorry. I know what it's like. And I really don't want to be another person always saying the wrong thing . . ."

"You've got a funny way of showing it," I say. I walk over

to the door and pull it open, holding out an arm. "I have to get to sleep."

Colin stands and collects the paper bag, shuffling across the shed. Outside, he waits for me to latch the door and follows me back to the house.

"Tam," he says when we reach the snow-covered deck.

"Would you please be quiet?" I hiss over my shoulder. "I don't even know what you're doing here."

"I told you," he whispers. "I wanted to make sure you're okay."

I stare at him through narrowed eyes, my scarf whipping around my face in the bitter wind. "I'm fine," I say. "I'm great. I'm sorry about your nose. Is that all?"

Colin stares at me, a sad slouch tugging at the corners of his lips. "Yeah," he says. "That's all."

He walks slowly into the darkness, toward the silhouette of his car. I watch him open the driver's door and slide in, the interior light glowing off the top of his cropped hair.

I quietly pull the sliding door open and carefully shut it behind me. Colin's car hums to a start and I glance outside to watch him drive away, but all I can see in the darkened glass is my own fuming reflection.

THIRTEEN

"YOU'RE SURE YOU DON'T WANT ME TO WAIT?"

Dad pulls into an open spot in the supermarket parking lot, and I reach for the backpack near my feet. It's jam-packed with everything I'll need for a night in the city, but I play it off like it's just the usual books and folders and quickly swing the car door open.

"It's okay," I say. "She's always late. I'll get a snack first or something."

Dad nods and taps the steering wheel with his fingers. "Tell Lula Bee I say hello." He smiles. "Skip and Diane, too."

"I will." I nod, and then remember the script I've rehearsed all weekend. "Oh, Dad? There's a chance we might be up late working. I know it's a school night, but we have this big project proposal due tomorrow, and it might be easier if I just stay the night. Hitch a ride to school in the morning with them. Is that okay?"

I see the conflicting emotions playing across Dad's face: not trusting me, wanting to trust me, wanting to believe I'm making friends and doing well in school. "Sure," he says. "Just call if you need a ride."

"I will," I promise, hovering at the door. Lately, there are moments like this, obvious hug-moments, when it feels like one of us should make some kind of an effort. But neither of us does, and I close the door with a wave. "See you tomorrow night."

Dad honks twice as he pulls away, and I exhale for the first time in hours. Across the parking lot, the ferryboat is gliding into the harbor, unloading rows of cars and hordes of travel-weary passengers.

I scan the parking lot for Ross's van, a big white utility vehicle with DAVIDSON ELECTRIC blazoned on one side. I check the time on my phone; I'm early, and rarely have the guys arrived for a boat reservation with more than a few minutes to spare.

Which is good, because I have plenty to do to keep busy. I start by ducking inside the grocery store, pulling up a list on my phone. I do a quick round, stocking up with the guys' snack favorites: gummy candies for Ross, hummus and crackers for Teddy, cut-up pineapple and cheese sticks for Eugene. At the deli counter, I order sandwiches, one for each of us, getting an extra turkey club on wheat with bacon and avocado for Noah, as a sort of tribute. I have no idea what Simone likes, but I take another spin through the produce aisle, piling my basket with apples and grapes and an armful of coconut waters. She doesn't strike me as much of a snacker.

Back outside, I lug my bags to a bench and prepare to get comfortable when I see a familiar figure whizzing by on a beat-up bicycle. Lula Bee dismounts at the corner and chains her bike to a lamppost before ducking inside the tattoo shop a few stores away.

I hustle up the block to meet her. I'd meant to call yesterday, to explain about missing class and to get our stories straight—the last thing I need is Dad finding some reason to call her house and learning I never showed up—but between last-minute show prep and sitting in on rehearsals, I never got around to it.

Now, I stare in through the shop's window and watch as Lula sits in the corner with a laminated book of designs, thoughtfully thumbing through the pages. I push the door open, the tinkling of chimes quickly drowned out by the angry, punk music piped in through speakers on the walls.

"Lula B—" I stop myself as she looks up sharply. "*Lou.* Hey."

There's a quick, confused scramble behind her heavily madeup eyes. "What are you doing here?" she spits. On the other side of the room, half-shielded by a curtain, is a big, bearded guy in his early twenties, every available inch of visible skin covered in intricate and colorful tattoos. He's hunched over a long table, and all I can make out of the re-clining client is her hair, long and curly and hanging down through a hole in the headrest. She cries out once, fast and muffled, and I wince.

"I—I was in town," I say. "Saw you riding by. Thought I'd say hi."

"Hi," Lula parrots abruptly, glancing at the door. "Anything else?" She crosses her arms, her eyes shifting quickly back and forth from me to the threatening buzz of the needle.

"Can we talk for a second?" I ask. "Outside?"

Lula huffs and closes the heavy binder. "Be right back, Gus," she calls out to the man behind the curtain. He looks up with a slow nod and Lula Bee follows me outside.

"Are you getting a tattoo?" I ask as soon as we're on the street.

"No," she says, leaning against the window and puffing her uneven neon bangs away from her face. "Maybe. I haven't decided." She waves me off. "What's up?"

"Well," I begin, shifting my heavy shopping bags from one shoulder to the other. "It's the project."

Lula bends one knee and plants her foot against the window, her head resting near a decal of a lotus blossom floating beneath the words TINY'S TATTOOS. "Yeah?" she prompts.

"We're supposed to present our ideas tomorrow," I remind her. "Only . . . it turns out, I don't think I can be there."

"Why not?" Lula asks.

I lower the bags into plastic heaps on the sidewalk and stretch out my fingers. "I'm sorry," I say. "Something came up, and . . ."

"Let me guess," she says. "The band."

I nod. "There's this show," I explain. "In Boston. I helped them get it, so I kind of have to be there . . ."

As my voice trails off, Lula stares at me hard. There's something familiar in her eyes, the same look she used to give me when we were kids, playing a game she was letting me win.

"I emailed you my notes," I tell her. "You can basically just get up there and read them. Tell Alden I'm sick or something. Can you do that?"

She keeps staring, long and intense, like she's seeing somebody else. Somebody she used to know but hasn't seen in a while. Or somebody she's been trying to avoid.

"Thank you," I say, reaching out instinctively to touch her arm. She looks down at my hand, like it's infected. I pull my fingers lightly away. "I mean it."

"Sure," she says, turning to go back inside. "Have fun."

"Lula?" I call after her as she pushes inside. "There's one more thing."

"Of course there is," she says, the chimes jangling as the door snaps shut.

"I kind of told my dad I was staying at your house tonight, so . . . you know, if he asks . . ."

Lula Bee smirks, the bottom of her black coat flapping around her knees. "You want me to lie for you?"

I look at her with pleading eyes.

"Lula, please," I beg. "I promise I'll make it up to you when I get back. I'll do the rest of the project myself, all right?"

Lula takes a breath, shakes her head once, and pushes into the door. "Sure you will," she says lightly. "Just don't forget to come home, okay? I was starting to get used to having you around."

I smile and lean down to scoop up my bags from the sidewalk.

"Tam?" she says, one foot wedged inside the door.

"Yeah?"

She nods in the direction of the open sea, and the mainland, the real world, beyond it. "Be careful," she says.

I try to wave her off but I don't really have a free hand, so I end up sort of shrugging, and Teddy's hummus topples out onto the curb.

"I'll be fine," I say, struggling to pick up the plastic container and hoping it hasn't spilled. "It's only one night."

Lula watches me as I awkwardly arrange the bags over my wrists and shoulders, before disappearing back into the shop. Through the glass, I see her walk to Gus and hover near his shoulder, admiring his latest commission.

I trudge back toward the parking lot, searching for Ross's van and praying we won't miss the boat.

. . .

The ride up to Boston is mostly uneventful, and it isn't long before we've all settled into our usual roles. Ross at the wheel, insisting on messing with the complicated sound system he and his dad have rigged up in the van, never getting through more than the first few bars of a new song before punching at buttons to find another. Teddy up front, mocking the GPS and giving us all minor panic attacks when he's sure we've missed an exit. And Eugene and me, crouched in the open backseat, our legs tangled in coiled wires, a toolbox clattering around behind us.

The only difference, aside from the glaring absence of Noah, is the just-as-glaring presence of Simone. Despite the frigid outside temperatures, she wears a flowery pair of short-shorts and a completely transparent white blouse (the better to see the flower print on her lacy black bra), and from the time we get off the boat she doesn't stop talking. She talks about a new crepe place near the venue that she wants to try. She talks about all the friends she has coming to see her debut. She talks about the logic behind her wardrobe, and the five other outfits she vetoed before settling on this one. Finally, Ross gently suggests that she give her vocal cords a rest, in preparation for the show. I try to stifle a smile.

Soon, it's just like it always was. Teddy whines about some girl he's been stalking and I tell him to try giving her space. "You're in a band," I remind him. "All you have to do is get her to a show. The rest takes care of itself."

Ross nags Eugene about finding a girlfriend, and I tell him

to back off. "Some people like to take their time before settling down," I pointedly tell him. "You know, make sure they've found the right person?"

Ross tosses me a glare in the rearview mirror and glances anxiously at Simone, but she's had her headphones on since he told her to stop talking, humming quietly as she stares out the window.

As we near the club, I break out the Bible and start going over logistics. "Sound check's at noon," I say. "Then we have a few hours to rehearse and get ready. I'll get the merch together"—I eye the box of T-shirts and CDs at my feet— "and meet you back in the dressing room around four-thirty. You go on at five on the dot, and the set can't be longer than forty minutes. So if you want to do the encore"—I flip to a page with the printed set list—"I'd say skip 'Elevator Girl,' and 'You and the Rest,' and go right into 'Feed Me, Friend,' et cetera. Sound good?"

The guys mumble favorable responses, and I see Simone slip out her earbuds. "Sorry," she says, lightly touching my knee with two fingers. Her nails are painted in alternating pastels with tiny flowers stuck on every other one. "But wouldn't it make sense to keep 'Elevator Girl,' and do that before the encore? It's just so powerful, you know? So intense."

I feel the skin on my neck burning and force myself to keep my breath steady. "Elevator Girl" was the first song Noah ever wrote about me, about the time I got stuck in an elevator on a middle school field trip to the science museum. He wasn't there, but he made up a story about it, about how I fell asleep and rode the elevator all the way to find him, in my dreams.

I rub my ring in tight, anxious circles around my finger. The idea of Simone singing my song—*our song*—makes me want to jump out of the moving van and hitchhike all the way home.

"She's right," Teddy agrees quietly, from the front seat. "It's a great song." I feel Eugene's eyes on the side of my face, Ross's glance in the mirror. Nobody says anything else and there's a heavy, loaded pause.

"Okay then," I finally agree, making a few quick notes in the margins of the set list. Ross inches up behind a big catering bus, into a temporary loading zone. Teddy turns around, a playful smile on his face.

"Let's do this."

FOURTEEN

THE BACKSTAGE AREA IS A SERIES OF DARK, LOW-ceilinged rooms, packed with performers and their attendants. I watch the show from the wings, reliving the familiar sensation of hearing both their actual voices and the sound system, staring at the bobbing backs of their heads and seeing the joy on the faces in the crowd, all at once. The set is flawless; nobody would have guessed that Simone hasn't been singing with the guys forever. It is surreal and sort of uncomfortable at first, but eventually, even I forget that things are different. It just feels right. And as much as it pains me to admit, she is a total natural in the spotlight.

I sneak deeper backstage during "Elevator Girl," but the strains I hear of Simone's clear voice are strong and compelling. The song sounds completely different; they'd been rehearsing it more up-tempo, and it has a new, sort of jazzy swing. Simone's voice is light and sweet, nothing like Noah's gravelly drawl, but somehow, even tucked far away at one corner of the makeshift bar and buffet, I can tell that it works.

When the show is over, the guys and Simone filter through the curtains, the crowd on their feet and cheering raucously behind them. One of the sound techs pats Ross on the back and a friend of Simone's, a dreadlocked drummer from another band, is tangling her in a hug. Eugene makes his way over to me, his black hair damp with sweat, and perches his bass against the wall. "What'd you think?" he asks. "Okay?"

"Okay?" I laugh, passing him a bottle of water from the cooler. "You guys were completely on fire!"

I grab a few more bottles and hand them to Ross and Simone, already snuggling on one of the ratty couches. Teddy pushes through a beaded curtain, sandwiched by a couple of older guys in expensive-looking T-shirts and intentionally beat-up blazers.

"You guys," he says, eagerly standing between us. "Look who's here."

It takes me a minute to place them—we've only met in person once, at a show in Providence, and most of our communication has happened on the phone or over e-mail—but then it hits me: the label guys, from LoveCraft. Jon and Jeremiah.

Lots of half hugs and pats on the back follow. Simone jumps in to introduce herself and is rewarded with fawning fanfare.

"The new sound is really solid," Jon or Jeremiah is saying. "Building on the same foundation, that authentic, rootsy feel. But, you know, also totally fresh."

"We're into it," the other one agrees. "All of it."

Teddy practically squeals. "They want us back!" The guys share quick, stunned smiles before the room is swallowed in chaos. There are laughs and hollers and high fives, and Eugene grabs me in an uncharacteristically enthusiastic hug.

"It's happening!" somebody shouts. "It's really happening!"

Around me, Jon and Jeremiah are already spouting through logistics. "I know you guys had a tour planned, before Noah . . ."

"We're so sorry, by the way . . ."

"And I know you worked hard on it, but the thing is, we've got this great band looking for an opener."

"Lucia and the Kicks?"

Ross's eyes bulge and Simone squeals like she stepped on a rat. *"Lucia?"* she repeats. "You're shitting me."

"We are not shitting you," Jon says.

"The thing is," Jeremiah goes on, "it starts in two weeks. The band that was supposed to open, well, they had a thing, some disagreement, yadda yadda. So if you're into it . . ."

"We're into it!" Teddy shouts.

Ross tousles Eugene's hair and now it's Teddy, hoisting me up by the waist and spinning me around.

"Okay, okay." I giggle. As soon as I'm back on solid ground, I steady my thoughts. If this is real, there's work to be done.

I reach for my binder in my bag, stashed on a chair in the corner. I crack it open and stand between the label guys, ready to talk shop. "Two weeks?" I say, making a show of pretending to check our calendar, confirming that we don't already have anything booked. "I think we can make that work. You want to just e-mail me the details? I can handle van rentals, hotels, that kind of thing."

"No need." Jeremiah beams. "It's all squared away."

"We have a great gal at the office, Rhea, she takes care of all that." Jon nods. Alarm and confusion must be spreading across my face at a rapid rate because he quickly puts a hand on my arm. "Don't worry," he says. "They're in good hands. I promise."

I swallow and take a step back as Teddy suggests a diner around the corner where they can all go to sit down and hammer out the details. Ross and Simone are engaged in some heavy celebratory petting on the couch, and Eugene packs up his bass. Suddenly, it's like they're all frozen, or I am, watching them as if they're projected on a screen, artificial and far away.

They don't need me. They're going to leave, and I'm going to stay. Just as my life was starting to feel the slightest bit normal, just when things started to make sense, I'm right back where I was eight months ago. Floating. Lost. Alone.

"Coming?" Eugene asks as they start to shuffle through the crowded hall. I'm hunched over my bag, packing up the snacks that nobody ate. I'm afraid to look at him or open my mouth to speak. I don't trust the throbbing pressure behind my eyes, the stinging tension in my jaw.

"Tam," he says lightly. "Come eat."

I shake my head quickly, staring at the threadbare laces of his boots.

"It's just one tour," he says. "It's not like we'll never see you again. And besides, you have school."

I surreptitiously wipe at an escaped tear in the corner of one eye. "I know that," I say, my voice thick with phlegm.

"It's what Noah would have wanted," he says. "Right?"

I look back at the floor. There's a burning in my stomach and I suddenly have the urge to punch him. It is *not* what Noah would have wanted, I feel like screaming. Noah would have wanted to be here. Noah *should* be here. The rest of you owe everything to him.

Instead, I clear my throat. "I think I'm going to meet up with some friends," I say evenly. "I'll catch you guys back at the motel. The room's under my name. You'll need to get a key."

I shoulder my bag and tug at the hem of my dress, a simple black V-neck with a belt that Noah loved, turquoise with a big silver buckle. I push past Eugene into the throng of musicians excitedly waiting to go onstage, or celebrating already-finished sets. My face is burning and my chest feels tight, but I keep walking, faster, faster, until I can see the door.

.   .   .

138

Outside, the air is sharp with cold. I walk a few blocks with my head down, tears stinging my eyes in the wind. I find a strip of seedy-looking bars and turn into the first one. There's a crooked sign swinging from a post that says LUCKY's, though it's fairly obvious that nobody has gotten lucky in this place in years. It's on a dark corner, across from a convenience store, the neon light of an outdoor ATM blurring through the snow-streaked window.

I choose it because there's no bouncer. There's an empty stool inside the door and a pool table along one wall. Rowdy country music blares from a jukebox in the back. It looks like a bar from a scene in a bad movie, where two brothers fight over a pageant queen or a drug deal goes predictably wrong.

The bar is crowded and hot. I take off my coat and hold it in front of me, like a shield. I don't know what I'm doing here, just that it's too cold to keep walking and I have nowhere else to go. The thought of cramming into a crowded booth with the band and the label guys, going over tour stops and set lists over plates of soggy fries, is, frankly, horrifying. On the other hand, nothing sounds more pathetic than sitting in an empty motel room, waiting for the guys to come home and tell me all about it.

I make a beeline for the restroom, because suddenly I feel like I might be sick. There's a line and I push to the front, ignoring the angry protests of the three women waiting. The door opens and I barrel inside, locking the door behind me.

The bathroom is tiny and has been painted bloodred, with

a single dingy bulb in a broken fixture over the mirror. I bend over the toilet and heave but nothing comes up. I wait, and I wait, and then I start screaming, because it feels like the next best thing. I scream until my voice is hoarse and my throat is raw. Then I run the faucet over my wrists and stare at my shadowy reflection. Mascara runs down my face, my skin is pale and dull. I look terrible. I feel terrible. I can't believe I'm here.

I take a few breaths and throw my hair in a messy bun. I walk back into the bar, skirting the glares of the women outside. I find an empty stool at the far end of the bar, next to a pair of middle-aged women with spray tans and low-cut blouses. One of them is wearing perfume that smells like a candy factory, or else she works in a candy factory. It instantly makes my head throb.

I look around the room and quickly realize that something in me wanted a bar because I thought it would feel familiar. I'm not sure what it says about me that my comfort zone is a place with loud music and sticky floors, but it is. So far, the only thing familiar about this place is the array of beers on tap. I miss Max, and would give just about anything to hear him behind me, calling me "Pickle" and giving me a hard time.

I drop my head in my hands. I don't know why but something about this feels worse than anything's felt in a long time. Losing Noah, like losing Mom, was miserable, but it was misery that made sense. That everyone could understand.

My insides burn and I kick the leg of the stool, slowly, again and again. The truth fills me up like cold concrete.

Who was I kidding? Did I really think I could tag along forever? Of course the band would move on, find another label, a real manager, not need me anymore. This is their life. Their big shot. I'm just a kid. How could I have been so naïve?

A new song comes on the jukebox, a sappy country ballad. I close my eyes again and for some reason I see Colin. A quick burst of shame tickles the tops of my ears. He was right. I thought I could just jump back into the way things were. *He was right.* I expect to be furious, to feel the familiar boiling rage that I felt when he confronted me after the first meeting. But instead, I just feel empty.

"Hey."

I look up to see that a guy has wedged his way between my shoulder and the candy factory lady. He's not bad-looking, maybe in his mid-to-late twenties, with light brown hair and a crescent-shaped scar between his eyes. It makes him look confused, or pissed off, but he's smiling, a sly, lopsided smile. He looks like his name might be Tucker.

"Hey," I say. I inch away from him on my stool, as far as I can get without falling. I turn my head but I'm stuck against the wall, and there's only so much staring at the framed health inspection certificates I can do before my neck cramps up and my eyes start to blur.

"There are hooks, you know," the guy says. I look back at him and he's pointing at a pair of silver hooks, stuck beneath the lip of the bar. He gestures to the coat in my lap. "If you want."

"Oh," I say. "That's okay. It's cold out."

The guy laughs. "You can say that again." He has nice, even teeth, and longish hair that curls around his ears. He seems like the kind of guy who has trouble talking to girls in bars, but is working on it. Or maybe he's on a dare. I glance quickly over his shoulder, half expecting to find a posse of whispering bros in the corner, monitoring his progress, egging him on.

"Can I get you a drink or something?" he asks.

I look quickly down at my fingers, locked together in my lap. I think of Molly, and I see the distance in her eyes, the fog of nothing that surrounds her. I blink and see Noah's face. My stomach twists. I want to feel nothing. I want a drink. A real drink. Just one, to make me numb again.

"Sure," I say eventually. "Vodka soda," I blurt, like I've done it a million times before. "With a lime. Thanks."

The guy smiles and bobs his head a few times, his hair flopping into his eyes. He leans across the bar and passes on the order.

The bartender mixes my drink and the guy pulls a twenty from his pocket. As he waits for his change, he turns to me, pushing the glass across the bar. "Here you go," he says.

I reach out, closing my fingers around the frosty glass. "Thanks."

He watches me raise the drink to my lips. "You're not twenty-one, yet, are you," he says with a smirk, more of a statement than a question.

I take a long sip, the bitter, fizzy cold sloshing into my belly. My head throbs, and I feel sick. Sick of being too young. I'm too young to live alone. I'm too young to manage a band. I'm too young to buy a drink, or have one bought for me by a guy I don't even like. "No," I finally sigh, with a pathetic little chuckle. "Is that a problem?"

He looks at me and there's something new in his eyes, something almost pitying and real. "Unfortunately for you, it's a big problem," he says quietly, reaching into his pocket again. This time he flashes a palm-size shiny badge. My stomach twists and drops as he gently grips my forearm and ushers me down from the stool. Without another word, he weaves me through the oblivious crowd, pushing the door open with one foot and leading me onto the cold city street, where the cop car is patiently waiting.

FIFTEEN

"BAIRD. TAMSEN."

I hear my name through a fog that must be sleep related, though I can't imagine I was actually sleeping. I roll over on the cardboard cot, the scratchy, standard-issue wool blanket bunched in a pile at my feet. I'm still wearing my shoes, my dress, even my jacket and scarf. I think part of me thought if I didn't disrobe the whole thing might be temporary, or a dream. But it's morning now, a gray dull light creeping around the bars in the windows, and I'm still here.

A broad-faced woman in uniform stands at the foot of my bed. "Ready?" she barks.

I thread my arms through my coat and kick my feet to the floor. Across from me is another cot, and the shape of a girl, still sleeping. She didn't move when I was brought in last night, just stared at me from her cocoon of itchy blankets, the whites of her eyes glowing in a square of the dusty light from a streetlamp that shone through the window between our beds.

It's not a jail, the cop had said, as he walked me to the door. He almost sounded sorry, explaining the spate of sorority girls he'd been snatching up undercover. He wasn't expecting a trip to the juvenile detention center, a ramshackle building in a broken part of the city, with rusted bars on the windows and rows and rows of runaways. I shuffled down the center aisle, wondering how many of them were grateful for a bed, and how many, like me, were just dumb.

"Ready for what?" I grumble at the woman impatiently tapping her foot in the hall. My head is pounding, hangover heavy, though I know it's not from drinking. It's worse. A life hangover, the muddy echoes of every idiotic thing I've ever done humming in my ears like an engine, stalled.

"Check-out time," the woman says drily, turning and stomping toward the stairs. "Don't forget to tip the bellman."

I keep my eyes on the crooked boards of the dusty floor, the shadows of sleeping figures blurring on either side of the aisle. Some are already awake, braiding hair, staring vacantly out the windows. I feel their eyes on me, hating me for leaving. *You go*, I want to tell them. *I'll stay.*

I'm buzzed through a series of doors and long hallways, until we reach the lobby, the same dingy room where the cop brought me in last night. A girl with a bloodied lip was flailing between two tired-looking officers, screaming about her rights and somebody named Dominic. There's no sign of the struggle now, just a neat row of yellow chairs, a table stacked with piles of brochures on health screenings and where to get free socks.

Standing by the door, lost inside a puffy black parka, is Judge Feingold. I look around the room, half expecting to see Dad sitting in one of the chairs. She must be here for somebody else, I reason, at the same time knowing how unlikely that would be.

I watch without speaking as she approaches the glass partition. The woman is now on the other side and passes over a thick envelope. "You'll get a notice about a court date in the mail," she says. "Don't throw it away. People always think it's junk and throw it away. It's not junk. It's important. Got it?"

She's talking to the judge but looking at me. "Yes," I say, though I'm not sure that I do.

"Is that everything?" Judge Feingold asks, gesturing to my bag, which is suddenly sitting in a heap by my feet on the dirty linoleum floor. It was taken away from me at some point last night, or must have been, because I haven't seen it since I got here.

"Yeah," I say, slowly bending over to pick it up. I watch as the judge starts toward the door, reaching into her pocket for a pair of thick wool mittens.

"Let's go," she says, nodding outside.

I follow her silently across the street, to where her car, a faded, moss-green Outback, is parked. She gets in first and leans over to unlock my door. I climb in carefully, clutching my bag to my lap, and don't say anything until we're moving.

"Why are you here?" I ask as we're pulling onto the highway.

"I think you mean *thank you*," she replies, her eyes glued to the road ahead. It's early and there's little traffic leaving the city, just open lanes and a dusty morning sky.

"Thank you," I say quietly. She flips on the radio, NPR, and doesn't say another word for the rest of the drive to the boat. I zone in and out of stories about rising gas prices, endangered ospreys, and political unrest in places I couldn't point to on a map. I stare silently through the window as the city fades and the sky expands, trying to figure out what went wrong.

• • •

An hour later we pull into the harbor and the attendant ushers Judge Feingold to a priority spot, near the front of the line. She gets out without saying anything and returns with a passenger ticket, which she hands to me across the seat.

"Should I walk on?" I ask. Through the terminal window I spy a huddle of passengers, taking shelter from the cold.

The judge jingles her keys in her lap and stares blankly through the windshield. The sea opens up before us, choppy whitecaps slapping against the hull of the giant boat waiting to ferry us back to the island. "I've never done this before," she says. "I need you to know that. I don't typically wake up at dawn to drive all the way into the city and clean up other people's messes."

I stare at my bare knees, the sharp hemline of my dress. There's something about still wearing it that feels like the worst punishment of all, like a walk of shame that lasts for hours, announcing to everyone that I'm a letdown, a disappointment, a *mess.*

"I'm here as a favor to a friend," she says.

"Max," I guess. She doesn't answer. Her hair is stuffed beneath a wool hat, a few dark curls flattened around her ears, and from this close I can see that her eyes are a warm, full brown. Without the robe, without the imposing desk, she looks much less threatening, though the flat, low tone of her voice remains detached and cool.

"I've talked to the clerk in Boston and arranged to have you released under my recognizance," she says. "Which means we will return to the stipulations of our original agreement. Only this time you won't screw up."

I feel a lightness spreading across my chest. Followed by a confusing muddle of thoughts. A second chance? Why would anyone think I deserve that?

The line starts moving and the car grumbles to a start. I pass my ticket back and the judge hands it through the window to the attendant. We pull onto the boat's clattering lower deck, squeezing into a spot between a horse trailer and a moving truck. I wait to see if she is going to get out; everybody's boat preferences are different. The trip from Woods Hole takes a little less than an hour. Some people like to sit in the snack bar, order an overpriced paper bowl of chowder and stare at the horizon through the smudged windows. Others insist on stepping outside, feeling the wind and brisk ocean spray, no matter the weather. But those of us who make this trip frequently usually like to stay in our cars, hoping to avoid the obligatory chitchat with fellow travelers, the occasional awkward run-in with somebody you'd rather not see. When Judge Feingold takes out a book of crossword puzzles and tilts back her seat, I realize it makes sense that she, of all people, would have reason to stay put.

I pull my coat closer around me and lean my head against the window as the boat jerks and jolts out of the harbor.

"You used to ask a lot of questions."

I open my eyes. Her pencil is poised above the black and white boxes, and she rolls it slowly between her fingers and thumb.

"When you were little," she says. "I don't think I've ever met a more inquisitive kid. You drove us all nuts."

Dad used to give me an encyclopedia every year for my birthday, an old, used volume that he made me promise to consult before asking him something he didn't know the answer to. Unfortunately, each book only covered a few letters, and it was hard to be curious alphabetically.

The judge taps the steering wheel with the eraser of her pencil. "But your mother was a saint," she says, with a smile.

"She would answer every one. Even when she obviously had no idea what you were talking about. *Where do words come from? Why is the moon following me?* She'd make something up."

The truck beside us rattles as the boat lurches over a patch of rough swell. I close my eyes again and try to see my mother. I used to be able to do it. I could close my eyes and draw from an endless bank of random memories. Bent over the community garden, pulling weeds in a floppy hat. Dancing in the kitchen with Dad or Max or Diane. Always holding out a hand to me, making room for me on her lap, brushing the hair from my face.

"You've been dealt some unfair cards," the judge is saying. "I know that. Nobody should have to know the things you know already. But you can't un-know them now. You don't get to pretend. You don't get to fake your way through this, Tamsen."

I swallow hard and stare at the glove box. I wonder if she gets reports from Bunny. Again, I hear Colin's voice. Was I cheating? Have I always been cheating? What more do I have to do?

"This is real," she says. "This is your life. It's the beginning, and what happens next is up to you. I won't presume to know enough to tell you what to do, or how to do it. But something needs to change. This is the end of second chances. Do you understand me?"

I close my eyes again, waiting for her, waiting for my mom.

But she's not there. I don't understand. I don't know how to change. But I know that I have to. "Yes," I say softly.

I put my hand on the door.

"I'm not here for Max," she says suddenly, as I climb out onto the car deck, loud with engine rumbles. "She was your mother, and she was my friend."

SIXTEEN

AFTER JUDGE FEINGOLD DROPPED ME AT SCHOOL, I assumed she'd gone straight to Dad to tell him all about my little city adventure. But that night at dinner, nobody seemed the wiser. Dad asked about our project proposal (which, since I didn't get to school until just before lunch, I still ended up missing), and I lied carefully, telling him it had gone well, and that Lula was really stepping up. The air felt charged and dangerous after I'd spoken, as if the judge had assumed Zeus-like capabilities and could strike me down at any moment. It would be the last lie, I promised myself, and anyone else who was listening. Only the truth, only *real*, from here on out.

The next widows group meets at the Agricultural Hall, and Dad and Juliet drop me off on their way out to dinner. Since I've been home, Thursdays have turned into "date nights," when Juliet's sister comes over to watch the kids and Dad takes her to one of the five mediocre restaurants open in the off-season. Tonight, I tell Juliet her hair looks nice (it does; new highlights, I think) and I see them share a surprised glance across the front seat.

The Ag Hall is packed with people and with goods, for the Annual Easter Flea Market and Antiques Fair. The long, cavernous barn has been chopped up into a grid, with narrow passages snaking between rows and rows of congested, craft-strewn tables. I stand inside the hefty wooden doors, unpeeling my scarf and stuffing my mittens into the pocket of my coat, while scanning the crowds for Bunny.

I have no idea why we're here for the Flea. I can only imagine what types of alternative therapies we will uncover among the overflowing aisles of recycled junk, the endless arrays of outdated electronics, and the blur of tapestries, clothing, artwork, and tchotchkes. But I'm sure that Bunny, per usual, has something up her woven poncho sleeves.

I see Liza and Karen the Librarian first, hovering in front of a wall display of neckties fashioned out of old comic books. I walk slowly over to join them, and soon I spy Bunny in a quilted, puffy coat, elbowing her way toward us through the crowd.

"Here you are," she huffs. "I knew I should have assigned a meeting place. I thought the end of the day would be quiet, but I guess everyone loves a good bargain!"

"I told you," Karen says, nodding knowingly at Liza.

Bunny bustles off to corral some other group members wandering aimlessly by a samovar of hot cider.

"Told her what?" I ask. Karen's eyes are red and puffy and I'm worried I've interrupted something.

"Bargaining." Liza leans over to explain. "It's the next grief stage. Karen thinks it's why we're here."

"I hate flea markets," Karen grumbles, crossing her arms. "Everything smells like my grandmother's attic."

Liza gives me a hidden smile. "One of those days," she says quietly, turning away from Karen's indignant mumbles. "But *you* look better." She gives me a quick once-over. "Not that you looked bad before."

"Thanks," I deadpan. "I showered."

I also dug out a few skirts and dresses that actually fit, and have been wearing them out in public, instead of the single pair of jeans and the selection of Noah's favorite shirts I've been living in. Plus, I brushed my hair this morning, which was new, and braided it to one side, which I can do again now that it's getting longer.

I don't realize I'm hoping to see Colin until I spot him by the door. He stamps snow from his boots and looks around, blinking and bewildered. I've thought about him more than a few times since I got back. I even found myself looking him up online, finding a few sparse profiles on networking sites, a smiley picture of him with a petite and bubbly-looking blonde, and a short bio on a law firm's website, listing him as a Junior Associate and volunteer Big Brother who runs marathons for fun.

Now, I watch as Bunny intercepts him on his way to a table of antique maps, clutching his shoulder and guiding him toward the ties.

"This is something," he says, as Bunny shoves him into our dedicated corner.

"Isn't it?" Bunny asks, vaulting her large, embroidered purse over one shoulder and rummaging through the open pocket. She pulls out a square yellow envelope. "I take it some of you have guessed why we're here today. The third grief stage is bargaining, that little vixen." Bunny winks and opens the envelope. "Bargaining is what happens when we start to feel useful again, but we're not fully prepared to face the new version of our lives. We may trick ourselves into trying something that we hope will make us feel better, or get us back to the way things were, only to realize it's little more than a distraction. Has anyone had any experience with this yet?"

Bunny scans the group. Karen crosses and uncrosses her arms. Martha feigns interest in a necktie bubbled in cartoon sound effects: "POW!" "CRRRRRASH!" "WHAM!" I bend down to retie the laces of my boots.

"Well, if you haven't yet, you will," Bunny continues. "And as practice, today we're going to do some bargain-hunting of our own." From the envelope, she pulls out a handful of bills, which she begins to pass around. "Here's ten dollars for each of you. The idea is to get as much as you possibly can for ten bucks. But there's a catch: you can't pay full-price for anything. No matter what they're asking, even if it's fifty cents, you get them down to a quarter. Got it?"

I see Karen rolling her eyes as she stuffs the money in the pocket of her coat. Martha delicately slides her bill behind a checkbook in her slim wallet. Liza actually looks excited, whispers something about soap made out of chocolate, and disappears into the crowd.

I take my bill from Bunny and watch as Colin pockets his. I try to catch his eye but he hurries off, his gray peacoat slung over the crook of his elbow, disappearing into the maze of vintage treasure.

I trail behind, scoping the wares from a distance. Colin stops first at a small, round table completely covered in buttons. I work my way through the frenzied patrons until I'm standing by his side.

"Hey," I say, pretending to examine the merchandise. There are buttons of all sizes, shapes, and colors, some laid out in neat rows, like they're transmitting a secret button code, and others grouped together in clear little bags.

"Hey yourself," he says gruffly.

"Looks better," I say, pointing to his now-healed face.

He touches the bridge of his nose gently. "Does it?" he asks. "It was starting to grow on me. I've got a pretty badass reputation at the post office now."

I laugh and shuffle along the edge of the table beside him.

"I have an idea," I stage-whisper. On the other side of the table sits a graying woman in a lime green housecoat. Every so often, she plunges her knobby fingers into a giant Tupperware full of . . . more buttons. "Let's make this interesting."

Colin lifts a sandy-blond eyebrow. "Oh yeah?"

"Whoever gets more for ten bucks takes the other out for coffee," I say.

Colin considers me carefully, and for a moment, I think it's too late. Whatever interest he may once have had in being around me has vanished. But then he smiles. "You're on."

Colin carefully lifts an envelope of green-themed buttons, some solid, some patterned, of various shapes and sizes. This woman not only loves buttons, I realize, she loves the potential of buttons. She loves imagining where they might end up; a sweater, maybe, or the decorative border on a pillow.

"You must be feeling generous," he says suddenly.

"Why's that?" I ask.

Colin turns to look at me, a mischievous gleam in his eyes. He palms the bag of buttons and shifts me slightly to the side, leaning over the table. "Excuse me, miss?"

I busy myself with a nearby display of instructional sewing books. "This is such a nicely curated display," I hear Colin say, his voice sticky-sweet.

The woman looks at him kindly over the tops of her reading glasses. "Thank you, dear."

"My mother loves to knit, and my brother just had a baby.

She's working on a sweater, I think it's just about this color," he adds, holding out the envelope of green buttons. "Do you think these would be the right size? I know she wants to make it big, so Leona—that's the baby—can grow into it."

"Very wise." The woman nods. "Children grow like weeds."

"That they do." Colin chuckles, nudging me subtly with one elbow. "So these would be all right, then?"

"Those would be perfect," she says, beaming.

"And how much will they set me back?"

The woman's eyes quickly scan the other would-be customers, before leaning in to whisper: "On the house, dear," gently touching the sleeve of Colin's cream-colored sweater. "Congratulations on the new addition," she adds with a wink.

Colin takes her papery hand and gives it a squeeze before slipping the buttons into his pocket.

"You have no idea who you're messing with," he says when he brushes past me, and though I laugh as I follow him deeper into the stalls, I have a feeling he's right.

Next, I follow Colin to a booth of belts and jewelry made entirely from bottle caps. He picks out a set of coasters and manages to convince the ponytailed guy behind the table to let him have them for a dollar. He never once appears to be anything less than perfectly polite and effortlessly charming. By the end of the transaction, the two of them are laughing like school chums, and the vendor is all but thanking Colin for taking the coasters off his hands.

"You're just lucky," I insist as we're swept back into the

current of dazed-looking shoppers. I point out another booth, this one a towering display of natural oils and perfumes, presided over by a militant-looking matron in a crisp, collared shirt buttoned to her angular chin.

A full hour and two armfuls of bargain-priced bounty later, and some failed attempts to haggle with a guy selling prints of vintage album cover art, I announce that Colin has officially won. This seems to be the only way to get him to call it a night, as he still has a couple dollars left. Out of the corner of my eye I spot the rest of the group, seated in front of the fire, and we make our way over to join them.

•   •   •

"Two Melt-in-Your-Mouth brownies, please. And one chai tea."

Colin returns from the refrigerator with a stubby bottle of organic chocolate milk.

"And one child's milk," I add.

It was my idea to stop at the Bake House after group. I called Dad and told him a friend would drive me home (*no more lies*) and hopped into the front seat of Colin's car.

The Bake House was Mom's favorite, a tucked-away café that specialized in vegan treats and dairy alternatives long before they were fashionable. There's a quiet corner stuffed with cushions and a small table, and I lead Colin there, grabbing extra napkins and a silver pitcher of soy milk on the way.

Colin struggles to get comfortable on a pile of paisley pillows, his sharp knees jutting out at awkward angles. "Nice spot," he says, attempting to sip from the miniature straw of his chocolate milk while balancing a brownie on his lopsided lap. "Cozy."

I laugh and take his brownie, setting it down on the table. "It's the best brownie on the island," I insist. "You'll see."

"I have to say, I'm skeptical," he says. "What if I don't want a brownie that melts in my mouth? What if I want a brownie that fights back?"

"Then you're out of luck." I shrug. "This brownie surrenders."

"That's what I was afraid of," Colin sighs. " 'Never surrender.' It's another one of my mottoes."

" 'Don't make sense, Never surrender,' " I list, breaking my brownie into gooey squares. "You have a lot of mottoes."

"Don't you?"

"I don't think so," I say, squinting in the light of a stained-glass lamp.

"Everyone needs a motto," Colin insists.

I consider this, swallowing a rich, velvety chunk of chocolate. "Okay," I say. "How about 'Just do it.' Can that be my motto?"

Colin laughs. "You might run into some trademark issues."

"You're a lawyer, right?" I ask. "You can represent me."

Colin raises his chocolate milk in a toast before narrowing his eyes. "How did you know that?" he asks, leaning against the sponge-painted wall and stretching out his legs. "How'd you know what I do?"

I feel my face flushing and try to hide behind my oversize mug of tea, making a show of blowing on it so energetically that the foamy top layer sputters back in my face.

"Your, um, sweatshirt," I finally manage. "You wore a law school sweatshirt one time. Plus all that sly negotiating at the Flea. Dead giveaway."

"Okay." Colin nods definitively. "You Googled me. You totally Googled me."

"I did not!"

"It's cool," he says. "Nothing to be ashamed of. I mean, if I hadn't looked you up, I'd never have known about your Cherry Garcia habit."

I stare at him, suddenly remembering an old profile I set up at the beginning of freshman year. I cringe, trying to remember what other fascinating bits of trivia I decided to share with the world. Probably a lot of Bright Eyes lyrics and e. e. cummings quotes.

"How was your trip?" Colin asks, slurping the last of his chocolate milk.

I pretend to flip through last week's edition of the local paper, discarded on the table between us. My cheeks are still burning and there are prickles of sweat on the back of my neck. "It was okay," I say.

"Good show?"

I take a sip of tea and wipe my mouth with the back of

one hand. "Yeah." I nod. "It went really well. Their old label wants them back. So that was exciting."

Colin looks at me carefully. "You sound thrilled."

I let my eyes glaze over a newspaper ad for a tackle shop near the harbor. "It means they leave for tour this week. With a new manager," I say. "They don't need me anymore."

"Ah." Colin nods. He takes a bite of brownie and stares up at the bulletin board, covered in flyers for meditation groups and pet sitters and tai chi workshops.

"This is where you say 'I told you so,'" I offer.

"It is?"

I nod. "You know," I prompt. "'It was a bad idea, life moves on and you have to move with it, times are changing,' et cetera."

"You make me sound like a Bob Dylan song," he says.

"You are nothing like a Bob Dylan song." I laugh.

"Ouch," he says smiling. "Okay. Well, you should probably know I wasn't going to say any of those things." He looks at me, his amber eyes softening. "But I am sorry you're upset."

"I'm not upset." I shrug. "I mean, I was. But I think you were right."

"You mean Bob Dylan was right."

"Sure." I smile. "Bob Dylan was right. Not that I have any idea what to do next."

"Nobody does," Colin says. "Why do you think I'm still here?"

"Your parents?"

"I can't blame them forever," he says. "Don't tell anyone," he leans in to whisper, "but I'm *twenty-six years old.*"

"No!" I gasp, pretending to be surprised, though of course my Internet snooping had already led me to assume just as much. "So why *are* you still here?"

"I don't know." He shrugs. "Everything made sense before. Anna and I got together after college. Our parents were friends. They planned our wedding before our first official date," he says. "The law firm I work at? It's my mother's."

"Really?" I ask, remembering a cover photo of a sleek-looking older woman with a severe bob.

"Really," he says. "I never had to think about a job. Never really had to think about anything. Until now. And I don't know, I guess now it feels like . . ."

"Nothing makes sense," I finish.

"Exactly." Colin polishes off the last of his brownie and wipes crumbs from his hands with a napkin.

"So?" I ask. "What's the verdict?"

"The verdict?"

"The brownie," I say. "Too wimpy?"

Colin smiles, tossing the empty carton of chocolate milk into the recycling bin across the room. "No. Sometimes it's good to give in."

I laugh. "New motto?"

"You can keep it," he says. "On the house."

SEVENTEEN

THE NEXT SATURDAY MORNING, I BORROW JULIET'S minivan and drive to Lula's house. Skip is out in the driveway when I pull in, spray-painting a new stencil onto the side of his faded blue pickup truck. SKIP'S GOATSCAPING, it says, in bright orange and red. He gives me a cheerful hello and tells me to go on in. "Last I checked she was still sleeping," he says. "All those vampire movies. She's nocturnal these days."

I smile and take the steps two at a time up to Lula's room. I knock quietly at first, and then louder. No response. I push the door open carefully, my eyes adjusting to the blackness.

Skip wasn't kidding. Lula has duct-taped blankets to her windows and there's a loud, static sound coming from a noise machine near the bed. She is buried beneath a pile of dark plaid blankets and barely stirs as I walk across the room.

I pull back the "curtains" and the tape peels off from the wall, the blankets tumbling to a messy pile by my feet. Sharp sunlight pours into the room and Lula tosses and turns, stuffing a pillow over her face.

"Why . . ." she grumbles.

"It's me," I say, switching off the noise machine with my foot. "I have an idea."

"Go away," she mutters, still mummified in sheets.

I pull the pillow from her head, her crimped red hair tangled and clinging to the case. "It's after eleven," I say. "And it's a beautiful day."

Lula opens one eye, studying me skeptically. "Who are you?"

I laugh. "I have an idea for the project . . ."

Lula kicks at me from under the covers. "No more project," she groans.

According to Mr. Alden, her proposal presentation went fine—in the middle of the week we got a formal report full of exclamation points and a note to include more "multimedia" in the final project. A few times, over lunch at our spot in a quiet corner of the cafeteria near a row of recycling barrels, I've tried to get Lula to talk about it, but she hasn't exactly seemed interested.

"I know that I bailed on you before and I know it was a jackass move," I say.

"Total jackass," she agrees.

"And I'm sorry, okay?" I say. "I'm trying to do better. Will you please just get out of this creepy lair and come with me down to the path?"

Slowly, Lula pushes back the sheets and lifts herself up to her elbows. She wears an enormous black T-shirt with red starbursts on the sleeves, and she stretches her thin arms up over her head dramatically. "The path? Your path?" She yawns. "Why? It's cold."

"Wear a sweater," I say, heading for the door. "I'm driving."

After I've had a prolonged chat with Diane about a water birth she attended and the power of pelvic tilts, Lula stomps downstairs and I drag her to the car.

"What's goatscaping?" I ask as we wave goodbye to Skip, now hosing down the gritty underside of his truck.

"Who knows," Lula murmurs. "Some new Skip scheme. He's going to rent the goats to people who don't want to mow their lawns. Apparently they eat poison ivy. He says it's the next big thing."

Skip is always after the *next big thing*. He loves farming, but it's never been enough to keep the family afloat, so he dabbles in whatever he can to get by. He's worked as a carpenter, driven a dump truck, offered carriage rides at weddings with the horses. For a while, he ran a farm stand out of their front yard, where Diane sold the skin care products she made out of seaweed and herbs.

I turn down the road to my house and pull into the drive-

166

way. We get out, but instead of going inside we walk around to the back, down the hill to where the trail to the beach begins.

The April sky hovers somewhere between winter and spring; thick gray clouds with patches of blue and stubborn bursts of sunshine. The ground is starting to thaw, brown and battered from so much snow.

Lula reluctantly follows me down the path. "Remember now?" I ask, trudging through cold, damp grass until I see the cave.

"Yeah, I remember," she says. "Still don't know why we're here."

The cave is a formation of ancient-looking rocks that's been here forever. After we all moved out of Max's, Lula and I would explore my new neighborhood, pretending to be ship-wrecked passengers, washed ashore and using the cave as shelter.

I kneel at the cave's opening, peering into the darkness. As usual, there are a few rusting beer cans and a handful of yellowed cigarette butts. There's new graffiti on the stubbly walls: "Kat + Zeb 4Eva" and "Go Wildcats!" I crawl inside, hunched in half, and start digging.

"How about now?" I ask, clawing at the hard dirt. I wish I'd thought to bring a shovel.

"Now what?" Lula asks, kneeling in the opening. "You're going to dig up the crap we buried when we were kids?"

I smile and pick up a thick, knotted branch. It's been years, but my fingers easily find the right spot. I use the stick to scoop out layers of tightly packed dirt, until at last I hear the familiar, tinny sound of wood on metal.

"Yup," I say. "Alden said he wanted us to think outside the box."

"I don't think he meant a literal box," Lula jokes as I dust off the broken metal latch. On one of our "shipwreck" missions, we decided we were stowaways, transporting precious gemstones and hiding from the authorities. We stole one of Mom's vintage jewelry boxes and filled it with candy necklaces, hair baubles, and a string of cheap beads we'd bought with tickets won at the video arcade. We buried it and made a pact never to tell another soul about our secret spot, as if anyone would care enough to dig it up.

"We're not going to write a paper," I say.

"I'm not doing anything," Lula counters. "This is your show."

"Fine." I shrug, passing her the box. "*I'm* not writing a paper. Everyone's always harping about 'Show, don't tell.'"

"So?" Lula asks.

"So," I say. "Let's show him. Show him what it was like for us. Show him how we grew up."

· · ·

"You're going to like it," Lula promises, flipping through channels on the boxy tube TV in her living room.

"I really don't think so," I argue.

"If you don't like it, there is something very seriously wrong with you," she says. "Something you should probably address. Just think of this as an important psychological test."

"Just what I need," I say, settling deeper into one corner of the couch. "More treatment."

Despite grumbling for the duration of the car ride back to her house, Lula insisted that I stay for a *Doctor Who* marathon on the Syfy Channel. I would much rather be working on our project—I have a billion scavenger-hunt-type ideas for ways to represent our island upbringing—but I know that I'm still in the doghouse where Lula is concerned, and I'd do just about anything to get out.

Diane brings us a bowl of homemade kettle corn dusted with rosemary and Parmesan cheese. I sit on the couch and Lula Bee sprawls out on the floor, clicking through channels. "Here we go," she says excitedly.

"Who's that guy?" I ask, pointing at a floppy-haired man in coattails and a bow tie.

"No questions," Lula barks, tossing a kernel of popcorn into my hair. "All will be revealed."

I roll my eyes and squint at the screen, doing my best to keep up.

Three episodes later, I have gathered enough basic information to differentiate characters and understand the general premise, which typically involves the good doctor himself (who also happens to be part alien) shooting through time and space in his magical phone booth, righting wrongs and saving civilization, as Time Lords are wont to do.

During a commercial, Diane says she's running out to a yoga class, and Lula asks her to bring us back burritos from the Mexican place next door. "There are like at least five more to get through tonight," Lula says, after Diane leaves. "You might as well stay over."

My first instinct is to come up with a reason to leave. Too much homework. Family dinner. It's not so much that I don't want to stay, just that I'm so used to leaving. To being alone. I call Dad and ask if it's all right. He does an admirable job of trying not to sound thrilled, as does Lula, when I tell her I've been given the okay.

After dinner, Lula brings the blankets down from her bed and we lay them out on the floor. We take the cushions off the couch and prop them up behind us, gorging on the no-bake peanut butter cookies Diane brought out on a tray.

"So the stuff with the band fell through?" she asks as the credits roll at the end of another episode.

"Why do you say that?"

"Why else would you be here?"

I'm not sure if she means "here on the island" or "here in my house." Either way, I feel like a colossal jerk. "They don't need me anymore," I say. "On to bigger things, I guess."

Lula shrugs. "Their loss," she says, turning the volume back up.

It's a commercial for men's antibalding cream. After a few

before-and-after photos and passionate testimonials, I grab the remote and mute the sound.

"I'm sorry," I say suddenly. Lula looks to me, confused, before rolling her eyes and grabbing again for the remote.

"You said that already."

"No," I say, pulling my hair away from my face. "Not just the project. I'm sorry for everything. Before."

Lula is quiet, and for a moment I think maybe she's going to pretend that nothing happened. Like it was completely normal for me to fall off the face of the planet just because I had a boyfriend and she didn't.

"Oh," she finally says. "That."

My heart thuds in my chest. "I don't know what happened," I say. "I mean, Noah happened, obviously, but I don't know why I was such a brat about it."

"Whatever." Lula shrugs.

"Not whatever," I press. I remember the way she looked at me outside the tattoo shop, the way she looks at me a lot. Like she's trying to figure out how much of me, the real me, is still left. "I don't want to pretend like everything's fine when it's not. You're obviously still pissed . . ."

"I'm not pissed," Lula balks.

I raise an eyebrow as she grabs again for the remote. I shove it behind my back, out of her reach. "Hey," she whines, before glancing anxiously at the TV. "It's starting!"

I shrug and bury the remote deeper into the cushions behind me.

"Fine," she huffs. "I'm pissed. Is that better?"

"Much," I say.

"But it's not about you," she says. "Not everything has to be about you, you know."

She lunges behind my back and steals the remote. I'm too stunned to fight back, too busy realizing that she's right. It never occurred to me that something else might be going on in her life. Her life that continued past the point where I left it, her life that belongs to her.

"Oh," I say. "Okay. Well."

"Well what?" she pushes. "You want me to talk about it? Tell you all my boy troubles so we can *bond*?"

I start to sputter an offended response, but stop myself midbabble. "Wait," I say. "Boy troubles? What boy troubles?"

"Forget it."

"Come on!" I say, standing up to block the TV, my arms spread out like wings for maximum screen coverage. "Or I'm not moving."

Lula rolls her eyes. "I could take you down in six seconds," she retorts. "But fine. There's this guy. At the tattoo place."

"The tattoo guy?" I laugh. "The big guy who works there?"

"He's not big." Lula frowns.

"Sorry," I say. "I just meant . . ."

"Whatever, yes, that one," she says, clutching a pillow to her chest. "Gus."

"Okay," I say. "Gus. So . . ."

"So what?" she asks.

"So what's up with you and Gus?"

Lula blushes and look at the ceiling. "Nothing," she groans. "Nothing is up with me and Gus. I'm in there all the time. I told him I want to apprentice."

"Do you?" I ask.

Lula shrugs. "I guess," she says. "I mean, it's cool, I'd never really thought about it before. But I like being there. He's nice. Funny. I don't know."

"Okay," I say again, treading carefully. "So what's the problem?"

Lula stares at me like I'm a pesky kid. "That *is* the problem," she says. "The problem is: That's it. Nothing's happening. It's been, like, months, and there's nothing else to tell."

I nod. "And you would like for something to happen?"

"Yes, Captain Obvious." She throws a pillow at me. "I would like for something to happen. Okay? Are you happy? Now can we watch TV?"

I bite my lower lip, trying not to smile, since I know I've pushed her as far as she'll go. For now. "Sure," I say, and I sit down beside her. She stares intently at the television, the blue-black lights of the screen flickering back at her in the darkness.

EIGHTEEN

"TAM, DO YOU HAVE A SECOND?"

Miss Walsh stands at the dry-erase board, wiping away words from this week's vocabulary quiz. The bell rings for first lunch and there's an eager stampede to the door. I stuff the pile of glossy *New Yorker*s I've been reading for our non-fiction unit into my bag and make my way to the front of the room.

"Sure," I mumble. I look through the collection of finger puppets Miss Walsh keeps lined up on her desk. They are mostly literary figures: Shakespeare, Dickens, a woman with a severe center part who could be any number of Victorian-era lady writers. Plus an impressive collection of cats wearing hats.

"It's not what it looks like," she says, attaching the eraser to its Velcro holster and pulling her wild red hair back into a knot. "It started with this one," she explains, holding up a whiskered puppet. "I said something about my cat and it was all over. As if it's not bad enough to be the crazy cat lady, somehow I've also become the finger puppet queen." She shakes her head exasperatedly. "It's a cross to bear."

I laugh. "Somebody has to do it."

Miss Walsh sits on a corner of her desk. She gestures for me to do the same. I lower onto one of the worktables behind me, letting my bag fall in a heap in my lap. "How's it going?" she asks eventually. "Everything okay?"

There's a dull flutter in my stomach. I'd almost managed to get through the week without somebody "checking in." In fact, in the last few weeks, school has quickly and surprisingly ascended to the ranks of places I don't completely abhor, simply because it's so easy to get lost here. At school, I'm just one in the crowd of faces, pushing through assignments and classes and routine. The very thing I used to hate most about it—the mindless flow of scheduled time—is the best part about it now. It's like being on one of those moving sidewalks at the airport. You get on, you get off, and all that's required in between is that you remain conscious and upright.

"I'm good," I say. I add a smile, with teeth, to be extra convincing.

It feels manufactured, but it's not a complete lie. Miss Walsh's writing elective is the one class I enjoy. I especially liked this last assignment, part of a unit on cultural criticism. We were given a list of critics and told to find their most recent published work. I chose Sasha Frere-Jones, a music critic for *The New Yorker*, and read a thing he wrote about Beyoncé. Then I wrote my own essay on Noah's favorite Dylan song, "Don't Think Twice, It's All Right." The essay took forever to write and felt clunky and weird. It was hard to find words to explain the way the song made me feel. I'm sure Miss Walsh is going to ask me to do it again, or choose another topic, but that's okay. The assignment gave me an excuse to think about Noah and do homework at the same time.

"Your essay was excellent," Miss Walsh says quickly, thumbing through a pile of graded papers on her desk. "I wasn't going to hand these back until tomorrow, but I wanted to get you while it's still fresh on your mind."

She passes me the pages I printed out in the library yesterday morning, only now there's a cheery, circled A on the top. "Don't look so shocked," she says. "You must have done this before."

I shake my head. "No," I say. "I thought it sucked. I mean . . ." I stutter, embarrassed.

"It does not suck," she interrupts. "Writing about music is hard. You know: 'dancing about architecture,' and whatnot . . ."

"What?"

"Somebody said that once. 'Writing about music is like dancing about architecture.'"

"How can you dance about architecture?"

"You can't. That's the point." Miss Walsh smiles. "Anyway,

I want you to email my friend. She writes for a bunch of websites and magazines and teaches music journalism at City Conservatory in Boston. We went to college together. I think you'd like her, and she might have more ideas than I do about what to do with this."

I look at the paper in my hands. "What do you mean, 'do with it'?" I ask. I wrote it, I handed it in, I got a decent grade. Seems like a fairly complete study in the life cycle of homework to me.

"I think you could submit it somewhere," she says. "If you want."

"Submit it?" I say. "You mean, try to have it published?"

Miss Walsh nods. "Yes," she says. "Don't tell me you've never thought about this."

"I've never thought about this."

Miss Walsh peers at me, like she's trying to see through me to some deeper truth buried deep in my soul. "What *do* you think about?"

I giggle uncomfortably. "Like, generally?" I ask.

"No." She crosses her arms. "Not generally. I mean what do you think about, when you think about next year? Where do you see yourself?"

I study the smudgy spaces between the black and white classroom tiles. In the weeks since I've been back from the city, I've been focusing on being present. Doing what I'm supposed to do, but not just because I'm supposed to do it. Turns out, it takes a lot of energy to live life to the fullest. There hasn't been much time left over for seeing into the future.

"I guess I don't, really," I say. "I mean, I haven't thought about it. Yet."

Miss Walsh nods. "You still have a semester to make up, is that right?"

I cringe. "Summer school," I say; another thing I've been trying to push far back into the darkest recesses of my mind. The idea of being cooped up in a temperature-regulated classroom while the rest of the world is pleasure-reading at the beach is enough to make me want to drop out all over again. "That's the plan, at least."

"Okay," she says. "And then what? Do you want to stay on the island?"

The answer to this question used to be so easy. I want to be where Noah is. If he's on tour, I want to be on tour. If he's here, I want to be with him. It's been a long time since I've had to think about what *I* want, where *I* want to be, independent of anybody else.

"I don't know," I answer honestly. "I don't know where else I'd go."

"What about college?" Miss Walsh asks. "Do you want to go to college?"

I remember the first time I saw a college brochure. It came in the mail for Noah when he was a senior, I think just because he had gotten on some list by signing up for the SATs. He ended up never taking the test, or visiting any schools—

he knew what he wanted and it had nothing to do with the inside of a classroom. But I stole the brochure and read it in secret, drooling over the leafy quads, old buildings crawling with ivy, and shaded cobblestone paths. Multinational friend-groups, drinking smoothies at picnic tables, textbooks open in their laps. State-of-the-art computer labs. Microscopes. Gray-haired professors behind stately, organized desks. It was glossy and posed, sure, but there was a secret part of me that thought it looked like the happiest, warmest, most invigorating place on earth.

"I used to," I say.

Miss Walsh looks at me for another long moment before scribbling something on a yellow sticky note and passing it to me. "Email her," she says. "Tell her you're one of my students. She'll probably want to see a few samples of your work, so get some pieces together. Who knows? Maybe she'll help you start thinking again."

NINETEEN

"YOU OKAY?" COLIN ASKS, SHUTTING THE CAR DOOR behind me. "You've hardly said a word since I picked you up."

Taking Colin to the Royal was my idea. I'd heard about a show I wanted to see—a solo act, a girl named Laurel Raynes that Max has been touting as the next Bonnie Raitt. I figured it would be a good excuse to get me to start writing again, something I might not be completely mortified to send to Miss Walsh's friend.

But the closer we got to town, the stranger I felt about bringing Colin to a place that breathed Noah from the moment I stepped in the door. It didn't matter that Max was my friend first, that the bar was my home away from home from the time I was old enough to crack a peanut shell. Ever since the guys started rehearsing there, I rarely showed up there alone.

And now, I'm showing up with . . . I'm not even sure how to finish the thought. A friend? A grief partner? A *date*? The idea sends a mixed-up muddle of nervous energy whirling around in my stomach. I swallow and try to focus on the hollow sound of my boots on the pavement.

"Sorry," I say meekly as we pass the old arcade. The streets are less empty than they were in the dead of winter, but nowhere near summer capacity. A few groups of kids huddle around the doughnut shop, a cluster of smokers stand outside the alehouse, shivering in their spring skirts and short sleeves prematurely dug out of storage.

The band is on tour—I got a postcard from Eugene saying they were staying in a bunch of Motel 8s and eating a lot of Denny's breakfasts. ("We're big time, now!" he'd joked.) It makes it slightly easier, knowing I won't run into any of them tonight and be forced into introducing Colin. And I have a feeling Max's Bonnie Raitt endorsement might draw an older crowd, not the usual twenty-something set of Ross's and Teddy's friends. But still. This was our home turf, Noah's and mine, and I have to remind myself to take long, calming breaths as we approach Max at the door.

"Pickle!" he calls out, shoving aside a few older gentlemen waiting in line ahead of us. "Get up here."

I push politely through, motioning for Colin to follow. "Hey, Max," I say, squeezing him in a hug.

"Who's the narc?" Max whispers, grinning over my shoulder.

"Max, this is my . . . friend Colin," I manage. "Colin, this is my . . . Max. He's the boss around here."

Colin extends a sturdy hand. "An honor to meet you, sir," he says.

I follow Colin inside and pretend not to notice the two raised eyebrows Max swings after us. The crowd is sparse but festive, and we manage to snag seats at one of the small tables up front. For the rowdier shows these are usually stashed in a corner, but tonight's scene is mellow and mature. I choose one of the tables off to the side, and am grateful for a quiet nook, where I can hide behind a column stuck with posters from past shows.

"Classy." Colin smiles, picking up a small, brass candleholder in the middle of the table.

"Max really pulls out all the stops," I say.

Colin leans closer, his face hovering near the candle, shadows crawling up the sides of his neck. He looks like he's about to say something when the rollicking house music abruptly switches off and a wide spotlight lands on a single chair on the stage. There's a quiet, uncertain patter of applause as a girl—she looks my age but moves like she's older—walks up from the back, a guitar under one arm and a bottle of water in the other. She is of indeterminate ethnicity—her skin is caramel colored, her hair a reddish blond. Her features are big and prominent, her lips full, her face heart shaped. She wears buckled boots, a long, gauzy skirt, and a scoop-necked top that hangs loose around her delicate shoulders.

"Thanks," she says humbly, before looking down at her fingers. There's something about the way she starts to play that instantly reminds me of Noah. She fills up the space around her so completely, just as he did. As soon as she starts singing, everything else is gone. Her voice is full and acrobatic, sometimes a growl, sometimes a whisper, sometimes a fluttering leap. She sings about trains, and I want to be on them.

She plays one hour-long set and it passes in a blissful blur. I hear Colin ask me if I want a soda. I see the shape of him walking toward the bar. Otherwise, I'm full of the warmth of her voice, my head swimming in lyrics, the tickling hum of her guitar. My heart feels like it's tripping to keep up with itself. I don't want anything more than this, I realize: to sit in a dark room with mostly strangers and hear something beautiful and new.

For an encore, Laurel Raynes plays a creepy and breathtaking acoustic version of "Heart of Glass," Mom's favorite Blondie song. There's a sudden aching in my chest and I feel like I'm being watched, but it's not a bad thing. I chew vigorously on the end of my straw to keep from crying, and somehow I make it to the end.

As the lights flicker on, Colin stands and holds out my coat. I put it on and follow him up the snow-damp stairs. My skin is still buzzing from the music and I take a few deep breaths, waiting for Colin to speak, but we walk all the way back to the car in a comfortable quiet. I wonder if he felt something, too, or if he can just sense that everywhere in me is someplace else. My fingers itch to be writing. My brain is flooded with ideas.

Colin starts driving. I barely notice when he turns the wrong way out of town, leading us toward the part of the island farthest from my house, where most of the summer residents live. The sky is bigger here, the trees less dense. The moon hangs low and full in the sky, constellations presenting themselves in bold, sparkling patterns.

"Where are we going?" I finally ask as Colin turns down a narrow dirt road.

"You'll see," he teases. "It's just up ahead."

At the end of the road is a small, grassy parking area, and Colin pulls over. He turns off the engine and we are instantly plunged into a thick, seaside silence, buzzing with crickets and the steady pulsing of the surf.

Colin gets out and I do the same, following him to a bench that overlooks a U-shaped inlet. "I've never been here before," I say, awed that there's a single square inch of this island I don't know like my own backyard.

"This was my favorite place to explore when I was a kid," he says, settling onto the bench and scooting to one end. "My parents' house is just over there." He nods to a row of stately summer homes with manicured hedges, layers of balconies, and million-dollar views of the bay and the ocean beyond.

"It's so peaceful," I say.

"You should see it during the day," he says, laughing. "It's a boat launch for the fishermen down here. And the shellfish warden always makes his rounds, demanding licenses from anyone in the water. It's a scene."

I smile, imagining the vacation set lounging on their patios with afternoon cocktails to the sound track of heated arguments over scallops and clams.

"I used to sneak down here all the time," Colin continues. "Sit on this bench and watch the action. My parents hated it, said it smelled *fishy*."

There's a splash in the water and I jump. It's been a while since I've been near the ocean at night. Noah and I used to camp out on the beach near his house, at least once a summer. We hadn't gotten around to it last year, and I don't think I've been back for more than a drive-by since he died.

"This is also where I proposed," Colin says, before clearing his throat. "It was the Fourth of July. I think somehow I managed to convince her that I'd arranged the fireworks, special. It did sort of feel like our own private show."

The wind picks up and I wrap my scarf closer around my chin.

"I haven't been back here since . . ." Colin crosses his arms. "The road loops around, and I take the long way now. Even though I only brought her here that one time. I don't know. It's like it's hers now."

I sit up straighter. It's exactly how I feel about the Royal.

It's funny how some places can just embody a person so completely. As if they're still there, as if they've been there the whole time, waiting for you to come back.

"Anyway," Colin says. "I could tell it wasn't easy for you to be there tonight. At Max's. I know it was a big deal to bring me. I'm glad you did."

I kick my feet into the sand, thick and damp with cold.

"It was pretty intense, huh?" He smiles. "The show, I mean. She was good."

"Mm-hmm," I mumble. I always have a hard time talking about music that I love. I guess it's part of the reason I like writing about it so much. I need a while to sit with whatever I've seen or heard. Musicians spend a lot of time with the songs they give us. It seems only fair to do the same with whatever we give back.

"It's like you were somewhere else," Colin says. "Like nothing else in the world existed. I don't think I've ever felt that way about anything."

It occurs to me that there was a time when I'd thought it was Noah that made me feel that way. He filled up the center of my universe so fully, there wasn't room for anything else. But maybe I was wrong. Noah was a part of it, but maybe it was music. Music was the first language I ever learned, from my parents and their records, from Max and his shows. It makes sense, I guess, that it would still feel the most like home.

"Tell me about him," Colin says suddenly. He turns to face me, the top of his knee wedging in against my hip.

186

"Noah?" I ask.

Colin nods. "If you want," he says. "Sorry. I just . . . sometimes I feel like . . . I know the group helps some people, but . . . sometimes I think it's easier, just talking. To one person. Does that make sense?"

"I thought you didn't care about making sense."

"You're right." He nods, straightening with mock confidence. "Strike that. I don't."

I think back to that first session in the theater, the way Colin distanced himself, the way he refused to engage. He seemed so aloof, as if he thought he didn't need Bunny, or any of us. But he's right. Bunny's methods probably aren't for everyone. I haven't decided yet if they're for me or not. The "real" me, that is. The one that isn't faking.

"Okay," I say gamely. This, too, must be part of the deal. If I'm going to really do this, if I'm going to do this right, I'm going to have to start talking. Might as well be tonight. "There's a lot," I say with an anxious laugh. Colin is staring at my fingers and I realize I'm frantically twisting my wedding ring against my middle knuckle. I squeeze my hands between my knees. "I don't know where to start."

"How did you meet?" Colin prompts.

"I've known him forever," I say. "Everyone knows everyone here, pretty much. And even if they don't, everyone knew Noah. He was kind of a prodigy. Always playing in talent shows, writing songs when he was in diapers, that sort of thing. But we didn't start officially going out until I was in the eighth grade. He was a sophomore. I sang in the joint chorus—middle school and high school—and he played in the band. I stayed after one day to try out for a solo—I didn't get it; I never got solos but I always tried out—and he was playing the piano . . ."

"I thought he played guitar?" Colin asks.

"He played everything. As soon as he picked something up he knew what to do with it. It's like it was inside him, already. Anyway, he asked me to walk home with him that day, which was weird. We didn't live anywhere near each other and it was like February and freezing. But we did it. And we were pretty much together all the time after that."

Colin stretches out his legs and sighs. "Isn't it strange?"

"What?"

Colin shrugs. "Like ninety-nine percent of people I can hardly tolerate long enough to get through the brain-numbing small talk, and then, with one person, all of a sudden, it's just so easy. Almost like you're not even trying. Like being alone."

"Yeah." I nod. "But better."

"Way better."

I sneak a glance at Colin's profile as he stares out at the moon, reflected in shimmering shapes across the water. All of his features are exactly as they should be; his nose, his forehead, his chin, all lined up in perfect proportions. It's one of those faces that's hard to remember at first, because there's nothing glaringly special or strange about it. But it's a pleasant face, I realize now; a face that would be hard to get sick of.

"So what happened?" he says softly, still hypnotized by the moon.

"To Noah?" I ask. "He died in his sleep. Some freak heart thing. The doctor said it could have happened to anybody."

Colin squints, as if he's trying to see more in the dark. His lips twist and turn, like he's in pain. "It didn't," he says. "It didn't happen to just anybody."

There's a breeze on my neck and a lump in my throat. I swallow it down and pull my coat tighter. "What about you?" I say. "Anna, right? You said your parents were friends."

Colin clears his throat. "But we didn't grow up together," he says. "Our moms were law school roommates, and they kept in touch. She grew up in New York. We were in Boston. I maybe met her four or five times on family trips. We'd go out to dinner and be forced into sitting next to each other. She was gorgeous. Way out of my league, from the beginning. Which, of course, made me decide she was also superficial and dumb."

I laugh and hug my knees to my chest on the bench. "Let me guess," I say. "She wasn't."

"Of course she wasn't." He smiles. "After college, our parents set us up at a wedding. Neither of us had dates and we spent the whole night talking and dancing. She was just as beautiful as I'd remembered, but also charming. Smart. Always said the right thing. Every time I'd put my foot in my mouth, which, as you can imagine, was often . . ."

"You?" I laugh. "No way."

"She fixed it. She'd call me on my bullshit, or turn whatever I'd said into something that sounded smarter. She was like a magician. She made my life . . . I don't know. Just right."

I chip at the purple polish I impulsively decided to try at Lula's house yesterday. It was a bad idea; all it does is draw attention to the fact that I am constantly gnawing at my cuticles, constantly picking at things and making them worse.

"We found out she had ovarian cancer a year after we got married," he says. "At first, it really didn't seem like a big deal. She didn't want kids, she'd always made that clear. We even joked that she was the perfect cancer candidate. She was young. In shape. Yeah, she'd lose her ovaries. So what? They were basically just taking up space."

Colin smiles sadly. "Then it got bad, fast. She stopped chemo last April and died in June," he says. "Everything you read about? It was worse. First she looked different. Then she acted different. It was a constant battle to keep her comfortable, but awake. Finally, she gave up."

I take a shallow, shaky breath. Colin pushes his hands into his pockets and leans back, tilting his chin up to the sky. We sit like this for a few minutes, without saying anything. I wait for it to feel too long, for the awkwardness to settle in, but it doesn't. It feels like we've closed ourselves into a bubble, a soft, cushiony air that breathes on its own, between us.

I lean back, too, and close my eyes. Colin shifts and I feel his elbow nudging my side as he slips one hand from his pocket. He reaches for mine, my fingers working over themselves in frantic circles. He holds my hand and we look out at the stillness of the water, the quiet of the moon, and finally I stop fidgeting, I stop thinking, I stop waiting for things to be weird.

TWENTY

"YOU THINK YOU'RE MAKING A STATEMENT, BUT you're not."

Lula stands in front of my closet, in a black lace bra and tight black jeans. It's Friday night and we're getting ready to go out, or Lula's getting ready to go out and I'm sitting on my bed, thumbing through a box of Mom's old stuff that I found in the basement. I was looking for records, something to get me going on the essay I told Miss Walsh I'd write and send to her friend in Boston. But there are a few loose photos scattered at the bottom of the box, and I spread them out in front of me on the bed.

"What statement?" I ask, fingering the faded shots of our parents lounging in hemp pants and hammocks, playing guitars, braiding each other's hair. It's alarming to realize how few of the "family photos" actually have any kids in them.

Back in the day, it seems, our parents weren't quite done being kids themselves.

"You think by not caring about whatever combination of dirty-pants-and-baggy-shirt you throw on, you're saying, 'I don't give a damn, I'm above it all,'" Lula says, emphatically tossing flannel after flannel into a pile on the floor. "When actually, the statement you're making is: 'I have no idea how to dress myself. I'm a little lamb that's lost in the woods. Please, somebody, help.'"

"How about this?" I ask, holding up a faded picture of Lula and me, age six, running around bare-bottomed at the beach. "Is this the kind of statement I should be making?"

Lula glances quickly over at me. "That would definitely be an improvement," she says. "I mean, do you need seventeen pairs of the same jeans? And these sweatshirts are big enough for three of you."

"They're Noah's," I say, without looking up. I can almost feel Lula cringe.

"Sorry," she says. "But that doesn't make them fit you any better."

"I told you. I will wear whatever you tell me to wear. I'm a lamb, lost in the woods."

This whole production was Lula Bee's idea from the beginning. She'd overheard during Free Study that a bunch of seniors were throwing a party at the Wind Farm, a secluded field near the island's tallest point and home to a towering pair of windmills. It was somebody's birthday—or maybe a few people's birthdays, Lula wasn't sure—but the important part was that Ava and Addison, who first bonded as kids in a hip-hop dance class and had been dancing together ever since, were rumored to be performing. Lula wasn't fully able to explain what this meant, but she made it very clear that there was positively nothing on the planet that would keep her, and by default, me, from witnessing what was sure to be a mortifying and calamitous spectacle.

She showed up after school and agreed to let me work on my essay as long as I would be her party-crashing companion later on. It was a steep price to pay, considering that standing around in the cold, ignoring and/or being ignored by everyone around us, and reeking of bonfire for days on end was pretty low on my list of weekend priorities. And I was excited about my essay. I had an idea about where I wanted to start, something about Laurel Raynes, and Blondie, and Ella Fitzgerald, and Mom. About the mixes Mom would make for us to listen to in the car: hodgepodge compilations that swung right from Ella's scats and sugar-sweet "A-Tisket, A-Tasket" to Blondie's bouncy "Hanging on the Telephone." I know she loved the music, all music, and wanted me to love it, too. But it was more than that. She wanted me to understand that I could do whatever I wanted. That I could sing soft or loud, in stockings and lace or black leather pants, and either way, I would be heard.

"You're not giving me much to work with here." Lula sighs. Finally, she pulls out a boxy white button-down shirt, left over, I think, from my school concert days. She throws it on; on her, it looks more like a sexy dress. She leaves it partially unbuttoned to reveal the lacy trim of her bra, the rounded tops of her bee-sting boobs.

For me, she selects a knee-length dress, gray with black horizontal stripes. "How do you feel about this?" she asks quickly, rummaging around for something in my desk.

I look up distractedly. "I feel nothing about it," I say. "Juliet made me wear it to her family reunion."

I turn back to the records, looking over the notes on the back of *Ella in Berlin*, the one where Ella charms the pants off her German-speaking audience by forgetting the lyrics to "Mack the Knife" and making up new ones on the spot. I hear a loud rip and look up sharply to see that Lula has cut the dress with crafting scissors and is now tearing it in an asymmetrical line.

"What are you doing!" I shout.

"I'm helping," she says. "Trust me." She throws the dress at me and rummages around for my black ankle boots, another Juliet purchase, after she read they were "in" one season. She was visibly annoyed when they promptly took up residence "in" the far reaches of my closet, and hasn't bought me much of anything since.

I drag myself from the bed and try on the dress. I pout in the mirror but am secretly amazed by how much better it looks at this length. My knobby legs look longer, but somehow not as gangly, and the stripes, which I'd assumed would

195

horribly accentuate my curvy hips and breasts, are actually distracting in an almost-flattering sort of way.

Lula does our makeup in the bathroom while the kids take a bath, which Grace finds hilarious and Albie finds the ultimate affront to his privacy. "No girls in the bathroom!" he shouts repeatedly, until Juliet reminds him that he is far outnumbered in the gender department. Finally, he wraps a towel around his waist, the way he's seen Dad do, and stomps to his room, muttering to himself about "no respect" and "personal space."

Dad and Juliet are sitting together in the living room as we leave, pretending to read magazines they must have dug out of the recycling box for the occasion. (Juliet's is an L.L. Bean catalogue, Dad's a backdated issue of *Sports Illustrated*.) The whole scene is clearly an excuse to make themselves available for last-minute guidance.

"No drinking and driving," Dad reminds us as he hands Lula her coat. "Call if you need a ride. And don't stay out too late."

I grab a scarf from the hallway closet and smile. It's like the time I spent at Noah's has left them brimming with parental sound bites and now it's all spewing out of them at once.

"You know what I used to do?" Juliet smiles over the flimsy pages of pullovers and monogrammed blankets. "Just take one beer and nurse it all night long. That way nobody gives you a hard time."

"So you want us to drink beer?" Lula quips.

"Fake it," Dad amends. "Just hold it and pretend to drink."

"This has all been really illuminating," I say. "But we're late."

I usher Lula through the door, make some more promises, and hurry out to the car.

"Fun, right?" Lula asks as we're driving. "Welcome to the world of the American teenager."

·   ·   ·

The Wind Farm is at the very top of a long and butt-bruisingly bumpy dirt road. A cluster of cars is gathered at one end of the field, near a crowd of kids and the smoky beginnings of a bonfire. Lula steers Skip's truck onto the grass and screams into a spot near the action. "So much for inconspicuous," I mutter as we climb out of the cab.

"Leave your coat," Lula commands. "I didn't spend all that time digging for a decent dress to have you mummy in a parka all night."

I groan and toss the coat onto the front seat, already shivering, and wrap my face and shoulders in Noah's scarf.

Lula makes a beeline for the cooler, where she wedges her way between two sleazy guys I recognize from Chemistry. They each hold a beer and share an expression of perpetually befuddled amusement. "Look," one of them says, laughing. "It's Little Lula."

Lula grabs the beers straight from their hands and passes me one. "True gentlemen," she beams, before grabbing my arm and steering me toward the fire.

We snag a spot near the windmills, and Lula insists we lie on our backs to look up at the enormous structures, looming overhead. "They look like robot dinosaurs," Lula muses, and she's right. They're prehistoric and futuristic at the same time, and it's easy to feel like a meaningless speck in their presence.

"I haven't been to a party since—" I pause to think. "I literally can't remember the last time I went to a party."

"Noah didn't like to go out?" Lula asks. She sits up, takes a long sip of her beer, makes a disgusted face, and pours the rest of it on the grass near her feet.

"We were always with the band," I say. "Rehearsing. Or just hanging out with Ross and his posse. Usually we did stuff by ourselves. Watched movies. Nothing special."

"And here I thought you guys were rock stars." Lula smirks.

"Hardly." I smile. "But it was nice."

Lula shifts inside her boxy shirtdress and musses up the back of her hair. "Every so often I'll crash one of these, just to remind myself why I don't do it more often," she says.

"Don't you ever feel uncomfortable?" I ask.

"About what?" she challenges. "Not being invited? Feeling uncomfortable means caring, and I don't care. I wouldn't invite any of these people anywhere I was going, either. This is a public field. I like windmills. The end."

I stare at Lula and wonder how much of what she's saying

is the truth. Clearly, she cares about some things. But she does do an impressive job of not letting on. I look around at the minigroups of familiar faces, joking and laughing, shoving and ducking, staring and pretending not to be staring. There's something nice about being surrounded by people, even if they're not technically your friends.

After a while, somebody turns off the muffled music blaring through a portable iPod speaker, and a spontaneous semicircle forms around the fire. There are some sporadic hoots and hollers, and suddenly, from between the windmills, two figures emerge. They are dressed in full-body metallic spandex, with tribal masks on their faces. If I hadn't known in advance that Addison and Ava were involved, I would never have guessed it was them.

They walk like machines to the center of the circle and stand in silence for a few bizarre moments. Lula whispers: "This. Is. Amazing." I nudge her to be quiet and sit up taller to see over the growing crowd.

The music switches back on, throbbing electronic rhythms, and the girls start dancing. Their movements are intentionally jerky and mechanical at first, but slowly they mellow out, into a tightly choreographed routine of impressive modern dance. One of them—judging from their heights I think it's Addison—does a sequence of front handsprings that sends everyone into a frenzied fit of cheering. At one point the music slows, and they dip and turn their way through a brief and graceful ballet.

For the finale, the music shifts again, to a raucous party song that everyone knows the words to. I'm not sure how it happens but Lula and I are both on our feet, clapping along as the girls jump and contort, before they fall to the grass in a silent, spent heap.

"Well that was disappointing," Lula says as we sit, over the endless cheers and thunderous applause.

"What do you mean?" I laugh. The routine was flawless, and inarguably entertaining.

"I mean it was awesome," she says. "And where's the fun in that?"

I nudge her in the shoulder and smile. "Maybe sometimes fun can be fun," I say.

"Gross." She rolls her eyes. Suddenly her posture shifts, and she ducks behind me.

"What?" I ask, looking around. "What happened?"

"Gus," she whispers from behind me.

"Where?"

"Don't look!" She digs into the small of my back with her elbow.

"Sit up," I say evenly. "You have to sit up."

"No, I don't," she says. "I'm perfectly comfortable and we can still talk and I'm not moving until . . ."

"Until he's five feet away from us and waving?" I say through clenched teeth, waving back at the bearded giant lumbering in our direction.

"No," Lula panics. "Nonono."

I subtly lug her into an upright position just as Gus approaches. He smiles and lowers himself to the ground with surprising control. "Lou," he says. "You made it."

"What do you mean I made it?" Lula practically barks. I attack the side of her foot with my toe. "I mean," she stutters, "did I tell you I was coming?"

"Nah." Gus shrugs. "Just figured you might be here. High school scene, and all."

"Which doesn't explain why you're here," Lula says with a smirk. I jab her with my elbow and she squeals. "Damn it. I mean, why are you here? The windmills?"

"What?" Gus raises an eyebrow. "No. Declan, you know, from the shop? He's into one of the dancer girls. The short one, I think. She invited us," he says. "Hope that's okay?"

Lula guffaws. "What am I, the party police?" she says.

"N-no," Gus stammers. "I just meant, since it's kind of like, your territory, or whatever . . ."

"I don't have a territory," Lula responds, and Gus shifts uncomfortably away.

"Hi." I lean forward abruptly, jutting an eager hand across Lula's lap. "I'm Tamsen. Lou's friend."

He introduces himself and smiles. His eyes, I can see now, are a deep, crystal blue, and when he smiles they crinkle sweetly at the corners. "Never met any of Lou's friends before."

"She's sort of a lone wolf. But we're working on it."

"We are?" Lula asks.

"Yup." I nod. "In fact," I say, tossing Lula a sly smile, "we were just talking about her birthday next week."

"No," Lula warns, "we were not."

"It's your birthday?" Gus asks. "You didn't tell me that."

"It is," I say. "And we were thinking about getting a bunch of people together to hang out. At the beach or something. You should come. Don't you think, Lou?"

Gus and I both look to Lula, who has either fallen asleep with her eyes open or is stunned into sudden and complete paralysis.

"Your birthday, huh? Sounds cool." Gus picks at a handful of damp grass. "I mean, as long as you want me there."

Lula tugs at the hem of her jeans and shrugs dramatically. "Whatever," she says, but I'm pretty sure I see the teeniest, tiniest hint of a smile inching its way across her face.

"Excellent," I say, dropping an arm around her shoulder. "Then it's settled."

Gus pushes up to his feet. "Nice meeting you, Tamsen," he says. "Lou. See you tomorrow at the shop?"

He holds out a hand and Lula offers a flustered fist bump/high-five hybrid. As soon as he's walked a safe distance, Lula is on her feet and pulling me with her. "I can't believe you," she seethes as we walk back to the parking area.

"I think you mean *thank you*," I say, remembering Judge Feingold on the morning she bailed me out.

Lula slams the door of the truck, and for a moment, I'm nervous that I've gone too far. But soon we're leaving the farm behind us, the windmills spinning in silent swipes in the mirror, and Lula is already planning her outfit for her big birthday bash.

TWENTY-ONE

THE NEXT MORNING, AFTER A LATE, CLASSICALLY Diane breakfast of tofu scramble and vegan nut cake, Lula drops me at home. There's a strange car in the driveway, a shiny sedan, and I assume it's one of Juliet's work friends coming to pick her up before the gym, her Saturday routine.

As soon as I open the screen door, I can tell that something is different. It's not just that the place is spotless; Juliet goes on weekly cleaning frenzies and it's possible I've managed to catch the twenty-minute window before the kid-tornado stirs it all up again.

There's a new quiet, formal and stiff, and I realize quickly that Grace and Albie aren't home. Juliet's sister must have taken them for the morning, which is odd, since Dad and Juliet are big about family time on weekends.

A floorboard creaks overhead and I hear a faraway chorus

of voices. I stop at the kitchen island to plug in my phone, in desperate need of charging. I'm on my way upstairs when I hear the phone buzz with an unread text and click it open. From Dad: *Ppl coming to look at house this morning. Should be cleared out by noon.—Dad.*

I leave the phone on the counter, wondering for the billionth time when he will stop signing off on his text messages. There's a patter of footsteps down the hall and I try to recall the condition of my room—did I leave anything weird out in the open? Lula's pile of clothing rejects are probably still in a tumble on the floor. *Oh well.*

I zip my coat and consider calling Lula to come back and get me, when the footsteps get closer and I hear the group— there must be three or four of them—starting down the stairs.

For some reason, instead of leaving, or staying to introduce myself like a civilized human being, I figure I should probably hide. I tuck into the coat closet, leaving the door open a crack, and crouch down between the neat rows of winter boots and labeled bins of hats and gloves.

"As you can see, it needs a lot of work," a woman's voice says as they reach the bottom of the stairwell. From my filtered slice all I can see is the swish of her dress, lime green with some kind of white design, and shiny, tall brown boots. Two people, a man and a woman, follow, holding hands. "But the location can't be beat. Just a short walk to town and a five-minute drive to the beach."

"Is it private?" the woman asks. I can see a sparkle of

diamonds on one hand as she rests it on the small of the man's back. "The beach?"

"Not technically," the agent says. "But very secluded. And there's a second entrance, a walking trail that only the locals know about. It picks up right in the backyard, here. I can show you on our way out."

There's a flutter in my veins. I think about the wooded path, the cave, the lazy walks I used to take with Mom, scouting beach plums for the jam she made each summer.

"The appliances are outdated, of course," the agent says, clacking around the kitchen in her boots. I hear the suctioning of the refrigerator door open and shut. "You could easily put in a dishwasher. How does anyone live without one these days?"

I roll my eyes. Juliet complains about not having a dishwasher every other night, but it's never bothered me, and dishes are usually my chore. There's something about standing at the sink, warm water running over my forearms as I stare through the window, that's sort of meditative.

"But I do love some of these personal touches," the broker continues. I can tell from her shadow that she's near the stove. "This backsplash is adorable. I think these are real Mexican tiles."

I hold back a laugh, remembering the month-long project of Mom painting cheap shower tiles and Dad hot-glue-gunning them to the wall. For weeks they would fall off and shatter on the counter, until Dad finally got somebody to come in and grout them. The one that I painted, yellow with bright purple flowers, Mom insisted on putting front and center, even though it clashes loudly with the others.

"And the built-ins in the living room are top-notch." I hear them rounding the corner as she points out the bookshelves Skip and Dad put in together, while Mom and Diane sponge-painted the hallway and Lula Bee and I made a fort out of moving boxes in my new room. "It's really perfect for a summer home."

There's another twinge as I imagine the house sitting empty for nine months of the year. There's no question that the island survives on its reputation as a tourist haven, but our house has never felt in any way part of that world. With all that it's seen, all the fights and tears and hugs and changes, it's more than just a place to visit. It's a home.

"To be honest"—the man speaks for the first time, his hands stuck in the pockets of his colorless pleated pants—"if we do make an offer, there's a good chance we'll tear it down. You're right, the location is ideal, but the rest of it . . ."

"It's not really our style," the woman says delicately.

I lose my balance and stumble back into the row of hanging coats. I perch on my heels and quietly lean into the wall. There's a pause, and my heart stops, until the footsteps resume and fade toward the door.

"Excellent idea," the agent is saying. "The property is really what makes this place so special. Think of it as a blank canvas. Paint your dream house however you like!"

I wait for the door to click shut and listen for the sound of the sedan's engine before crawling out of the closet. From the picture window in the living room I watch as the car rolls down the road, my pulse raging in my ears. *Tear it down?* My eyes well up as I walk past the bookshelves, still stuffed with Mom's favorites—Victorian classics, airport mystery novels, cheesy beach reads.

In the kitchen, I run my hand along the smooth tiles behind the stove. The whimsical designs Mom selected, the dancing skeletons in cowboy hats she copied from a book.

I think about my room, my bed. Mom's bed.

I pull my phone out of the wall and shove it deep in my pocket. I run outside and leave the door open behind me. What does it matter now? What does any of it matter? All of it, all of this, everything we ever were, will be gone soon. Demolished. Forgotten.

. . .

"I should have called."

Colin stands inside the door, in the same Harvard sweatshirt he was wearing the day I almost broke his nose. There's a reddish-brown stain near the collar that I pretend not to notice. "Where's the fun in that?" He smiles. "Come on in."

A small brown dog with wiry hair and a long, sausage-link body yips and jumps around my ankles. "Down, Gertie,"

Colin commands sternly, which only adds to Gertie's enthusiasm for my lower legs. "Gertie, go!" he orders, and surprisingly, the dog trots to a nearby cushion on the floor, quickly curling into a neat, boot-size ball.

I follow Colin through an open foyer. The house is a sprawling, modern series of connected boxes, with a lofted living room and one full wall of floor-to-ceiling windows overlooking the bay. "Nice place," I say, and hope this understatement of the century will pass as an excuse for any dropped-jaw staring.

Colin leads me through the kitchen—a shiny space with bronze fixtures, built-in chopping blocks, and *two* dishwashers—toward a pair of leather upholstered armchairs in front of an imposing stone hearth. "My mom reads a lot of design books," he says, gesturing at a coffee table stacked high with glossy magazines and thick, hardbound art books. "Not those," he adds. "Those are just for show."

I laugh and glance at the books on the table. I recognize a few of them, a book on island farms and one on a local landscape artist that everyone adores. This is a summer home, I think. This is a place to be visited.

"What's up?" Colin asks, settling into one of the chairs. He wears mesh running shorts and his cheeks are flushed in a way that looks like he's recently worked out. "I mean, not that something needs to be up. But you look sort of . . ."

"Sort of what?" I scoff. My head throbs, my eyes burn, and

the skin around my fingertips is raw from chewing it during the long walk from my house to Colin's. I can only imagine what kind of impression the overall package is making.

"Worked up," Colin says gently. "Everything okay?"

I try to nod, but somehow the simple movement of tilting my head up and down sets off a cascade of tears, and soon I'm sobbing into the handful of tissues Colin passes over in a wicker dispenser shaped like a conch shell.

"Sorry," I eventually manage. "Yeah. I'm good."

Colin laughs and squeezes next to me on the couch. "Oh, thank God," he says with a dramatic sigh. "For a minute there I thought you might be upset about something."

"Nope." I smile, wiping at my damp cheeks with the sleeve of my coat. "Just peachy."

Colin leans back into the crook of the couch, one arm resting lazily behind my neck. I stare at the wad of tissues in my hand and take a few deep breaths. "They're selling the house," I say. "My house. The house I grew up in."

Colin nods. "You just found out?"

I shake my head. "No," I say. "I've known. But I didn't think I cared. I thought I'd already be gone by the time it happened. With the band, or whatever. And now . . . now I don't know where I'm going, or what I'm doing, and they're tearing it down . . ." I feel myself relaunching into blubber territory and try to breathe slowly through my nose.

"Who's tearing it down?" Colin asks.

"I snuck in while it was being shown this morning," I say.

"This horrible summer couple, with shiny shoes and pleated pants." I glance at him sideways. "No offense."

"None taken." He shrugs. "Pleats do nothing for my figure."

I manage a choppy laugh and shake my head. "It's stupid. I know it's stupid."

"It's not stupid," Colin says. I feel a tickle and realize that he's playing with the back of my hair. It falls softly out of its bun and I comb it away from my face. He pulls his arm back and scratches a spot on his elbow, as if maybe my head had just gotten in the way, en route.

I clear my throat and stare into the fireplace. The stones are smooth and pristine, as if it's never been used. "You know how everyone says it's like a part of you dies?"

"Sorry?"

"I mean, after something . . . when somebody . . ."

"Oh," he says, smiling. "Just one of the hundreds of gems I get on a daily basis. My favorite is 'One day at a time.' I mean, what, exactly, is the alternative? Is there a way to get through it faster? Month by month? Year by year? Because that would be awesome. Sign me up."

"Totally." I realize that with Colin, it doesn't feel like talking about this stuff is just what's expected of me. Hoops to jump through. A chore. It feels like something that might actually help.

"I don't know," I go on. "I guess . . . I sort of wish it was true. I wish a part of me died when Noah died. But it didn't.

I'm still here. All of me. And everything's still so screwed up. No matter how many times I promise to change, to be better, to do better. At the end of the day it's still me, trying to figure out all the same shit." I wring my fingers together in my lap. "It just seems unfair. Like I should get a pass or something." I laugh. "Is that normal?"

Colin leans forward. He puts a hand over my worrying fingers. "Nothing is normal." He closes his hand over mine, giving it a quick squeeze before pulling his fingers back. "Which is really the best thing we have going for us."

My eyebrows cinch together. "It is?"

"You do get a pass. It's like a license to do whatever you want." He leans back, resting his head against the couch. "You can feel whatever you want, however you want. If you want to stay in bed, stay in bed. If you want to make a change, make a change. You can be exactly the person you want to be, with zero regard for anybody else. At least for a while."

I consider this. It's so new, so opposite from everything I've been taught. Up until now, it's felt like everyone—Dad, Juliet, the judge, even Lula Bee—has expected me to grieve in a certain way. To stay busy. To move on.

"How long is a while?" I press.

"It's been almost a year for me," he says. "At first, I went right back to work. But eventually I realized it wasn't helping. I wasn't happy, and I was useless in the office. I needed to just . . . check out.

"Listen, people are going to give you all kinds of advice,

but there are only two things to remember: everyone is trying to help. And not one of them has any idea what they are talking about. Not your dad. Not Bunny. Not me. You are the only person who knows how you feel, or what you want. Trust *that*. Be *that*."

Colin's arm has found its way back along the edge of the couch and I let myself lean back into it. I try to think about the times I've done exactly what I wanted to do. Most of them have ended in disaster. "Remember when I punched you?" I ask.

"Punched me?" He laughs. "Nudged me, maybe."

I steady him with a smiling glare and point to the stain on his sweatshirt.

"No way," he says. "What happened, see, was I had this wicked cold, and . . . and my nose was already broken, so when I ran into your glove with my face . . ."

I'm laughing now. "Okay," I finally say. "Whatever helps you sleep at night. But we both know the truth. And the truth is that you got your ass kicked by a girl."

Colin sits back. "Are you saying you want a rematch?" he asks, his voice bold and challenging.

"Maybe." I shrug. "We'll have to work out some kind of handicap, though. So we're even."

Colin pulls me closer into his shoulder. "I can live with that."

I laugh and then it's quiet, and I feel him staring at the side of my face. There's a force, like a magnet, that pulls my face toward his, like everything in me wants to be as close to him as it can get. I turn and I see him, patches of red still blooming on his cheeks, his gold-flecked eyes soft and searching. Our noses are inches apart and soon my hands are moving on their own. One falls on his knee, the other lands gently on the side of his jaw, his skin smooth and warm beneath the gentle graze of my fingers.

There's a flicker in his eyes and his jaw tenses, like he's seen something that's scared him, but then he softens slowly into my palm. He leans into my hand as if my fingers are a part of him, like they're holding him in place. I'm afraid of breathing, afraid of any small movements. It's been so long since I've felt attached to somebody. The weight of his face on my hand feels calm and exciting at the same time. Like it's old and new, at once.

The side of my leg sinks into his. His hand is on my coat, near my hip. My other hand floats to his chin, and then I'm falling forward, the shapes of our mouths opening around each other, his lips against mine, no space between us. It's bumpy and strange at first, with some wobbly teeth clatter, but soon I feel my body melting, the warm, familiar release. I had no idea how much I missed it. How much I'd missed being touched.

I'm still falling when Colin jolts away. He wedges out of the corner of the couch with sharp, awkward movements and I lurch toward the space where he was sitting, like I've tripped in midair.

His face is still and suddenly pale.

"I'm so sorry," he says. "I'm . . . this wasn't . . ."

It takes me a moment to realize what's happening, and then hot flashes of shame are crawling up my neck. I drop my head into my hands. "No," I say. "I'm sorry. I'm the one . . . I thought . . ." I hurry to my feet. "I'll go."

"No," he says quickly, grabbing on to my elbow. "Don't go."

I peel his fingers from the fabric of my coat and keep walking. "I told you," I say. "All I do is screw things up."

"You didn't screw anything up," he says. "I was just . . . I didn't want you to think . . ." He's chasing after me now, I'm through the kitchen, almost to the door. "Will you please stop walking and listen?"

I stop with one hand on the knob, my shoulders heaving, my breathing short and broken.

"I can't stop thinking about you," he says, from over my shoulder. "I don't mean metaphorically. I mean like in the actual sense of every time I have a thought, you're in it. And I'm sorry, but it kind of freaks me out."

I let my hand fall from the doorknob. I feel a hand on my shoulder, and the muscles in my neck instinctively tense up around it. "Hey," he says. "I'm sorry. I didn't want you to think I planned this."

"Planned it?" I turn to face him. "I showed up here, like a mess. I cried on your couch. I kissed you. What did you do?"

I don't mean for it to sound like a challenge, but it does.

Before I know what's happening, his hands are on my face and we're kissing again, only this time there are no bumps. No teeth. We kiss like it's what we were always supposed to be doing, like it's the only natural thing, like everything else is just noise and space.

TWENTY-TWO

"WE'RE GOING TANNING?"

Karen the Librarian climbs out of her minivan and looks back at an address scribbled on a piece of paper in her palm. Bunny texted me the same address earlier in the week, and now we're all here, in front of a run-down duplex in a weird industrial park near the airport.

Martha stands beneath a graying sign with a cluster of yellow cartoon suns. "We're not really sure," she says, smiling at me. After Martha, I was first to arrive; Colin and I drove separately, even though we spent the afternoon together at the beach near his house. Which is how we've spent most afternoons since the day I showed up at his place unannounced. At the beach, or hiking with Gertie (if you can call lazily strolling in the woods and waiting around for a shuffle-footed hot dog to catch up *hiking*), or just hanging out on his deck.

It's almost impossible to imagine that there was a time when I did other things after school. If I think about it too much it's scary, but mostly I'm too happy to think.

I try not to smile too stupidly as he pulls the old BMW into a spot across the grass. Bunny and Liza pull in just behind him, and soon we're all huddled on the stoop, awaiting further instruction.

Bunny reaches into her bag and pulls out five blindfolds. I hear Colin laugh and nudge him gently with my elbow. He tickles the bottom of my rib cage and I try not to squirm. It seems like flirting during widows group would most likely be frowned upon.

"Today's Active Grieving is all about depression," Bunny says, passing us each a blindfold, hygienically wrapped in plastic. "I thought long and hard about how to tackle this bad boy. Usually I like to find an activity that illustrates the grief stage—you know, bring it to life. But I have a feeling you all are pretty familiar with living depression, and I'm not about to put you through any more of it."

"Thank God." Karen sighs dramatically, and we laugh.

"So I figured, why not do the opposite?" Bunny huffs up the steps to the main entrance. Part of the building is an electronic repair shop, and the adjacent window display is stuffed with refurbished laptops, tablets, and smart phones. I wonder for a moment if the opposite of depression is a new iPad or Kindle.

Bunny ushers us past the entrance to the repair shop and

down a narrow hallway. As we approach a second door, I notice more cartoon suns, stenciled on the wall at eye level. Bunny takes out a key and fits it in the lock, swinging the door open to reveal what appears to be a computer lab.

"Welcome to Light Therapy," she says. We file into the space, which is small and dark, with thick white shades covering the few high windows. The room smells like lavender, which I soon realize is coming from the many oil diffusers placed strategically near the heating vents. It's warm, but not too warm, and in front of each strange-looking monitor is a soft reclining chair.

"What is this place?" Liza asks over my shoulder.

"I know, I know." Bunny smiles. "It looks a little kooky. These are light therapy boxes. There's a lot of science that says they help. This is my first time using them with the group, so I'll be interested to hear your thoughts. Take a seat, get comfortable, and let's see if we can't figure these doodads out."

I choose a seat across from Colin and tuck my jean jacket under the table. The monitor is a blank screen, and as Bunny speed-reads through the list of instructions laminated in a frame by the door, it becomes clear that there isn't much to them. There's an on/off button, and when I press it, the screen flickers to life, a dull white light slowly intensifying to a steady, strong glare.

"Now put on your blindfolds," Bunny says. Colin gives me an exaggerated wink from behind his screen and I kick him under the table, my shin accidentally digging into a jumble of extension cords instead. Bunny glances in my direction before continuing: "And bring your chairs up nice and close. That's right. Now just relax. Try to quiet your mind, and let the light wash over you, like a warm bath. I'll be back in half an hour, but you're welcome to stay longer. Enjoy." Bunny flips another switch by the wall, and soft white noise shushes from speakers overhead. The door clicks shut and we're left alone, with our baths of light and quiet.

At first I'm twitchy, my stomach fluttering as it has been every day, any time Colin is within arm's reach. But soon I settle down, my limbs melting into the comfortable fabric of the seat. The light does feel warm, and my skin starts to tingle, but not in a scary, chemical way. It's like my pores are each opening and light is seeping in, trickling down inside me to all the dark, angry places even I can't always reach.

When Bunny returns, I'm almost disappointed, and if I didn't hear Colin shuffling to his feet in front of me, I might have been tempted to stay. I remove my blindfold, sitting for a moment while my eyes adjust to the room. The others are gathering their things and shuffling, zombielike, to the door, except for Liza, who stays in her seat, still glowing in front of her screen.

Outside, Bunny sits us down for a quick chat on the stoop. Martha is noticeably mellowed out, using words like "floating" and "free," and Karen is actually smiling. Bunny, despite not having light-boxed herself, is apparently riding a contact high, and touches each of us tenderly on the head as she walks around us in a circle, a bizarre, grownup game of Duck Duck Goose.

Eventually, Martha gets up to leave and Karen follows. While Bunny is wrapping them each in long, meaningful hugs, Colin shifts over beside me, so that the sides of our legs are touching.

"What'd you think?" he asks.

I smile. "I don't know yet," I say. "It definitely did something."

"Yeah?" He raises an eyebrow. "I couldn't get comfortable. Kept thinking about how funny it would have looked if somebody took our picture. Like a creepy cult of sun worshippers that were inconveniently afraid of the sun."

I push my knee against his. "You missed out," I say. "Some of this stuff actually works, you know."

Colin shrugs and stands, offering me a hand. "You'll probably need to convince me," he says. "Over brownies."

I smile and start to follow him to the parking lot when I realize I've left my jacket inside. We arrange to meet at the Bake House and I hustle back down the hallway and into the therapy room.

Liza sits with her back to the door, the screen still beaming in her face. I notice her blindfold first, discarded on the desk beside the monitor, and then I see the familiar, tight jumps of her shoulders. I bend down to retrieve my jacket and am halfway to the door when I hear the unmistakable sniffling of a controlled sob. I linger, wondering if she'd rather be alone, before turning back toward her.

"Liza?" I ask carefully.

She startles, her hands flying to her face. She slaps clumsily at her cheeks. "I'm sorry," she says with a sniffle. "Do we need to leave?"

"No," I say, lowering into the chair beside her. "No. I just, I forgot my jacket, and I . . . I wanted to make sure you're okay."

Liza manages a smile and runs her fingers beneath her eyes, scooping up the puddles of mascara that have started to gather there. "I don't know why I bother," she grunts, a laugh escaping through the sobs as she wipes the dark smudges on her shirt. "It's not like I've made it through a day without crying. I mean, you'd think I'd learn. Mascara just makes it worse."

I smile and inch my chair closer, but not too close. I've never been a good comforter. Mom was world-class. She always knew exactly the right amount of pressure to apply to exactly the right spot. A gentle stroke of my forehead. A firm squeeze of my shoulder. A rhythmic pat on my back. Whenever Noah was upset about something, I did what Dad does. I gave him his space. It seemed like it was what he wanted, but now I'm not so sure.

"This thing really works, huh?" she says. "I mean, it did. For a few minutes. For a few minutes I actually felt . . . good. Like I used to. As if none of it happened. Sort of like those first few moments, right when you wake up. When you can't totally remember what's real and what's not. I love those moments. I live for those moments," she says sadly. "And then I get up, and I make breakfast, and lunch, and I hug my kids and I tell them stories about their dad. The ones I think he'd want them to remember, times when he was the most fun, or the most brave, or the most attentive. And I do it all because I want to be there for them, I want them to know they can be sad, and I'll be there. That's my job," Liza says. "But, to be honest? If I could just stay under the covers, and live in those few moments? Before they get up? Before they need me? I would. I would stay there forever."

Liza digs a tissue out of her pocket and wipes her nose. "That probably sounds horrible," she says.

"No," I say quickly. "It doesn't. It sounds like the truth." My mind scans back to all those mornings waking up in the cabin, after the funeral. I'd blink from my sleeping bag on the floor and glance around at the unpainted walls, the untrimmed windows, the long, open hallway. I'd wonder when Noah would get around to putting in the doors, and then I'd remember: it was just me. I was alone. It was, without fail, the worst part of my day.

I reach out and put a hand on Liza's forearm, the soft cotton of her V-neck shirt moving as I rub gently back and forth. She holds my hand and gives it a squeeze.

"I can usually keep it together until nighttime," she says. "That's the hardest, for some reason. When the kids are asleep and the house is too quiet. I guess today's just been a bad one."

"Anything specific?" I ask. I don't want to pry, but I remember the way it felt to talk to Colin, that night by the bay. Maybe there is something to be said for just letting it all out.

"My stupid landlord." She waves me off. "He's raising our rent for the summer. We've been year-round there for seven years, and now, all of a sudden, he says either we pay more or move out." She shrugs. "I know it happens all the time. He could get ten times what we pay, by the week. But still. What a pain. To move three kids and all our crap for a few months? And where will we go? My mom lives in a shoebox."

Liza shakes her head and sits forward. I remember the first time we talked, on the bench outside the gym. She seemed so together. And I was so lost. They say it comes in waves, grief, that it never really leaves you. I wonder if you ever get used to it, or if it hits like a tsunami every time.

"I'm sorry," Liza says again. "I don't know why I'm laying all of this on you."

I smile. "It's better than being alone," I say. "Isn't that the point? I mean, isn't that the only reason we keep coming here? Those of us who have a choice?"

Liza reaches out and gives me a long, hard hug. She pulls back and smiles. "Can I tell you something else?" she says. "Something actually horrible? Sometimes I look at you, and I get jealous. You're so young. This, what happened to you, what happened to Noah, it's a nightmare. But you're going to get through it. You'll never forget him, but you'll get through it. It kind of makes me want to hit you."

I laugh. "Go ahead!" I say, putting up my fists in mock defense. "Worked for me."

Liza lightly swats me on the side of one arm. "Nah," she says. "I like you too much."

"I like you, too." I smile.

"Thanks," she says.

I grab my jacket and start for the door. "Coming?"

"Think I'll sit for another minute," she says. "You know. Really get my money's worth."

She wipes her eyes again and flips the screen back on. I walk into the hall and pull the door shut behind me, leaving Liza and the dull, gentle hum of healing light.

In the parking lot, I toss my coat across the front seat of Juliet's van. I'm about to climb in when I hear a voice behind me.

It's Bunny. "Over here," she calls out from the front seat of her toy car. Spread out across her lap are a pile of knitting tools and a half-finished scarf. She nods back at the duplex. "Is she okay in there?"

"Yeah," I say. "I mean, not really. But getting there."

Bunny leans across the seat and pushes open the passenger door, waving me in. I hesitate for a moment but slowly climb in beside her. "How about you?" she asks. "How are you doing?"

I shrug. "Okay, I guess," I say. "Better. I think."

"I'm glad." She nods. "I was worried about you at first. You seemed like a tough nut to crack."

"I did?" I laugh.

Bunny raises an eyebrow. "Hoo boy," she whistles. "All that armor. Seemed like you had some practice with this."

"Yeah," I mutter. "You could say that."

"I'm glad you're giving us a chance, here," she says. " 'It works if you work it.' Isn't that what they pound into you in AA?"

"I'm not sure."

"I think that's it," Bunny says. "Anyway, I just wanted to let you know that I've noticed. And also tell you to be careful."

"Careful?"

"With Colin," she says. "He's sweet. Really. But he's not where you are. Not yet. I would never tell anyone who to consort with, that's not my style. And besides, what do I know? You two could be a perfect match someday. But I do know when people are ready, and he's not."

I sit stunned in the passenger seat. Bunny pats my knee, a pair of bulbous, crystal rings clattering on her thick fingers. "Just my two cents." She shrugs. "See you next month?"

I nod and scramble out, watching blankly as the car shifts noisily into reverse and sputters away.

TWENTY-THREE

"MAY I SPEAK TO TAMSEN PLEASE?"

The voice on the other end of the phone is formal and un-familiar. I quickly rush to turn down the volume on Dad's old record player, newly cleaned and repositioned in the middle of the living room. Whenever I'm alone in the house, I've taken to going through all of Mom's albums and playing them so loud that the photos on Juliet's beloved gallery wall shake in their Pottery Barn frames.

"This is Tamsen," I say. I rarely, if ever, get calls on the house phone anymore, and I can't imagine who would be looking for me on a Saturday afternoon. Dad and Juliet took the kids to a matinee, a rainy day tradition, and won't be home until bedtime. They invited me to join them in town for dinner, but the thought of pretending to care about their ongoing search for the perfect "family house" and ideal slice of suburbia does little for my appetite. They're still waiting to hear back from the pleated-pants people about an offer, and didn't seem at all phased when I told them what I'd overheard about tearing the house down. "That would be a shame," Dad said, an indifferent glaze clouding Juliet's eyes. And that was that.

"Tamsen, this is Valerie West, from City Conservatory," the woman on the phone is saying, and my stomach drops. *Vwest1@cityconservatory.edu.* The email I sent last week, the one with two attachments, the Dylan paper I wrote for class and the more recent essay about Mom and her favorites. I sent it Sunday night and spent the next four days obsessively checking my inbox. When nothing came, not even a curt acknowledgment of receipt, I did my best to push the whole thing from my mind. It was a silly idea to begin with. What would a college professor want with a few random notes I'd made on some songs I thought were worth listening to?

"I'm sorry to call you on a Saturday," she says. "We're in the middle of finals and it's pretty much anarchy around here."

"That's . . . that's okay," I stammer.

"Carla gave me your number," she says. It takes me too long to realize that Carla is Miss Walsh's first name. "I thought I'd try to catch you, before sending an email back. I still prefer chatting on the phone when I'm getting to know a person, though I seem to be in the minority on that." Valerie chuckles and I laugh along with her, although my heart is still thudding in my chest and I'm pretty sure she can hear it.

"Anyway," Valerie continues, "Carla's an old friend, and when she sends a student my way, I know enough to pay attention. I read your pieces." *Pieces.* It sounds so professional when she says it, and I'm suddenly racked with anxiety that I didn't proofread well enough.

"You really have a great style," Valerie says. "Very natural. It's clear that music means a lot to you. That you're passionate about the experience of seeing it live. I love that. Writing about music can be such a challenge."

"Like dancing about architecture," I interrupt.

I can almost hear Valerie smile. "Right," she says. "Everyone's favorite quote. Though I have to say, I've never really understood why."

"Me neither!" I blurt out. "I actually don't get it at all."

She laughs but doesn't say anything else, which I take as permission to keep talking. "I mean, writing about music is just like writing about anything. I'm just trying to explain what I hear, what I see, and why I respond to it, or not. You know?"

Valerie takes a breath. "I do know. And that's why you should keep it up. There are so many great journalism programs these days—many, like ours, affiliated with conservatories. Sort of like the best of both worlds. What are you thinking about for next year?"

"Next year?" I repeat. "I'm not sure yet. I . . . I don't know if Miss Walsh, if Carla told you, but I . . . I took some time off, and . . ."

"She did mention some of your troubles," Valerie says. "And I know you have work to make up. But I have an idea. As soon as you finish your application, drop me a line—or give me a call—and let me know. I'll flag it with a note, recommending acceptance once you've taken the required tests and completed your summer classes. Then we can see where we're at. How does that sound?"

A car whizzes past on the rain-slicked road in front of our house, suddenly stuck in slow motion. The air around me buzzes. *Application?* "I'm sorry," I stammer, "do you mean . . . application to the conservatory?"

Ever since my after-class conversation with Miss Walsh about college, I haven't given the idea much thought. And I certainly haven't considered applying to a music conservatory, considering that I can barely play an instrument and singing is something I've been told I do best in the shower.

"Tamsen?" Valerie asks. "Still there?"

"Yeah," I mutter. "Yes, I'm still here. It's just . . . I'm not actually sure, I haven't really decided if I'm going to apply or not, yet."

"Oh," Valerie says briskly. "I'm sorry. I just assumed—usually when Carla sends a student my way it's because she wants my help with admissions."

"No," I say. "I mean, not just the conservatory. I haven't decided if I'm going to college at all."

"I see," Valerie says.

There's a slow tightening around my chest, and I keep talking, too fast, like maybe if I just say a lot of words she'll understand that I'm not just another screwup. "I guess I just hoped you'd have some ideas about . . . publications." I try to sound like I've thought this through. "Maybe somewhere online where I could send the stuff I write? Or even just some . . . contacts, in the industry? Anything you think might help point me in the right direction."

I hear a shuffle of papers before Valerie clears her throat. "Tamsen," she says. "I hate to sound like a broken record, since I'm sure you've heard this before, but the right direction is college."

The skin on my neck starts to itch. I perch at the edge of the couch and try to steady my ragged breathing.

"But maybe not for the reasons you're thinking," Valerie adds quickly, almost preemptively, as if she's expecting me to protest. "If you're really interested in journalism, and writing about music in particular, you need to surround yourself with other people interested in the same thing. Your teachers, your classmates, these are the people who will one day help you with your career. Like any industry, this one has certain . . . stepping stones. And sure, it's possible to skip them, but I'm not sure why you'd want to."

It feels like there's more I should say, more to convince her that school might not be for me. But the truth is, I don't know what's for me and what isn't. I haven't given much thought to college because I assumed it was too late. What if it isn't? I remember the brochures I stole from Noah. All that, *and* music? What if I still have a chance?

"I'm not saying I won't read your stuff. And I can try to put you in touch with a few editors. If what you write is good enough, nobody is going to care if you go to college or not. But that's not a good enough reason not to do it."

I look across the room at the unfinished record, still spinning on the table, noiseless except for the rhythmic *click click*.

"It's up to you, Tamsen," Valerie says. "But I hope you'll change your mind."

· · ·

"What's in the bag?"

Colin kicks off his rain boots and leans them against the wall. He carries a hefty-looking paper bag into the living room and sits beside me on the couch. "You said we were celebrating," he says, digging through the bag with a noisy crinkle. "I went with the theme."

First, he reveals a chilled bottle of sparkling apple cider.

"Cider?" I chuckle as he runs into the kitchen for cups. It's still early, before six. I sent Colin a text as soon as I hung up with Valerie. I figured he'd stop by to pick me up and we'd go back to his house, but he arrived bearing gifts and seems to be making himself comfortable.

"Listen," he says, smiling as he lays out two champagne

flutes, an anniversary present Juliet got for Dad one year. It's possible this will be their inaugural toast. "Let's just say I'm feeling a little bit . . . scandalized. It's one thing for you to seduce me in the light of day . . ."

"Seduce you?" I laugh.

"But I think it's best we keep this in a PG-13 zone," he says, pouring the golden cider and passing me one. "At least under your parents' roof."

"Fair enough," I say, holding up my glass and clinking it against his.

"Wait." He pulls his glass back. "What are we toasting? Your message was cryptic."

I smile. *Good news,* I wrote. *College bound. I think?* "I got a call from a professor at this music school in Boston," I explain. "She says they've started a dual-degree program, music and journalism. She said as long as I do okay on the SATs and finish summer school, she'll help me get in."

Colin sits up straighter. "Wow," he says. "That's . . ." His face is open and his smile broad and eager, and I watch as he forcibly flattens out his features. "I mean, is that what you want?"

Over the past few weeks, despite everything in me that tells me it's a mistake, I've done a lot of Noah/Colin comparisons. In many ways, it feels like I'm taking a page straight out of the Dad-and-Juliet book. Where Noah was quiet and reserved, Colin speaks his mind. Where Noah was offbeat, Colin is predictable. But there's one thing they have in common, one thing so big that I can't believe I haven't seen it yet: neither of them has ever told me what to do.

Whenever I'd have an argument with Dad, or a tough day at school, Noah would ask me what happened, and listen. Then he'd ask a question back, something like: "What do you think you'll do next?" or "Anything I can do to help?" Sometimes, when I wanted him to get as worked up as I was, it drove me crazy. But most of the time, it was just what I needed to push me out of my rut. To get me thinking in a new and better way.

"I think so," I say now to Colin. "I mean, it feels really fast. Like it's too easy, or somebody's going to call back and tell me it's a joke." I roll my eyes. "I'll probably bomb the SATs or fail summer school now."

"That's the ticket." Colin nods. "Pessimism. Gets you *everywhere.*"

I knock his knee with one of mine. "I know," I say. "I should just be excited."

"You shouldn't be anything," he says. "Remember? This is a *should*-free zone."

I look at the sharp pattern of the rug through the glass coffee table. What if things were different? I suddenly hear myself thinking. What if Noah were still here? There's no question I'd be with the band, on tour when they were, building a life on the island with Noah when they weren't. Would it all have just been a lie? Was I just too afraid to admit that I wanted something else? Something just for me?

"I don't know," I say. "What if I get there and I hate it?"

Colin sits back. "You will," he says. "Sometimes. I thought about transferring like every other week, first semester. But then you'll get used to it. You'll meet some people you like. Or you won't, and you'll do something else."

Colin reaches out an arm and tucks a wayward piece of hair behind my ear. "So I say let's celebrate. Because whatever you decide, it's good news. Okay?"

"Okay," I agree. Colin reaches into the bag and pulls out a cardboard to-go box and two plastic containers. He opens one clear container to reveal a dozen oysters, shucked in their shells, with all the required condiments in individual covered cups. The other is full of warm steamed littlenecks and a foamy bowl of melted butter. In the box are two enormous lobster rolls, overflowing with juicy pink and white meat. "Let's eat."

"What *is* this?" I ask, dumbfounded.

"I told you." Colin shrugs. "It sounded like a special occasion. And what's a special occasion without shellfish?"

We take the feast out to the back porch, sheltered from the warm rain that drizzles on Mom's forgotten garden and Albie's death trap of a swing set. I find some linen napkins and even an old scented candle, which I lay out on the patio table. I light the candle, and Colin looks impressed, until we realize it smells exactly like a Creamsicle and doesn't exactly go with the meal.

After dinner, we clean up the wreckage of shells and sauces

and tie them all up in plastic bags. Colin pulls me onto his lap and rubs out the goose bumps on my arms. I lean my head into the side of his neck and breathe him in. He always smells so clean, fresh and soapy, like he's perpetually drying off from the shower.

"Are you smelling me?" he asks.

I bury my face deeper into his shoulder. "Is that not allowed?"

"I don't know." Colin looks up at the underside of the decking above us. "I'll have to check."

"Check what?"

"My manual for dating teenagers," he says.

I sit up abruptly and perch on the end of his knee. I grab his shoulders, each with one hand, and stare into his eyes. "Can you do me a favor?" I ask.

"Anything."

"Stop."

He tilts his head to one side. "Stop what?"

"Stop obsessing over this," I say. "Us. There are so many things that should make this weird. We can go over every one of them, every time we see each other, or we can just . . . not."

Colin looks up at me, a wrinkle of concern spreading between his light eyebrows.

"Personally," I continue, "I have enough to worry about. I would really like for this to be the one part of my life that doesn't require analysis. Is that okay?"

Colin's stare is long and focused and gives nothing away. For a terrifying moment, I think I may have ruined it. By saying it out loud, what we've both been thinking, the elephant on the patio, I took it too far. I took *us* too far. He'll change his mind. He'll leave.

But he doesn't leave. Instead, he wraps his solid arms around my waist. He picks me up, and stands, and walks us both back through the kitchen, into the living room, and lays me down on the couch.

"What time is it?" I whisper. I lunge with one arm to the coffee table, grabbing for my phone. Again, it's dead. I look across the room to the cable box—6:27. The movie is just ending. They won't be home for at least an hour.

"Good?" Colin asks, as I rest back into the pillows.

"Better than good," I say. I bring him back to me, unbuttoning the top of his striped shirt. It feels good to mess him up, to pull the crisp fabric of his clothes away from his body. I push down his sleeves and run my hands down the smooth backs of his arms, the strong lines of his triceps, the warm dip between his shoulder blades.

We kiss and he relaxes on top of me, his hands moving up my sides beneath my shirt. It tickles at first, and I wait to see Noah, to feel confused, to feel wrong. But I don't. I close my eyes, as if to test it, and still, all I see is Colin. All I feel is Colin, the clean, warm smell of his skin pressed against mine.

I shift his hips and inch out of my skirt, pushing it down toward my ankles with one foot.

"Are you sure?" Colin asks.

I nod and kick the skirt to the ground. I fumble with his belt, unlooping it from his pants. The buckle knocks against the leg of the coffee table with a sharp clatter. I unbutton his fly and he squirms, his pants in a huddle at the end of the couch. He fumbles with the hook of my bra for so long that finally I reach back and do it myself.

"Sorry," he mumbles into my neck. "It's been a while."

There's a cramp in my neck and I try to shift positions, accidentally kneeing him in the crotch. He winces and I laugh. "Me too," I say.

His hands, my hands, are everywhere, and we're kissing, so soft and deep that it feels like there's no end to either of us anymore. There's just the new, moving shape of our bodies together. I close my eyes again and try to feel nothing but the warm, gentle pressure of his hands on my skin.

Outside, there's a muffled click.

"What's that?" Colin asks, bolting upright.

I sit up behind him, frantically peering over his shoulder from between the closed blinds. There's the unmistakable sound of muffled footsteps, but I don't see Dad's car. I race to put on my bra but the straps are tangled and I toss it to the ground, deciding instead to just throw on my shirt without it. I stumble into my skirt and motion for Colin to clean up as I tiptoe toward the hallway.

There's a knock at the door, and soon after, the doorbell.

Dad would never ring the doorbell. I feel a quick flash of relief. Whoever it is, they'll leave.

"Tam?" I hear a voice. My stomach lurches and drops. "Anyone home?"

Through a narrow window beside the door I can just make out the slickered silhouette. Noah used to borrow that coat, a vintage fisherman's jacket, whenever it so much as threatened rain. He said it was a *classic*.

It takes less than half a second for me to decide that ignoring Mitch would be a bigger admission of guilt than simply opening the door. I pull the knob toward me and take a deep, useless breath.

"Mitch," I say, with a smile so wide and phony it hurts.

Noah's dad stands with his hands in the pockets of his coat, the rain pelting the back of his neck. "Hey, kid." He smiles, a Noah smile, crooked and sweet. "Mind if I come in?"

My heart crumbles and a sharp panic vibrates in my veins. I glance hurriedly over my shoulder. Colin is out of sight, the living room tidy and quiet.

"Uh, sure," I say, stepping back toward the stairs.

Mitch peels out of his slicker, careful not to drip too much on the rug. "Sorry to just show up like this," he says. "It's been a while, and I just wanted to let you know . . ."

His voice trails off and I feel him studying me. A tag tickles my collarbone. My shirt is on backward. Mitch's eyes wander over the back of my head, and a shadow creeps across his face. He glances quickly at the boots, Colin's boots, leaning sideways against the wall.

"I just wanted to tell you I finished the house," he says, his voice soft and muffled. "Your house. It's ready. If you still want it."

Mitch bunches his coat up under his arm and pulls the door open. He pauses for a moment, and it looks like he has more to say, but then he's leaving, hurrying back into the rain.

"Mitch, wait," I call after him. I have no idea what I'll say if he stops. I don't know if I want him to. Before I can decide, he's across the wet sheen of pavement, opening the door to his truck and climbing clumsily in.

TWENTY-FOUR

"WHAT DO YOU MEAN YOU DIDN'T SEE IT?"

The room is spinning. Colin hovers near the fireplace, still shirtless, his arms wrapped protectively across his chest. My bra is looped over the armchair, hideous, misshapen cups and stupid tangled straps in plain sight of the front door. I scoop it into an angry ball.

"I'm sorry," Colin says. "I thought I got everything."

"I can't believe this!" I screech. My voice is piercing and primal. Colin takes a few steps toward me but stops.

"It's okay," he says gently. "Everything is . . ."

"Everything is completely and totally fucked," I interrupt. "Is that what you were going to say? Because there is only one way to finish that sentence, and that's it."

Colin carefully lifts his shirt from behind the couch and

slips it on. He slowly and silently pushes each button through its corresponding slit, smoothing out the wrinkles near the bottom in a way that makes my blood burn. My life is ruined, I've disappointed the one person who was never anything but kind to me, and all Colin cares about is keeping his clothes wrinkle-free?

"You should leave," I say, soft and vicious. My head throbs and I need to be alone. I need to think. I feel like I'm drowning and I need to swim to shore.

Colin scans the floor. He loops his belt around his hand in tight circles, the buckle snug against his palm. Without a word, he passes into the hallway and stands beside his boots.

"I know you're upset," he says.

"You think?"

"I'm sorry," he says again. "And I'll go if you want, but I don't think this is fair."

I laugh, harsh and loud. "*You* don't think this is *fair*?" I bellow. "Do you even know who that was? Who just walked in on me half-dressed? That was Noah's father."

"I sort of figured . . ."

"Oh, good," I say. "Then this must be a joke. Because there's no way you could understand that, and still not think it's *fair*. What's unfair is that he came here to tell me the house is ready. The house he and Noah were building. The house that was left to me. *My house*," I'm shouting, and hot tears pool in the corners of my eyes. "It's ready. And I've screwed everything up. Again."

Colin takes a tentative step toward me and puts a hand on my elbow. I'm crying hard now, snot and tears melting down my face in a sticky, soupy mess, and I don't care.

"Tam," he says. "I don't want to go. I want to help."

I shake my head. "You can't," I say. "I thought . . . I thought this was . . . it wasn't real, okay?" I wipe my face sloppily with the back of my hand. "I was confused. You were confused. We were both . . . we were trying to make this something it wasn't."

Colin pushes my hair away from my face and pulls me into him. I bury my wet cheek into the starched corner of his shoulder. "You're wrong," he says into the side of my face. "You're so wrong. I'm not confused. I've never been less confused. This is real. You know that. I know you know that."

I take a few clean breaths of him and slowly pull myself away. "You're not ready," I whisper. "Bunny was right."

"Bunny?" Colin scoffs. "What does that wackjob have to do with us?"

"She's not a wackjob!" I shout. "You don't give anything a chance. You're too afraid to actually feel anything that happens to you. All you want to do is lose yourself, in the island, in me. All of your *not making sense* and *should-free zones*. It's all just a way to keep yourself from dealing with anything real."

Colin takes a step back, like he's lost his balance, standing up.

I glare at him. "What are you even still doing here?" I

243

demand. "You have a job! You have a life! You can't hide out with me forever."

There's a long, painful silence, and then a weird, dark smile is creeping onto Colin's face. He shakes his head slowly. He steps into his boots one at a time and turns toward the door.

"This is a lot," he says, with his back to me. "It's a lot for you right now, and . . ."

"It's a lot for anyone," I say. "Except, apparently, you."

Colin swiftly turns to look me in the eye. "You don't know anything about what it's been like for me," he says. "You don't know, because you're so busy with your own shit. And that's fine. But don't expect me to sit here and be lectured about how I'm not *grieving* right, that I'm not *real* enough, just because you insist on living as if nothing has changed."

I cross my arms. "Nothing has changed?" I bark. "What does that mean?"

"It means that first, you were Noah's girlfriend, and then you were Noah's wife," he says. "Now, you're Noah's widow, and if you're not careful, that's all you'll ever be." He stares at me, steely and unmoving. "Is that what you want?"

I look at the tops of my bare feet, my shoulders heaving as I struggle to keep my breathing calm.

"Maybe you're right," he says, gentler now. "Maybe I am too scared to move on. But don't pretend you're any different."

I close my eyes. "You should go," I say. "Now."

He waits a moment longer. I feel his eyes on the top of my head. I hear the door creaking open and sliding shut.

When he's gone, I stare through the wall, waiting for the sound of his car door closing, the grumble of the engine, the squeal of his tires in the rain.

．　　．　　．

I pedal along the soggy streets, gusts of midnight wind rustling through leaves in the blackness.

I couldn't sleep. I heard Dad and Juliet and the kids come home, heard them race through their bedtime routine and settle in for the night. I kept my door firmly shut, hoping they'd think I was studying. I sat up in bed in the darkness, playing over everything that happened, everything that was said. All I could see was Mitch's face, the slouch of disappointment that pulled at every one of his gentle, Noah-like features.

Finally, after tossing and turning, my mind churning in an endless, punishing loop, I made a decision. I had to leave. I had to go back home.

The gears of my bike are rusted and the back tire is low, making a repetitive *thwap thwap* sound as I push through the wooded trails that lead from my house to Noah's. Albie's backpack, stolen from the closet, shifts awkwardly from side to side, the Creamsicle candle from our dinner table I threw in as an afterthought slapping heavily against the back of my ribs. From my room, I took the framed photo of Noah and me, and, for some reason, an extra pair of pants. I have no idea how long I'll stay, but suddenly it feels like I'm being beckoned. Like there's no other place in the world I should be.

I glide silently down the wet, hilly driveway and dismount where the pavement turns to gravel. I hide my bike in a space between the rosebushes and walk carefully up the path to the cabin. Mitch has put stones in, smooth and level, and they wind around to the new, covered porch.

I push the front door open carefully. The house is dark and still. I'm afraid to turn on the neat row of track lighting that runs the length of the living room. Instead, I open the backpack and light the candle with matches I stole from Dad's not-so-secret study stash.

I do a quick tour of the kitchen, running my fingers along the concrete countertops, the polished breakfast bar, the brand-new oven and farmer's sink. I let the palm of my hand sink into the cool of the freshly painted walls, the smooth grain of the sturdy banister that leads upstairs to the open second floor.

The candle throws a flickering arc against the exposed beams, the cozy sitting loft, the washer and dryer perched in a tower against one wall. I pad softly down the hall to the bedroom, with a new, full bed, tasteful lamps, a walk-in closet with a door on each side, just like Noah always imagined.

I climb out of my clothes and I lie on top of the soft comforter. A breeze rustles through the open windows and I feel a tickle on my forehead. Curtains. Molly must have helped. There's no way Mitch could have done all of this on his own.

My eyes are heavy and I let them droop, my head melting into the pillows. I let my hand wander to Noah's side of the bed, imagining I can feel him, the slender line of his torso, the soft curve of his chin. I imagine he's curling up beside me, an arm flung over my waist, a kiss, like always, for the top of my head.

Tears slide down my face and I let them fall. My body trembles from exhaustion, like I've just climbed a mountain, or swum in stormy seas. The dreamlike visions stop and soon there's nothing, just me and the darkness, an empty space to float in before I fall asleep.

TWENTY-FIVE

THE SCREAM OF SIRENS.

"I've got you."

Orange. Red.

Black.

The wall. Moving.

Throbbing heat.

"You're okay. You're safe."

Folded in half.

Over his shoulder.

My lungs, clenching.

My throat, raw.

"I've got you."

Hands on my back, my legs, the sky spinning in darkness.

Orange.

Help.

Red.
Help.
Help.
Help me.
Black.

TWENTY-SIX

"YOU'RE UP."

My head feels like it's being knifed and clawed and fanged all at once. My eyes blink open, burning and blurred. Instinctively, I try to press my hands against my temples but moving my arms causes more hot stabbing, only this time in my chest. I'm in a room with pale yellow walls.

"Careful," Dad says, lurching forward.

"What?" I cough. I try to sit up but don't get much farther than straining my neck. I lie back down. My mouth tastes like something foreign and unnatural, grease or poison or gunmetal.

"Just try not to move too much." Dad pats the top of my leg like it's a sleeping cat. "You're okay. Thank God, you're okay."

"What happened?" I can comfortably move only my eyeballs so I do that a lot, hungrily searching my periphery. There are two big windows surrounded by a series of framed photographs. Sailboats. A girl with a balloon by the ocean. Still life with fruit and teapot.

"You're in the hospital," Dad says. His fingers play imaginary piano keys on the armrests of his chair.

"I know that," I say. I try to guess the time by staring out the window, but I can't quite see where the sun is and anyway I have no idea how that would help me. Sudden, horrific flashes wash in and out. I close my eyes again.

Fire. Smoke. Mitch.

"Mitch," I croak.

"He's fine," Dad says. "Everyone's fine. It was an accident."

"What was an accident?" I demand.

Dad looks at me like he wishes he could blink and make us both disappear. "The fire," he says softly. "You left a candle burning. The curtains caught. Thank God Mitch got to you in time."

I open my eyes. There's a water stain on the ceiling. It's shaped like a croissant.

"Do you want anything? Something to drink?" A pink plastic tray swivels in front of my chest. Dad tilts the pink straw of a matching pink cup toward my lips, and I take a sip. "There you go," he says, and I stop.

I wiggle my toes. Inspect my arms. Nothing and everything hurts.

"You're fine," Dad says, reaching for my hand. "You'll feel achy and sore from the smoke. But you're fine."

Sweat pinpricks my armpits, which is odd since beneath the thin hospital sheets I'm wearing only a square-shaped paper gown. Patches of tiny goose bumps pepper my skin.

"Dad," I say.

"Just rest," Dad says, his voice soft and thick with emotion. "There's plenty of time."

I turn my head to look at him but my neck throbs, and I'm relieved because I can feel a threatening tightness in my cheeks and I know if I see the way he's looking at me, I'll cry.

"I ruined everything," I say, a whisper. "The house. Mitch."

Colin.

"Everyone is fine," Dad says again, rubbing my knuckles with his thumb. "The house is fine. The fire didn't spread beyond the bedroom. And all that matters is that you're okay. Right?"

I know he's trying to make me feel better, but I don't want to feel better. I want to get up. I want to yell, and scream, and smash things. I want this sterile room, these painted walls, the whole happy world to look as worn out and broken as I feel.

I close my eyes and a few lost tears squeeze out. I breathe slowly, testing the limits of my tender lungs. I wait for the fury to pass.

"How did you do it?" I ask, my eyes still pressed shut.

"Do what?" Dad asks.

"When Mom . . ." I say. "You never fell apart. You were strong."

I hear Dad breathing, in short, shallow pulses. I open my eyes and see him gazing vacantly out the window. A ferryboat is passing, quiet and majestic. "I wasn't strong," he says. "I fell apart every day."

My mind snaps back to our house, empty, too quiet. Buried sobs behind the walls. His eyes, red and tired as he made me breakfast. Then lunch. Then drove me to school, remembering my backpack, soccer practice, play tryouts. Easy conversation at dinner. *How was your day?*

I was a kid. I was a kid without a mom. I didn't care how his day was. I never thought to ask.

"What changed?" I ask. "What happened?"

Dad thinks for a moment. "Nothing, really," he says. "Time. And Juliet." He looks down at the tops of his loafers. "I know you think I was impulsive. Forgetting who I was. But she saved me. She found me when I was completely lost, and she brought me back to life. Without her, I never would have been able to be the person I am today. The father I am today." He shrugs. "Maybe that's not saying much, but it's true."

I close my eyes again and see Colin. I see the way he looked at me when I said those horrible things. The hurt in his eyes just before he turned away.

"There's no right way," Dad says. "There's no trick. This stuff . . . it's the worst of the worst. I should have . . . I shouldn't have made it look so easy, with your mom. I sent you to that doctor, and I thought it was enough. I thought we were okay."

"We were okay," I say.

"We weren't." He shakes his head. "We're not."

Dad pulls at his chin, the spot where his beard used to be. It's one thing I don't miss. He looks more like himself without it.

"I'd like to be," I say softly. "I'd like to be okay."

"Me too," Dad says. "I'd like that, too."

TWENTY-SEVEN

LULA'S BIKE IS WEDGED AGAINST THE FENCE WHEN Dad drives me home the next day. In the last forty-eight hours, there's been a lot of drugged-up day-sleeping, and I've had some strange dreams. Mostly, they've been about Lula. She's standing over me somewhere, scowling. She's walking past me in the halls at school like we're strangers. We're little kids again, and she's locking herself in her room, refusing to come out.

As soon as I see her bike, I remember why: her birthday. I missed her birthday. Sure, I was in the hospital, but whose fault was that? I push out of the car before it's fully stopped and hobble toward the door.

"Easy, Tam," Dad calls after me, but I ignore him.

I lurch upstairs, my lungs sore and throbbing. The door to my room is closed. I push it open slowly and see Lula before she sees me. She's at my closet, neatly hanging up a pile of clothes I left on the floor and carefully returning them to the rack.

"Lula?"

She whips her head around and drops the dress she's wrangling in a puddle.

"I'm so sorry," I blurt. "I'm so, so . . ."

Before I can finish she's scurrying across the room as fast as her tiny legs will take her, and throwing herself at me. Her arms are tight around my ribs and it's hard to breathe, but I don't say anything. I hug her neck, her coarse, over-processed hair scratching my chin. I hear a sniffle but I'm not sure if it's her or me.

Lula pulls abruptly back, slaps at her damp eyes, and then shoves me, hard, in the shoulder.

"Hey!" I howl.

"What the hell were you thinking?" Lula shouts. "You could have died. Didn't you watch that fire safety video in health class? Candles and curtains? That's, like, an after-school special!"

My skin still crawls at the memory of Mitch hauling me out of the bedroom, the window engulfed in smoke and licking flames, but there's something about the shrill pitch of Lula's voice that makes me almost smile.

"I'm sorry," I say. "It was . . ."

"It was totally moronic and you will never do anything like it again," she says. "The end."

"The end," I agree.

Lula nods as if we've made a pact and slumps on the edge of my bed. I crawl to the pillows behind her, stretching out my long legs.

"So what happened?" Lula asks.

I bury my face in a pillow, the soft fabric cool against my hot skin. Amazingly, I don't have a single burn, though there are parts that still feel raw and prickly. "Your birthday," I start to say, soft and muffled by the clean sheets.

"My birthday?" Lula nudges my foot with the side of hers. "Who cares about my birthday?"

"I do," I say.

"You were busy." She rolls her eyes.

"I shouldn't have been."

Lula hops down abruptly from my bed and starts rummaging through the contents of my dresser drawers.

"I wanted to be there."

"Seriously?" she scoffs. "Forget it." She kneels down to push through a pair of boxes still shoved against one wall.

I lift myself up to my elbows, a twinge of pain shocking the base of my neck. "What are you looking for?" I ask.

From a pile of school stuff beneath my desk, she pulls out the tin box we dug up for our project. She dusts it off and sets it at the edge of the bed before whipping her phone from her pocket and snapping a picture.

"He doesn't need the real thing, does he?" Lula asks.

"Who?" I inquire. "Alden?"

"Let's go, Firestarter," she quips. "I've got an idea."

She pulls open the door to my room and starts into the hall. "Wait." She stops. She shuffles back to my closet and grabs one of Noah's flannels. It's one of his favorites, green and blue and white. Before I can protest, she finds the scissors on my desk and cuts a small patch from the bottom.

"Okay," she says. "Now we're ready."

I follow her silently downstairs and through the kitchen, where Dad is checking work emails on his phone. He watches us scurry past with one eyebrow lifted, but says nothing. Lula slides open the door to the deck and runs across the lawn, toward the path.

When we get to the cave, we kneel in the dewy grass and Lula opens the box. There's one picture already inside, one of the ones I found with Mom's things. It's the shot of the two of us, Lula holding me on her hip at a parade. I'm practically twice her size and my legs almost touch the ground but her face is set in a look of serious determination. We both have lollipops and patriotic face paint. In the background, our moms look on, young and long-haired and carefree.

"Your dad told me about the house," Lula says.

I rub the piece of Noah's shirt between my fingers, faded and soft. "Yeah," I say. "Pretty lame."

Lula shrugs. "Things happen," she says. "Things change. It doesn't mean you forget."

She digs into her pocket and pulls out two small figurines,

Doctor Who and the time-traveling police box. She drops them both in the box and holds out a hand to me. "Your turn," she says.

I hold on to the fabric a moment longer before passing it over. She lays it neatly on top of the toys and the photo, like a blanket. She closes the box and latches it shut.

Together, we start digging, until our fingers are caked with mud. Lula wedges the box in the ground. Just as she starts to fling handfuls of dirt on top, I reach for the box.

"Wait," I say.

Lula watches as I struggle to twist my wedding ring off my finger. I haven't taken it off once since Noah pushed it on, and it sticks stubbornly at my knuckle. Finally, it slips free. I stare at it in the palm of my hand, the simple gold band we picked out at a jeweler in town, the cheapest one we could find.

"Are you sure?" Lula puts out a hand to stop me as I start to open the box. "You don't have to . . ."

"I do," I say.

I do.

Lula nods and waits for me to drop the ring in the box with a sharp *clink*, and together we throw dirt in the hole, burying it deep in the ground.

"One day, we'll come back," Lula says. "No matter what. Okay?"

"Okay," I agree.

Lula sits with her back to the cave, the sun shining in

filtered rays on the top of her feet. "Aren't you going to ask what happened?"

I stare at the pale stripe of skin where my ring used to be. "With what?"

"My birthday?" Lula prompts. "Gus?"

I look up sharply. "You hung out?" I ask, searching her eyes for a clue. For the first time in as long as I can remember, she isn't wearing any makeup, and I can actually see the natural sparkle of her eyes, blue and with a glimmer of something new.

"Of course we hung out," she says, aiming for nonchalant.

"What happened?" I smile, sitting up straighter. "Tell me everything."

Lula smiles, too, despite her best efforts to keep cool. "He called and asked if we were still going out. I said I didn't think so—I'd already talked to your dad, and I didn't feel like doing much—but he was weirdly persistent." Lula laughs. "It was . . . I don't know, it was definitely awkward, at first. He invited Declan and Ava, and . . ."

"Ava?" I ask, dumbfounded. "From school?"

"No, the other Ava," Lula jokes. "Yes, from school."

"Yikes," I say. "Now I'm really sorry I wasn't there, at least to run interference."

"She's not so terrible on her own. We went to the Thai place. It was actually kind of fun."

Fun? "Okay." I shake my head. "And Gus?"

"Gus," she says. "Gus was . . . I don't know. He was great."

Her voice is strange and guarded. Lula busies herself with some dry twigs in the grass, leaning them against each other in the shape of a small fort.

"Lula," I prod, with a smile. "Did something happen?"

She smiles back. "You could say that."

I laugh and nudge her with my bare foot. "Something good, right?"

"Yeah." She nods carefully. "Something good."

We sit in the quiet for a bit and then she tosses a twig at my lap. "Okay," she says. "Your turn. What exactly went down that night? I mean, why were you so upset?"

I groan and lean back and close my eyes. "I'd sort of . . . I don't really want to talk about it," I grumble.

Lula stops fidgeting and turns to look at me. "That's funny," she says. "I sort of really don't care."

It's hard, at first, but eventually I tell her everything. I tell her about the conservatory and Valerie West. I tell her about Colin, how it all went from the best to the worst, in a flash. I tell her about Mitch, and what I remember about the house. The fire.

Lula draws with a stick in the dirt and listens, and she doesn't say a word. And when I'm done, we keep sitting, in the same spot we sat in as kids, in the same backyard, under the same island sun, until it's time for lunch.

TWENTY-EIGHT

"HOW'D IT GO?" DAD ASKS AS JULIET AND I GET OUT of the car. It's one of the last Saturdays in May, and spring is everywhere. Dad stands with a hose at his hip, a spray of water soaking the new shrubs Juliet planted at the realtor's suggestion. The fence has also been repainted, a sharp, gleaming white, and it's amazing how much better the house looks with just a few improvements.

"I'm not sure," I answer honestly. I thought I'd be one of the only ones taking the SATs so late in the semester, but the high school cafeteria was crowded with what felt like much of the island's teenage population. The instructions and endless rows of identical bubbles were overwhelming, and some sections felt like they were written by nonnative English speakers, but there were parts I felt good about, too. "Have to wait and see, I guess."

Dad walks the hose to the side of the house and turns off the metal spout. Juliet kisses him on her way to the door. "I'll make lunch," she says. "Ready in ten?"

Dad nods, and I linger on the front steps as he winds the hose around the new decorative reel Juliet brought home last week. I watch him in his weekend clothes, loose-fitting shorts, leather belt, short-sleeved collared shirt with a mock-Polo emblem on the pocket.

I've been thinking a lot about Mom, and Noah, and where they are now. I've never been much of a believer in the afterlife. Even when I was little, as much as I wanted to believe Mom wasn't really gone, I could never work it out in a way that made sense. But sometimes it's nice to imagine them watching us. I wonder what Mom would think of Dad if she could see him now. I have to think she'd at least get a kick out of his restored commitment to chores around the house.

"You ready for next week?" Dad asks.

It's the last week of classes, and graduation is in a week. Lula Bee and I have our project to present, but other than that school as we've known it is pretty much over. There are lots of assemblies, and yearbook parties, and distribution of graduation materials. Mostly, I just can't believe I made it. I can't believe I'm graduating, even if it won't be official until I finish summer school in a few months.

"I think so," I say. Dad wipes his hands on his shorts and joins me on the stoop. "Are you?"

"You mean the house?" Dad asks.

The teardown couple's offer fell through; apparently they found something else up-island, move-in ready with better views. But our house has been shown nonstop, and the agent is certain we'll have another offer coming this week. This time, from a local couple. I wasn't here when they looked around, but Albie told me all about it. They have a little boy, Grace's age, and are expecting another baby in the fall. Albie, as always, had a few complaints: the woman's belly was too big and weirdly shaped, the man didn't take off his sunglasses. But they sounded nice, and enthusiastic. They loved the trail to the beach, and there was even talk about beach plums and making jelly, which I know would have made Mom happy.

Dad puts a hand on the old wooden decking. I'm surprised it hasn't found its way onto the list of home-improvement projects yet. "Actually," he says. "I've been wanting to talk to you about that."

I squeeze my hands between my knees. I've known this was coming. Juliet's been raving about a house she saw closer to town, with a big kitchen and a playroom for the kids. They're waiting until our house sells to formally put in an offer, but the house in town has been empty since the owners left last year. I know Juliet wants to get a jump start on moving, and, if possible, be in by the summer.

"I know," I say. "Moving is stressful, and you'll need my help." Between classes and packing boxes, I'm not expecting the world's most relaxing summer break. But I'm okay with it. It will be good to be busy. The busier I am, the less I think about Colin, and the fact that he still hasn't returned any of my calls.

I've even tried driving by his house some days after school. At first, his car was there. I watched him once through the big windows, throwing a ball for Gertie across the living room. Lately, the driveway's been empty and the lights turned off. It seems like a cruel joke that I'll never see him again, but I know that it's possible. Likely, even. After the things I said, I almost don't blame him for wanting to disappear.

"We're not moving," Dad says. At first, I'm pretty sure I haven't heard him correctly.

"What do you mean?"

"I mean, I've done a lot of thinking, and Juliet and I have talked about it, and this house is plenty big," he says. "And, more important, it's your home. It's where you grew up, partly, and I know it's important to you."

"Dad," I start to interrupt, but he puts a hand on my shoulder.

"This has been a real crap year for you, and I haven't always known the right thing to say, or do," he says. "To be honest, the whole thing, Noah . . . it reminds me so much of your mom, what I went through . . . it's not the easiest thing for me to live again."

"I know, Dad."

"But that's a lame excuse and I know it." Dad shakes his

head. "You're my kid. And it's my job to make things easier for you whenever I can. And if keeping this house makes things easier, or less confusing, at least . . . I want to do that for you."

I look down at the scarred skin around my fingernails. Three weeks with no biting. All it took was a little willpower, and a trick Juliet showed me involving hair spray and Scotch tape.

"No," I say quietly. "I mean, thank you. That's . . . really nice. But . . . you don't have to."

"I know I don't have to," Dad says. "I want to."

"We want to." There's a voice over my shoulder, and Juliet pushes through the screen door. I look back to see that she's smiling. "Really." She nods. "The kids love this house. And they love you. We love you. Whatever you decide, next year, whenever, we want you to know that you always have a home. Your home."

Juliet moves to stand behind Dad and he reaches around to loop one arm between her legs. I remember what he said in the hospital, when I first woke up. It's true. She saved him. She may not have been my choice, or in any way a replacement for Mom, but nobody would have been. And that's not what he needed. What he needed was a reason to keep going. A reminder that life is long and full, no matter how you fill it.

"No," I say again, firmly this time. "I mean it. I've been thinking a lot about it, too. This house isn't big enough for

266

the four of you. You need a house that makes sense for you. For the family," I say. "All of us."

Dad stares ahead at the new fence. He leans back into Juliet and looks up at her. Juliet narrows her eyes at me. "You're sure?" she asks.

"I'm sure," I say. "It's just a house."

I feel Dad watching me, his gaze piercing and doubtful, but Juliet leans over his shoulders to give me a lopsided hug. "Thank you," she whispers in my ear. I hug her back, mostly just patting her forearms and breathing in the scent of her flowery perfume, until she lets me go.

Juliet swings open the door. "Lunch is ready," she says with a grin, before disappearing inside the house.

Dad and I sit quietly for another moment. He clears his throat. "This is really what you want?" he asks.

I shrug. "Who knows?" I smile. "But it's what you want. And if all goes well, I won't even be here very much."

"Don't say that." Dad pouts, nudging me with one shoulder. "You'll have breaks. You'll visit."

"Of course I'll visit," I say, nudging him back. "And besides, you're really going to need a house with a dishwasher. You know, since you're losing yours." I hold up my hands and flaunt them like they're prized possessions. Dad laughs and pulls me in for a sideways hug, and together we go inside to help Juliet set the table.

·   ·   ·

"This came for you."

After lunch, Juliet rifles through a stack of mail on a table by the door.

"With all the excitement, I forgot." She smiles apologetically and I reach for the package, a square orange envelope with my name scrawled in Sharpie on the front. The weight and bubble-wrapped shape are instantly familiar, and suddenly I'm back in Ross's basement, stuffing demos into envelopes and passing out preprinted stickers that I typed up at home, every label, radio station, and booking agent the Internet could find.

I take the package up to my room and peel it open. A single CD in a paper sleeve slides onto the bed, followed by a flimsy piece of hotel stationery from a Nashville Holiday Inn. *Tam,* the note reads, in Eugene's careful print: *Just something new we've been working on. The label guys are "super into it." Hope you are too. —E.*

I smile and pop the CD into my computer, untangling Noah's headphones from a drawer and pulling them over my ears. There's a scratchy whisper, and then Teddy's lazy voice as he counts off on his drumsticks, *One two three four . . .*

The song is surprising, definitely Simone-inspired, with a lilting melody and easy beat. But every so often there's a pop of Ross on the keys, or a soulful few bars of Eugene on the bass, and it all makes sense. They've found a way to hold on to the band they were trying to be, while sneaking up on the band they became instead. Simone sings about diving underwater, swimming with all her clothes on, dragged down and held up, all at once. I realize that Eugene must have written the lyrics.

I close my eyes and remember that night in the pool. I feel the pressure of water around me, the cold feeling of wanting to disappear, the strong sensation of being tugged to the surface. It's all there, in the music, a story with ups and downs, but no clear beginnings and just a hint of something better at the end.

When it's over, I sink into the pillows and start the song again, already composing the letter I'll write back.

TWENTY-NINE

OUR LAST GROUP MEETING IS HELD IN THE THEATER, back where it all began. Bunny has transformed the stage into an altar of sorts. We were each told to bring a photograph of the person we lost, and we lay them out in the center of the circle, along with the pile of candles and colorful scarves Bunny threw in for sacred effect. Bunny says the idea is that we are comfortable with each other now, and can be trusted to "hold space." She says that a lot—"holding space." I guess that's what it's called when you let somebody talk without interrupting, or asking questions, or trying to give them advice.

I sit next to Bunny, with an empty space beside me, waiting for Colin to walk in. For the past three weeks I've wondered what it would be like to see him again. Would we pretend that nothing happened? Would it be uncomfortable opening up in group knowing that the other person was listening?

I never find out. "Colin had to be out of town, unexpectedly," Bunny announces, after she's finished readying the circle. "He wanted me to tell you all how sorry he was not to be able to say goodbye, and that he sends each of you light and healing."

I look down at my hands in my lap, a complex swirl of emotions bubbling up inside me. I'm furious he couldn't be bothered to see the group through. I'm relieved he's getting back to his life, his real world, if that's what he's doing, where he's gone. Mostly, I'm suspicious about whether or not Bunny talked to him at all. It seems unlike her to lie, but there's no part of me that believes he said anything about light and/or healing.

Bunny asks if we're ready and we nod, a somber calm settling around the circle. Liza goes first. She talks about how much she's afraid of forgetting the little things. How she walks a line between wanting her kids to remember their dad, and wanting them to be normal and happy. She also talks about not knowing what to do when they're kicked out of their house at the end of the month. She says she's grateful to have made so many good friends. She says she knows if she's patient, things will work out. I close my eyes and try to silently tell her how brave I think she is, what a good mom she must be. I wish I could give her a hug.

Karen talks about wishing she and her husband had

traveled more, and vows to take the trips they'd always wanted to take together, on her own.

Martha, who rarely says anything, surprises us all by talking the longest. She tells a long and rambling story about her husband, who was a dentist, and the summer they first moved to the island and opened up his practice. She talks about being young and in love and all the things that changed over the years and all the things that didn't. She talks about missing the sound of his car door slamming at the end of a long day, his footsteps on the gravel. She cries and talks about how she's sorry her kids haven't gotten married yet, how she can't imagine thinking about them starting families that won't ever fully know hers.

After each person has finished, nobody says a word. The speaker lies down in the center of the circle, and everyone else gathers around them and touches them—just puts their hands on a part of the person's body, their arms, their legs, whatever. There's lots of crying and quiet. It sounds sort of maudlin, but it's actually surprisingly nice. There's never anything to say in these moments anyway. *It's going to be okay. You'll get through this. Life goes on.* They're all just words that mean well but say nothing, and nobody ever believes them until after they've come true.

Everyone else has already had a turn, so when Bunny asks if I'm ready, I don't have much of a choice. "Sure," I say. There's a shift in the room, and I know it's up to me. This is my space and I have to fill it with something. It's strange—I still don't know these people at all. I know their names. I know how each of their spouses died. I know little bits about what they do, the ways in which they struggle. But I don't know any of the intimate details I would of a friend, or a boyfriend. And yet somehow I feel more comfortable talking to them. As if purely the fact that we're all damaged in the same way makes it easier to understand each other. Like we really are a club: a weird, random club of sad and mostly middle-aged young widows.

"I guess I'm feeling okay, today," I begin, because that's how everyone else has started. "I mean, I'm feeling better. It's been a . . . it's been a really bizarre year."

There are a few soft chuckles and I glance quickly around the circle. It feels so unnatural to talk to a group of people who aren't allowed to talk back. Like shouting into a canyon. I decide it's easier to look at the floor.

"I don't like doing this," I say finally. "Talking. I'm not good at it. I never have been. I mean, you wouldn't guess it, because I do it a lot. It's sort of . . . I guess it's a defense. I learned it when my mom died. I was young, and everyone told me it was wrong to keep things in. So I did a lot of talking. Processing. I learned to say the things that people wanted to hear. But it didn't mean I knew what I was talking about. Or believed what I was saying. It didn't mean I was healed."

Bunny makes an *mmm*ing sound and I look up to see that a few people are nodding. I've noticed that these little moments of connection are people's way of letting you know they're still there. Just because they're not responding doesn't mean they don't get it. They want you to know you're not alone.

"I guess one thing I'm learning is that it never goes away," I say. "I've thought more about my mom in these last few months than I have probably since she died. And Noah . . . I know that I haven't even begun to understand what losing him has done to me. I keep thinking I'm getting better, that I'm figuring things out, and then, *wham*. I do something stupid, or somebody says something that pisses me off, and everything feels hard and hopeless and unfair again. Like I'm stuck on a track, going around and around, and no matter what I do, I can't get off."

My voice cracks and I swallow. I take a few jagged breaths. "Somebody once told me I was lucky, because I'm so young. Because I have so much time to start over." I look up and see Liza smile. "But listening to all of you, all of your stories, I just wish I had more. Noah was . . . I know I'll never meet anyone like him, ever again. I know I'll meet someone, maybe a few someones, but none of them will be him. I'll never know what it would have been like, if we'd had more time. And that . . . it makes me really, really mad."

I look around the group. Karen's eyes are closed and Martha nods to her lap. There's a long silence and I feel Bunny staring at me from across the circle. I take a big breath and continue.

"I'm trying to go to college in the fall," I say. "If I get in. It feels . . . I don't know. I'm excited. But it also feels weird. Like I'm letting Noah down. Not that he wouldn't have wanted me to go to college, if that was what I wanted. But it's just so different. Different from the life we would have made. And sometimes I wonder how he'd feel about it. How he feels, if he knows."

Tears fall onto the tops of my hands and I wipe them away. I thought I was feeling strong today. One by one, I watched the others break down, convinced I'd be different. But now, I know, I'm not.

"I guess I'm still working on everything," I say. "I thought if I could just get through all of this, the group, school, the way everyone wanted me to, I thought I'd figure some things out. Evolve, or something. But it hasn't happened yet. Most of the time, I feel the same way I've felt since I was ten years old. I miss them a lot. I miss Noah," I manage, my throat tight. "I really miss my mom."

Before I know it, my head is hanging and I'm sobbing, big, ugly sobs that sound like they're coming from somebody else. There's a shuffling and I feel them closing in around me. I feel hands on my knees, on my shoulders, on the top of my head. I never make it to the middle of the circle, but nobody seems to mind. Sometimes, people meet you halfway.

·   ·   ·

"I liked that," Bunny says, after most people have filtered out. I forgot my photo of Noah and came back to find Bunny alone, blowing out candles and packing up her scarves. The theater feels somehow smaller without us circled up inside it. "What you said about being on a track. That felt very honest."

"It was," I say, trying not to sound annoyed. I've come a long way with this group, with Bunny and her culottes and incense, but I do sometimes wish she'd just talk like a normal human being.

"You know, sometimes I wonder why I do this," Bunny says. "These groups. I think they do help, just getting together, being around people who know something about what you've been through, but like I said in the beginning, the books, the theories . . . nobody knows what to say."

I nod. I think about Colin, the first night we kissed. He knew that nobody had the answers. I remember Bunny in the car, warning me he wasn't ready. But I wanted him to be. I needed him to be. I needed him to be okay, so he could tell me I was going to be okay, too. But he wasn't, and it wasn't his fault. It was mine, for not giving him the time to get there.

"These grief stages, depression, anger, acceptance, they're more like phases. They're not levels," Bunny says. "And they don't go in order. They happen all at once. Sometimes all together, sometimes taking turns. And they never go away. But eventually, they get all jumbled up in the mess of every day. 'I hate my husband for dying, I'm in love with a new pattern for a quilt. I'm pissed at my kid for not returning my calls, I'm scared of getting older alone.' It starts to even out, like everything else, and soon it's not the *only* thing. That much, I can promise."

"Thank you," I say. I wrap my arms around her cushiony middle. She seems taken aback and I wonder when the last time was that anybody held space for her.

THIRTY

FRIDAY, THE LAST DAY OF SCHOOL, IS A HALF DAY. Lula and I finally present our Social Sciences project, which has turned into an old-school slide show of childhood pictures and artifacts, coupled with some research about identity and place, and set to a sound track of Mom's old records. Islanders, it turns out, are similar in many ways to small-town mainland kids. We explore. We connect. We make friends, lose them, and make them again. And sometimes, we leave. But wherever we go, the island is with us. Maybe everyone feels that way, but it seems to me that growing up here put a special imprint on all of us, on the people we've turned out to be.

After school, I'm supposed to meet Lula at the tattoo shop. Things with Gus have been going well, and Lula has been helping him out after school. It's funny to see her with a boyfriend. She has an amazing way of letting him in without shutting out anyone else. I've been taking notes.

On my way to town I find myself taking a surprise turn. I've been thinking about Mitch, and Molly, and the cabin. Mitch came to visit in the hospital the first day I was there, and I spent most of our time together sobbing into the paper sleeve of my ugly hospital gown. It wasn't pretty, and I'd like to try again.

The driveway has been repaved and the grass in the lawn is freshly mowed. There's a new, fenced-in vegetable garden, and I wonder for a moment if Mitch has taken over landscaping duties. Then I see Molly, hunched over a six-pack of baby lettuce plants. Even from the determined shape of her shoulders, the way the muscles move in her arms, I can see that something's changed.

She turns as I slow the car to a stop and stands, taking off her gardening gloves and tossing them to the ground. "There you are." She smiles.

I take a deep breath and walk slowly to the garden. I keep my back turned to the cabin. I can't bear to see it. Not yet. "I just wanted to stop by to say sorry," I stammer, when I reach her. "Again."

Molly looks at me for a long, charged moment and puts an arm around my shoulder. "Come on," she says, leading me up the shell path to the big house. "There's pie."

Inside, Molly sits me at the dining room table. It's a circle— Molly is a firm believer of eating in the round—and there's a blue vase with orange and gold tulips in the middle. I tried to stay out of the house as much as possible after the funeral, but on the few occasions I did go inside Molly was usually asleep on the couch, buried under a puddle of blankets, or going through old photographs, a glazed, semiconscious look in her eyes.

The blankets are still in a heap on the couch, and the floor looks like it hasn't been cleaned in months, but the curtains are open and light streams boldly in. Molly washes her hands at the sink, and I remember the first meals I ate here. I remember Molly showing me how to clean a cast-iron pan. I see the same pretty, floral message pad by the cordless phone, the kiln-fired jar of blue ballpoint pens. I remember how full and warm it felt to be in a room where everything had a place.

Molly cuts two pieces of pie—strawberry-rhubarb, her specialty—and brings them to the table. She sits across from me and passes over a fork. "Summer's here," she says with a smile. "At last."

I nod and take a bite. There's so much I want to say. I want to tell her that I haven't forgotten. Any of it. I haven't forgotten her or Mitch or everything they've done. I haven't forgotten Noah, even if sometimes I've acted like I wanted to. I think about telling her how much her family has brought to my life, how I'll be forever changed by the time we all spent together.

Instead, I eat pie. Molly tells me about her garden, the new varieties of tomatoes she's trying this year. She's excited, but there's a darkness in her eyes, a shadow that hangs and hovers, like a force field of familiar despair. There may be flowers on the table and pie in the oven, but grief hums all around her, a constant reminder that she'll never really be whole again.

I must be staring, because eventually she sighs and says, "I'm going to meetings again." I take her hand and want to hug her, but I don't because she's still eating and it's hard to compete with Molly's pie.

Mitch comes home from work while I'm clearing the table. He hugs me at the sink and doesn't let me apologize, even though I keep trying.

"This is the way it is," he says, squeezing my shoulders. "It gets better. It gets worse. It gets better again."

"And it's just so damn big," Molly sighs. "It's bigger than all of us." We're all standing around the kitchen island, the butcher's block chopping board where I used to help Molly cut vegetables for a salad while Noah and Mitch worked late outside. "It's living with a hole you keep trying to fill up. Nobody knows that better than me," Molly says.

"But the house," I say, a terrified quiver in my voice. "After all the work you did . . ."

"It's a house," Mitch says. "And believe it or not, it doesn't look so bad."

He motions for me to follow him to the front window, where he draws back the blue-and-white-striped curtain and points across the driveway. I steady myself and peer out over his shoulder. One upstairs window is missing, covered in paper and ringed by layers of charred wood.

Other than that, there is absolutely nothing wrong with it.

"We could have lost the whole thing," Mitch says. "But the fire department got things under control quickly. We lost a window and we'll have to redo a couple walls and part of the ceiling. It'll take a week or two. After that, like I said the other night . . ." I see Mitch pull in a breath and my heart sticks. *The other night.*

"Like I said before," he goes on. "It's still yours. Noah wouldn't have wanted it any other way."

I turn back to the open living room. Molly perches on an arm of the couch and Mitch is at my shoulder. "I can't live here," I finally say. "Not because I don't want to. I loved living here. I love that house. But I'm leaving. I've decided to go to school in the fall."

Molly and Mitch share a glance over my head. "I know." I smile. "It's been a shock for me, too."

"That's wonderful, Tam," Molly says. She stands and wraps me in a hug. "That's great news. Right, Mitch?"

Mitch nods, standing near the window. "Sure it is," he manages. "I mean, we'll miss you around here."

"I'll come back," I promise, just the way I promised Dad.

Mitch looks out again, at the leafy woods surrounding the land they've lived on, built on, worked on since he inherited it from his grandmother, so many years ago. "It's a hard place to leave," he muses. "For good, anyway." He turns again to look at the cabin. "And it'd be a shame not to have anyone out there, after all this."

I feel for my phone in my pocket and swipe it to life. "Actually," I say, "I've been thinking about that. I've been going to this group, sort of like a support group for people who . . . for widows." Molly looks at the floor and Mitch clears his throat. "I've met some really great people, and one of them, Liza, she's a single mom. Three little kids. They've been renting from the same guy for years, and all of a sudden he's jacking up the price, just because he knows he can get more for it in the summer."

Molly clucks her tongue and Mitch runs a hand through his hair. "You're kidding." He shakes his head.

"I know," I say. "And she's just . . . I think you'd really like her. I was hoping maybe . . . I know it's a lot of people in a small house, but it would just be until fall, until they can find something bigger."

I feel Mitch and Molly looking at each other over my head. "Sure," Mitch says finally. "We'd love to meet her."

I smile. "I was hoping you'd say that."

Molly tears off a page from one of her notepads and I jot Liza's number down from my phone. They walk me to the door and we say goodbye and I promise not to leave for school without coming over for dinner. I hug them both and promise myself that I will, no matter what.

On my way out to the car I stop into the cabin. Immediately the faint smell of burnt wood stings my nostrils, and a pit forms in the bottom of my stomach. I force myself to climb the new steps, to stand inside and look around. Downstairs, there's hardly any evidence of damage, except for a pair of damp and dirty rags slumped in a heap in the corner.

I close my eyes and see Noah, lugging the mattress up the stairs with Mitch the first night we slept out here. We didn't have a formal move-in date, since we hardly had anything to move, but that night was special. We ate pizza on the living room floor, listening to Noah's favorite playlist on my computer, dreaming up where everything would go. The couch, when we got one. The table, when we got one. The piano, when we got one. (A piano, though totally impractical in the small space, was high on our list of priorities.)

I open my eyes and try to hear the clamor of tiny footsteps, pounding back and forth between the rooms upstairs. Racing through the screen door to the little yard. Liza making breakfast in the kitchen and watching them through the window over the sink. I imagine Liza helping Molly with the garden, anticipating the easy way they'll know each other without even trying. The secret, unspoken language of people who have already seen the worst, and know what it takes to keep going.

Mitch was right. Noah would have wanted me to stay here. He built this house for us, and couldn't imagine anything better than growing up together inside it, near the family that he loved, his refuge from the constant motion of touring and being onstage.

But Noah also wouldn't have wanted me to be tied down, chained to his memory by a house that would never be ours, especially not if I had other dreams, other places I wanted to be. And if he knew I was helping somebody like Liza, someone who loved the island as much as he did, I know he would be proud.

I pull the door shut and walk back to my car. I wonder if that's it, then. If that's what I'll do. Colin was right. I can't live for Noah. I can't be his widow forever. But I can make him proud. I can make my mom proud, too.

Or at least I can try.

THIRTY-ONE

THE BLACK CLOUD INCHES UP FROM THE HORIZON, gradually eating away at more of the piercing blue sky. Lula and I nudge each other anxiously as we join the rest of the graduation crowd, turning our heads to monitor the storm's progress.

The forecast called for "drownpours," a seemingly new weather-related phenomenon invented especially for today. Yet Principal Morris and the superintendent insisted that the ceremony be held outside as always, on the green in front of the town hall.

"You'd think they'd skip through some of the speeches," Lula mutters under her breath, and I laugh. Chip Lassiter, the valedictorian, is drawling through a forgettable account of the many ways in which he's changed over the last four years. I remember Chip as a freshman, the gawky kid in glasses who kept running for student council on a platform of healthier vending machine options and the addition of Frisbee Golf to the athletics program. As far as I know, he never won, but every fall he'd try again, and I liked that about him. I've heard he's going to Stanford on a full scholarship, and I find myself hoping that he'll quickly find a happy cohort of gawky Frisbee golfers out there.

"Don't they know we're wearing white?" I ask through clenched teeth. For some reason, instead of caps and gowns, school tradition dictates that all graduates wear white. Girls in white dresses, boys in white shirts and khaki pants. There are, of course, the few kids who insist on standing out. One girl even showed up in a white bikini top, which a teacher promptly made her cover up.

Shockingly, Lula adhered to the dress code, though not without her own special flair. She wears a pair of white spandex leggings and a big, lacy white tunic, with a thick white headband in her hair. Juliet bought me a new white dress for the occasion. It's nothing special, but I don't hate it, and I even dug out the ankle boots she bought me last year to wear with it. Juliet said I looked "very grownup," and Lula approved, which is all I can ask for these days.

A clap of thunder booms in the distance and we all jump and giggle. There is some frenzied conferring onstage between the presenters, and one speech is cut as they decide to move right into the diplomas. Mr. Peterson begins reading out the names in alphabetical order, and one by one we file out of our seats and toward the temporary stage as fat raindrops begin to fall around us.

They're just getting to the Bs when the rain picks up. It's a hot, muggy day, and at first it feels nice, but soon the grassy lawn turns to a mess of mud and shallow puddles, and worry spreads from one row to the next. Girls start looking down at their dresses, the clean white fabric sticking to their bodies, the suggestive shapes of undergarments becoming more visible with every new, revealing drop.

The teachers huddle onstage, but Mr. Peterson keeps reading. There's a dull panic rising in my belly; I don't know why, but it's important that they get to my name, and fast.

"Anna Bachman," I hear, and watch as she splashes up the steps and slides across the stage.

"Brent Bagley."

"Tamsen Baird."

I smile and Lula leans forward to give my waist a squeeze. I trudge through the soaking field and up the slippery steps, my wet ankles sloshing around in my boots as I walk across the stage. Mr. Peterson hands me my diploma—or the piece of blank paper rolled up to look like a diploma—and we share a smile.

I turn to look for Dad and Juliet and the kids. I know they're sitting somewhere near the back, but all I can see is a mad rush of people racing to shelter, huddling under awnings or scrambling to their cars.

My eyes wander to the side of the stage, where a small

crowd of spectators has gathered under the cover of a big maple tree. I see somebody waving, and I have to squint to realize that it's Judge Feingold, standing alone beneath a red umbrella. She's too far away for me to make her face out clearly but I imagine that she's smiling, and I hold a hand up to wave back before scurrying out of the rain.

From over my shoulder, I hear the principal interrupting to announce that all students should meet inside the town hall, and the rest of the festivities will be postponed. I hold up my fake diploma, even though I'm sure nobody can see me. My name was the last name called.

•   •   •

Inside, the town hall is stuffy and chaotic, as parents and kids try to find each other and the giddy energy of finally being done starts to settle in. After we're formally dismissed from the proceedings, Lula and Gus try to goad me into coming with them to the beach, where, as soon as the rain stops, a bunch of kids are having a catered graduation party that everyone has been invited to crash. Dad and Juliet are hovering under a window waiting for me. They mentioned something about going out for lunch, and I know they'll be hurt if I leave without them.

"I'll catch up with you guys later," I say. "Besides, doesn't it kind of defeat the purpose of *crashing* if it's sanctioned in advance?"

Lula shrugs as Gus reaches for her hand and pulls her toward the door. "Fun is fun?" she jeers at me, pausing to plant a hard, sloppy kiss on my cheek before they run out in the rain.

Gracie tugs at the hem of my dress and I scoop her up into my arms. "Wet, yucky," she mutters in disgust, patting my sleeve with cautious, chubby fingers.

I join the adults near the windows and hug Skip and Diane, catching the tail end of what sounds like an invitation to their house for a pig roast later in the summer. Juliet looks horrified, but Dad eagerly agrees before turning to lay a firm hand on my head.

"The reluctant graduate," he says. "How's it feel?"

"Wouldn't you like to know," I tease.

He laughs. "There's still time."

"There's always time," I hear over my shoulder, and turn to see Max, beaming from ear to ear.

"You came!" I shriek, wrapping my arms around his neck. Max hates ceremonies of any kind, and I thought for sure he wouldn't make it.

"Your graduation?" he asks. "I had to be here. Bet your dad twenty bucks you'd bolt before they called your name."

Dad smiles. "I never doubted you for a second." He laughs.

"Who's hungry?" Max asks. "You all want to come to the bar for some burgers? I got a band in there rehearsing that I think you'll really like."

I watch as Juliet squirms over the idea of the kids in a bar, but Dad and Max are already making plans. They walk together, hunched over in the rain like nothing's changed, the way it is with friends remembering younger versions of each other, settling into old jokes and routines like no time at all has passed.

"I'll meet you guys there," I say. I borrowed Dad's car to get to town early and it's parked on the other side of the green. I sprint through the relentless spray of rain, jostling against wet white figures on all sides. It feels like one of Lula's science-fiction movies, where all the characters dress alike and some catastrophic event turns a community upside down.

I weave through rows of slow-moving traffic, waving to familiar faces as they cheer through open windows, horns blaring, music competing from one car to the next. In this movie, I decide, nobody is an alien, and nobody dies. It seems only fair that for a few hours, the big news is just that everyone has something to celebrate, and people are feeling good.

I hurry to open the car door and at the last second glance back toward the green. I thought I heard somebody calling my name, but there's so much hooting and shouting it's impossible to tell where it came from. I search the passing cars for Lula, but I don't see her anywhere.

Just as I'm about to climb into the front seat, something tells me to look up again. And I see him. Standing under a tree, a sport coat balled up and held over his head, is Colin.

I think about crossing the street, but before I can move

he's pushing through traffic toward me. A car skids to a stop, its bumper inches from his kneecaps, and he waves a hurried apology through the windshield.

"Get in!" I call across the roof of the car as he splashes through a puddle. I duck into the driver's seat and unlock the passenger door. The seat squeals as he sloshes inside, pulling the door shut behind him.

"Nice day," he says, running a hand through his newly cropped hair. Suddenly the car is full of quiet, just the squawking of Colin's wet shoes and the hard patter of rain on the hood. I'm grotesquely aware of my see-through dress, and position my arms strategically across my chest. There's something about being exposed in clothing that's almost more uncomfortable than being completely undressed.

"I didn't know you were still here," I say finally.

"I wasn't," he says. "I mean, I left. I came back."

"Just for this?" I ask.

"No." He presses his hands against the tops of his wet jeans. "Had to pick up the rest of my stuff. Get the house ready for renters," he explains, staring at sheets of rain through the glass. "Those are lies."

I smile. "You didn't have to come."

"I know," he says. "I had a hard time deciding if it was weird or not. I wanted to see you. I always want to see you, but . . ."

"It's not weird," I assure him. "I'm glad you're here."

"Me too," he says.

"I tried calling. Texting," I say.

"I know," he interrupts. "I was an idiot. I hung around for a while, moping. Then I decided I was being pathetic and I forced myself to go home."

"I'm sorry," I say. I wonder if I'll ever stop apologizing. I wonder if there's a quota of lifetime apologies and if by now all of mine are used up. "I shouldn't have said—"

"Everything you said was true." He turns to me. "I just hadn't heard it out loud in a while. When Anna died . . . I don't know. It had been such a long few months, and there was a lot in me that was just glad it was over. In a lot of ways, she had already been gone for a while. I missed her, I miss her, of course I miss her, but . . ." He shakes his head. "Part of me just thought that it was going to be different for me. I was going to be the guy who kept it all together. I didn't need help. My parents kept pushing, and I pushed back. There were times when I honestly believed they were more broken up about it than I was . . ." He laughs. "I was dumb. Everyone tried to tell me there was more there. Stuff I was too scared to see. They were right. You were right." He takes a deep breath. "It's been a not-so-fun couple of weeks."

His hand rests on his knee and I reach for it. "I know what you mean."

Colin smiles. "You know a lot of things," he says. "But not everything."

"Is that so?" I challenge.

"You were right that I was hiding," he concedes. "But you

were wrong about everything else. I've had lots of time to think, I mean, *really* think, and even with all the rest of it, even after I got back to the grind, missing Anna, missing the way my life was supposed to be . . . I knew. Whatever this is." He holds my hand in the air. "Whatever it was, it was real."

I feel a knot pulsing in my throat and I look away, the trees bent by the weight of wet branches, the crowd smaller now, as the rain keeps falling.

"The timing couldn't have been worse," he says lightly, squeezing the tops of my fingers. "But it's real."

I manage a small laugh. "I know," I say quietly.

We sit like that for a few long minutes, hands locked together between us. I see a version of us together and it starts like this: we drive off, right now, and never look back. We start over somewhere new, where nobody knows what's happened to us, what we've been through, or where we've been. We live in a little house and we have jobs that we like and we take Gertie for walks at sunset. It's a good life. It's a real life.

But even as I'm seeing it, dreaming it, I know: it's not my life. My life is here. No matter where I go, it will always be here. There's no running away from that.

"So what now?" I ask timidly.

"I don't know." Colin shrugs. "I've decided to leave the firm. Take the summer off. Might go on a trip, the kind I wish I'd done after college, before everything happened so fast."

Colin stares through the windshield, into the rain. "And then, in the fall, you go to school," he says. "You *are* going to school, aren't you?" he asks.

"Fingers crossed." I sigh.

Colin nods. "We see what happens, right?"

I smile. A piece of my hair falls out of my braid and I reach up to tuck it behind my ear. Colin does, too. He holds the side of my head in his hand and I turn to him. We kiss, soft and quick.

"See what happens," I agree, after he's pulled away.

I offer to drive him to his car but he says he doesn't mind walking. He gives my hand a squeeze, and I promise to call once I'm settled in the dorms. Campus is only a few T stops away from where he lives, and he knows a great sushi spot in between.

"We can meet there," he says.

"It's a date," I say, even though I can tell we're both not sure that it will be.

I watch him walk away in the rain, imagining what he looks like in the city. People take on a slightly different shape on their home turf. Taller, or maybe just more solid, whether they like it or not.

I search for the keys in my squishy bag. I think about Dad, and Juliet, and the kids, and Max, all huddled around a booth, listening to some new band Max can't wait to show off, and Albie dousing his French fries in ketchup and Gracie pushing all the buttons on the jukebox, and Juliet passing out napkins while Dad and Max laugh over foamy beers about the time they closed the bar early and Max got out his guitar and Dad played drums and Mom sang every Blondie song she knew all the words to, and a few that she didn't, and I danced by myself in circles until I fell asleep on the sticky, peanut-studded floor, my head just inches away from the vibrating wall of giant, echoing speakers.

And then I start the car and I drive.

ACKNOWLEDGMENTS

THIS BOOK WAS WRITTEN UNDER THE GUIDANCE OF two of the world's most patient and insightful editors: Wesley Adams at Farrar Straus Giroux and Joelle Hobeika at Alloy Entertainment. Precisely the right number of cooks in this kitchen. Thank you.

Thank you to my agent, Faye Bender, for continuing to answer my emails, even when they all say the same things.

Thank you to my high school boyfriends. One of you died too young. One of you introduced me to Donald Byrd and Ella Fitzgerald. I learned so much from you all.

Thank you to Veronica Conover, for loving my kids and for reading my books.

Thank you to my family: Maria, Bruce, George, and

John. My children, Evie and Wiley. My in-laws, Madi, Bugs, and Cali. And my family of friends on Martha's Vineyard. I couldn't imagine a better place to call home.

And thanks most of all to Eliot, for everything.